Pride Publishing books by M.C. Roth

Single Books
The Drumbeat of His Heart
A Song for His Heart
Karma's Kiss
Greedy Boy
Feral Woods

It's a Kink Thing
Kinked Up
Unkinked
Kinks and Crosshairs
Dupli-Kinked
Getting Kinky

Collections
Secret Santa: Daddy's Secret

I0658892

It's a Kink Thing

GETTING KINKY

M.C. ROTH

Getting Kinky
ISBN # 978-1-80250-518-4
©Copyright M.C. Roth 2023
Cover Art by Kelly Martin ©Copyright March 2023
Interior text design by Claire Siemaszkiewicz
Pride Publishing

Published in 2023 by Pride Publishing, United Kingdom.

Pride Publishing is an imprint of Totally Entwined Group Limited.

GETTING KINKY

Dedication

For Q

Chapter One

Elliot

"That was amazing, baby." Hunter rolled to the side, nuzzling into the pillow as he let out a breath. There was cum leaking from his ass and dripping between his thighs in pale rivulets. Elliot reached for it, smearing it until the slickness turned tacky. It clung to his fingers, thick and smelling almost purely of him.

"Ew, gross. Why would you do that?" Hunter turned his head, making a face as he shuffled away.

Letting out a sigh, Elliot bit back the urge to growl out exactly why he wanted to see his husband marked with his cum. Instead, he pressed his dirtied fingers together, watching the cum slowly start to flake away.

There were two reasons really, and he knew Hunter didn't want to hear either of them. He had tried to tell him before, stuttering through his answers before Hunter had turned his nose up.

Turning on his back, Elliot stared at the ceiling and the small silver fan making slow laps in an attempt to dry the sweat from his soaked skin. His flesh prickled as his heart started beating normally again, his thighs still burning from the workout.

"You okay?" asked Hunter, reaching for the cloth by the nightstand that he'd put there in advance. It was dark and probably cold, still ready to wipe away every trace of their love in a few quick strokes.

Always the planner.

Hunter wasn't one to let them sit and just *steam* after sex. He seemed to hate the feeling of cum on his skin or inside him. Most days he asked Elliot to use a condom, treating it like going bare was some kind of special occasion.

Elliot let out a grunt, rolling to watch his husband. Hunter started with the cloth between his thighs, where the smeared layer was mostly dry. In a few moments, there was no evidence except the slight redness to his hole and a softness that Elliot longed to reach out and touch.

He wondered if he could slide right back in there, soft cock and all. *Too bad it's off-limits.*

Hunter leveled him with a look, his dark hair sticking to his skin. A few strands had come loose in their lovemaking, lost in the bedsheets, only to tickle them later. "What is it? Was it not good? I thought it was great—your best yet—and that's saying something."

What is this? A pep rally? Elliot really didn't want to be one of those guys who said 'it is what it is', but that was the only thing that came to mind. He wasn't boasting when he said he had the stamina of a champ. And he always made sure he kept up his two-to-one ratio—for every orgasm he had, he made sure Hunter had two.

"Uh...yeah." Elliot looked to the side. There was a picture of them on the nightstand from their last trip to Disney. Their smiles had been brighter than the fireworks that night, and he'd felt like a kid again for the first time in years. They'd made love on the balcony of their room when darkness had fallen, the stars and the creepy guy two floors up, their only company.

"Wow, thanks," Hunter deadpanned, dropping his feet to the ground and marching to the bathroom. "I don't think I've ever had such a rave review before. If you weren't in the mood, you could have just said so."

The funny thing was, Elliot *had* been in the mood, almost voraciously so. He couldn't seem to get enough, and no matter how many times he came, he always craved more.

But each time he thrust home with Hunter beneath him or riding him, the joy and expected pleasure dulled to a faded whisp of something that never quite lived up to what it was supposed to be.

"It's not you, Hunt. You're beautiful and amazing. I just..." He couldn't say it. Their sex life was active, if not a touch on the boring side, but it lacked everything that he wanted and needed. "Maybe you could top next time?" *And every time after?*

Hunter made a face from the doorway to the bathroom before running a hand through his messy hair. It only looked wilder when he was done, sticking up in directions that defied physics. He really was the most beautiful man Elliot had ever seen.

He often wondered why Hunter hadn't taken the modeling gig he'd been offered years before when they had just been starting a life together. He belonged on the cover of magazines, not working from home and hidden away in an expensive condo.

"You know I'm not really into that," said Hunter, shrugging his naked shoulders. There was a love bite on his pec that was quickly turning from red to purple, a vivid reminder of what was left of their passion. "I have a hard time topping you, baby. Even thinking about it gives me weird vibes. I can try, though."

Elliot's stomach sank like it so often did after they were intimate. Hunter didn't have to explain the weird vibes because it was the same thing he felt every time. It wasn't supposed to be a chore, but that was exactly what sex had become. Yet, somehow, he craved it.

"I don't want to push you to do something you aren't comfortable with." Elliot turned away as his chest went tight, trying to hide his face. The truth was, Hunter topping him was only the tip of the iceberg of his sexual desires.

The sheets rustled and the bed dipped as Hunter returned, leaning over and placing a kiss on Elliot's cheek. "Tell me what's bugging you, baby. I can't help if you won't tell me. It's you and me against the world, right?"

"Yeah." Threading their fingers together, Elliot closed his eyes, forcing his tears back. He was tall and built, and some guys mistook him for a gym rat, but he was really a huge softie. The simplest insult could ruin his month, and Hunter had been the only steady thing throughout his adult life. Hunter had picked up the pieces so many times he'd lost count.

He owed him everything.

"I need more," said Elliot, biting his lip as everything threatened to come pouring out of his mouth. He could barely hold it back. It had been building for so long, that he was surprised it hadn't burst free already. The images were there, though, plaguing him at night when he was supposed to be sleeping.

"Okay? Like more sex? We can do that, baby. As much as you need." Hunter placed another kiss on his cheek, and Elliot fought the urge to flinch. There was no warmth to the touch, only bleak helplessness.

"No, not like that. I need *you* more. Some days I just need you to just take over and look after things. You know what I mean?" *God*, he wasn't saying anything right, but he couldn't make sense when everything was a jumble in his mind.

Hunter paused, flexing his hand. Elliot could only wonder what he was thinking and what the look on his face was. Disgust? Confusion? Or the '*no*' that he really feared? None of it would be new. They'd gone down this path a dozen times, Elliot testing the waters and Hunter screaming 'shark' before they'd even put a toe in.

"Like the banking and stuff? I can do that, too. I know you have a lot more responsibilities at work than I do, so I can definitely take care of some extra things around the house. If you need more free time or 'you' time, then I can help you with that."

We are getting nowhere. He gritted his teeth in frustration, wishing he had something to bite down on. It was almost terrifying how quickly the rage came on lately. "I need you to take control," said Elliot, his voice almost a growl. "In sex...in everything."

He blinked his eyes open as he felt Hunter pull away. When he turned his head, he met Hunter's confused and hurt gaze. The beautiful blue he'd fallen in love with was there, distorted beneath the fresh glaze of tears.

He'd promised himself never to hurt Hunter or be the cause of any pain, but it was plain as day in front of him.

"Never mind." He forced a smile on his face, pulling the covers up to his chin. He was exposed and naked, suddenly afraid of what Hunter would see if he looked too hard. "Forget I said anything. I'll make breakfast if you do the dishes."

"You sure?" Hunter scratched at a flake of something on his stomach that he'd obviously missed. His relief was almost palpable.

Sitting up, Elliot brought their lips together in a brief kiss. "I'm sure. Sorry… I shouldn't have brought that up. You're perfect, Hunt. A man wouldn't ask for more unless he were crazy."

There was that cute flush across Hunter's cheeks that made him look ten years younger. Sometimes, he still looked the same as he did during their college days. It was only when he smiled that Elliot could really track the differences.

"Can I have French toast?" Hunter perked up, grabbing his robe and throwing it over his shoulders. The front draped open, showing off his abs and his perfectly soft cock.

Elliot's cock stirred again, and he pressed the heel of his hand to his groin, squishing it into submission as he rolled out of bed. He grabbed boxers and jeans, jamming his cock up along the waistband so Hunter wouldn't see. If they rolled back into bed now, they'd get nothing done all day.

He swept his hands inside Hunter's robe one last time, trailing down his smooth skin that had him fully hard in moments. Letting out a shuddering breath, he placed a kiss against the side of his neck, licking the sweat that was still lingering there. Hunter let out a giggle, squirming in his hold.

"I'll make you whatever you want as long as I can have this," said Elliot as he grasped the robe's tie and tugged it free before tossing it on the bed. "You get the juice and I'll get the rest."

It was domestic bliss at its finest, even with a gaping hole in his gut and an unsatisfied arousal that thrummed beneath his skin. Hunter lounged on one of the stools at the end of the kitchen island, his housecoat open and his naked ass on the leather surface. He scrolled through his phone as Elliot gathered ingredients and started up the stove.

The kitchen was small for the two of them, especially since the price tag of the condo had been so large, but Elliot secretly loved it. There was no elbow room to speak of and some of the cupboards didn't open because the handles would have run into an adjacent drawer, but it kept everyone in the kitchen close. He only had to reach out and he'd be able to touch Hunter, who would send him a smile with every caress.

He cracked an egg into a bowl, grumbling at the shell that escaped and slipped right to the bottom. He dragged his nail against it, but it foiled him until he promptly gave up. *Nothing a little cinnamon won't fix.*

Hunter made a choking sound behind him, the chair squelching as he shifted. "Oh my God. Look at this, baby. Can you believe it?"

He spun his phone to Elliot who grabbed it, turning the stove down a touch before he looked to the screen. His jaw almost hit the floor as his heart came to a brief stop. *This is... It's...*

"Some kind of swingers club or something? Alice sent me an invite to the open house." Hunter chuckled, leaning his cheek on his hand. "I don't understand how people are into that kind of thing. All that leather and skin, and people getting spanked and stuff? How humiliating."

The crackling of the toast in the pan dimmed to a quiet haze as Elliot stared at the invite on the screen. His palms were suddenly slick, fresh sweat breaking out along his spine. It was no swingers club.

Unkinked. Of course, he recognized the name of the place hosting the open house. The dim picture of a white unmarked door that Alice had included didn't do the place justice from what he'd heard.

He'd been dreaming about it for the last year — everything from the supposed leather attire, mysterious rooms and the people within its sound-proofed walls. When he closed his eyes, he could almost imagine the smell and the taste that would roll across his tongue.

He'd learned about the kink club almost by accident when a co-worker had mentioned that they were into BDSM after they'd gotten a little tipsy at an office party. One Google search had left him hard and wanting, fresh dreams haunting him about the kind of life and dynamic that he'd never have.

The hole in his chest was suddenly gaping, its maw open wide and ready to swallow him whole. His mouth was dry, his eyes burning as he struggled to look away. There was no information — not really — only a time and a date, when he craved so much more.

"We should go." The words were out of his mouth before he even knew he was saying them. Elliot flushed, dropping the phone on the table before turning to the fridge and grabbing a few more slices of bread. "It sounds fun, I mean. They have a dress code and everything. It would be like Halloween."

He was sure that if a kinkster ever heard him say that, they'd be insulted. If their thoughts were anything like his, it wasn't so much dressing up as revealing a part of themselves that they'd kept hidden at their nine-to-five. He'd figured that out when he'd splurged on a pair of leather underwear. He still had them, hidden at the bottom of his filing cabinet beneath their old mortgage papers.

Hunter stared at him, his jaw slack and his eyes wide. His cheeks had flushed, the rosy blush creeping down his neck. "You want to go to a sex party?"

Oh fuck. "It's not a sex party, and look... It says that the public is welcome for one night only, and they have a demonstration about Dominance and submission. You're always looking to try new things, so why not go out on a limb?" *Please, please, please.*

Hunter leveled him with a look, pulling his lips back over his teeth. He could probably see right through Elliot's lie. Elliot was the one who was always on the search for new things, like his tropical garden, which he'd moved to his office after Hunter had complained.

"I mean, I like new foods and stuff. I'm in love with that Indonesian restaurant we found, but I don't know if we're going to fit in with this kind of crowd. It doesn't seem exactly natural." Hunter took his phone back, squinting down at the screen.

Elliot had heard that one before more times than he could count, but never from Hunter. It stung, lancing into the coolness of his chest like an open wound.

"You're sounding a lot like your mom there," said Elliot, his heart sinking even lower. "It hasn't been that long since your family considered you and me 'unnatural'. Hell, some of them still do, even if we get a Christmas invite. It's like they think I woke up one morning and said 'hey, I want to be homosexual now so people can tell jokes about me and threaten me with bodily harm'." Elliot shook his head, trying not to grit his teeth. At the rate he was going, he would wear them down. "I love you, and you happen to have a penis." *Penises are the best.*

Hunter flushed, biting his lip. "I'm sorry. I really didn't mean it that way, and that was terrible of me. If you want to go, we can absolutely go. I'll even dress up."

Elliot looked up as something on the stove started to burn, black smoke puffing into the air. Grabbing the spatula, he flipped the toast out of the pan, the charcoaled side landing face-up on the counter. *Shit.*

"When is it? I didn't even look." His heart pounded, his hands shaking as he pulled a few paper towels free from the roll to clean up his mess. Egg and cinnamon swirled under his hand as he tried to wipe them away.

"This Friday. Oh, don't you have that work thing?" asked Hunter, seeming almost relieved.

"Nope. That's next Friday." *It's absolutely this Friday.* He could miss one meeting without any sort of penalty, especially when it was an after-hours one. It was one benefit of being one of the best in the company.

"Oh." Hunter's face fell and he clutched at the edge of the robe, tightening it across his chest. "I guess we can go then."

"We don't have to." Elliot cracked a fresh egg into the French toast mix, not even trying to retrieve the shell this time. His hands were so unsteady that he wouldn't have been able to pull it out, even if he managed to trap the tiny piece against the wall of the bowl.

"No, I want to. I'm really excited," said Hunter with the enthusiasm of someone marching to their doom. Running his hand through his hair, he let out a long sigh. "Just help me pick out something to wear. I'm terrible at that kind of thing."

Chuckling, Elliot placed a fresh piece of bread into the pan, the egg mixture sizzling as it hit the surface. The sharp scent of cinnamon and vanilla almost covered the burnt charcoal still clinging to the air.

"You are right about that," said Elliot, his smile real for the first time in ages. "You wore a plain gray T-shirt to a concert. I mean, come on, it's a concert! It's the only time you can wear all black with a spiky collar and do your hair in a pink mohawk and people don't give you a second look."

Hunter stuck his tongue out, shifting on the chair with another wet sound. His ass must've still been leaking. Luckily the chair would wipe clean easily, not that Elliot really cared. As far as he was concerned, he was okay with a bit of cum on every surface except for the table, and even that could be bargained for.

"Or, you could just wear this," said Elliot, sliding his hands back into Hunter's robe. "Put on a little G-string and maybe tape some Xs over your titties." He pinched Hunter's nipples, grinning at his squeak. "Sounds like a perfect dress code to me."

Hunter slapped him playfully on the hand when he pinched him a second time. "You are insatiable, baby. Maybe a sex party is exactly what you need."

Elliot wasn't going to bother correcting him again, not when he was finally going to Unkinked in the near future. "Oh, but I have you all to myself until Friday. What am I going to do with all that time?"

He mouthed at Hunter's neck, sucking a bruise in the same spot he had before breakfast. Hunter shivered, no longer trying to push him away.

"I think your toast is burning," Hunter whispered, tilting his head back to give him better access.

"No, it's not—oh shit." Elliot lunged for the pan, dousing it under cold water as smoke rolled from it. He sent Hunter a wink, trying to play off every bit of nervousness. "Saved by the pan."

Chapter Two

Elliot

"Did you have to wear that?" whispered Hunter as they stepped through the door of Unkinked and into another world. Every dream and moment researching the place had been for naught. Nothing could have prepared Elliot for the sheer reality of it.

Outside, it was crisp like fresh spring, but inside it was hot, dark and gut wrenchingly amazing. Between the leather and the amount of skin on display, Elliot wasn't sure where to look. One thing was for certain, though. No one was looking at them in the same way Hunter was staring around with wide eyes and judgment written in every jerky movement.

"Yes." Elliot shut his mouth, running his hands over his chest and belly. His shirt was tight and black, hugging his abs and pecs in a way that he hoped would dazzle. He'd gone with something simple up top to try to calm his nerves. He'd let his inner self shine through with his pants, though, dressing in the bathroom at the last minute and going straight for the door so Hunter wouldn't have a chance to stop him.

Leather cupped him from ankle to hip, especially around the groin area where he'd slipped his leather underwear beneath. It was tight, uncomfortable and absolutely glorious. He wasn't sure how such restrictive material could make him so free, but it did.

"It's embarrassing," Hunter hissed, clutching at Elliot's elbow. "Can we just leave?"

They were barely two steps through the curtain after signing their lives away on non-disclosure and consent forms, and Hunter was already trying to back out? He'd dragged his heels the entire night, claiming a headache and a sore throat before he was miraculously cured when Elliot went to leave without him.

"You look great, Hunt. Just relax."

Hunter's black shirt and slacks didn't stand out at all. There were a few people dressed just like him, moving comfortably throughout the space with a fluid languidity that Elliot longed for.

"I'll get you a drink, and we can leave soon, okay? I just wanted to look around and see what all the hype is about," said Elliot. The half-lie was putrid on his tongue, accumulating with the rest of the acidity that had started piling higher over the last few months.

Looking around was as dangerous as it was alluring. It meant adding to the fantasies that had been building in his mind. Maybe his disappointment would only be stronger once it was all torn away from him.

He'd already asked his kinky co-worker way too many inappropriate questions when she said she wouldn't be able to make the open house. She'd said she was allergic to newbies, whatever that meant, but was more than happy to fill him in on a few details.

"Of course, I look great. I dressed like a normal person." Hunter crossed his arms, dragging Elliot to a stop from where they were still looped together at the elbow.

Elliot swallowed, clenching his teeth as numbness radiated from his core. So, maybe he wasn't dressed for going out to a restaurant, or work, but there was nothing wrong or abnormal about a little or a lot of leather. Saying it to himself did nothing to halt the consuming shame.

The lights were low in the main area, making it seem larger than it probably was. To his left was a well-stocked bar that was packed with people coming and going, and to his right were booths that were filled to the brim. The far end was even darker, fading away from his vision—but he *knew* what was there, and it called to him.

His co-worker had talked about the rooms at length, going into details while leaving him salivating for more. There was *Wet*, a place that he wasn't sure he would ever want to step into. *Impact* was another one that made the hairs prickle on the back of his neck, and not in a good way. *I don't need a room*. It wouldn't make him feel whole. He had an abundance of those at home.

There were more people than he could have guessed, some dressed like Hunter and others closer to him with a touch of leather. There were a few men who were shirtless except for a harness of thick leather straps decorated with silver loops, and one woman whose corset exposed the entirety of her breasts. Between all of them, their heads were held high, except one who knelt to the side of one of the booths, his eyes partially closed with a drunk look on his face.

Elliot stared with longing at the kneeling figure, swallowing at the bliss that met his gaze. The voices dimmed as he watched the slow rise and fall of his breaths, and the tiny shifts he made, wiggling his ass as if he couldn't be more comfortable. His knees had to hurt against the hardwood floors, but he looked as if he didn't feel a thing.

He led Hunter to the bar, still unable to take his eyes off the kneeling man. *Submissive* a voice whispered in his mind. A happy submissive, with a Dominant who looked like he was on top of the world. Elliot barely had eyes for the Dom.

What am I doing here? He couldn't avert his gaze — not when they reached the bar, leaning against the sparse few inches of space left behind when someone carried their drinks off, and not when the Dominant leaned down to give his submissive a sweet kiss. It was a private and exposing moment that had Elliot on edge in an instant, his longing almost palpable.

He vaguely heard someone asking for his drink order, and he mumbled out a reply, his staring growing so obvious that even Hunter seemed to have pulled himself out of his ass to notice.

The blond Dom looked up, catching Elliot's gaze with a knowing smirk. He leaned across the table, speaking to a man sitting across from him, who Elliot hadn't noticed.

He must've been another Dom, just from the way he nodded and looked around the room. He was a full head shorter than the blond and was thin and wiry instead of muscular. When his blue eyes flashed to Elliot's, he had to look away. He'd never seen a look so heavy and intense before, filled with so much promise that it had to be a lie.

Elliot whirled toward the bar, grabbing the drink that was placed before him a second later. He took a sip as the back of his neck burned and his body flushed hot and cold. Hunter was on the stool next to him that must've been vacated at some point, pouting over his glass of what looked like Sprite.

His drink wobbled as Elliot lifted it, pausing when it touched his lips again. He couldn't remember for the life of him what he had ordered, but he could smell the bitter alcohol wafting from the glass and taste it on his tongue. He wasn't sure if he wanted to dull any more of his senses and face his fantasies with only half of his wits.

"First time in here?"

Elliot whirled toward the sound, coming face to face with the intense gaze that had caught him from across the room. A few drops of his drink spilled over onto his hand, and he let out a gasp at the cold shock of it.

A pulsing exhilaration flowed through him, something moving in his chest as he stared at the stranger—a stranger who was talking to him and wasn't just a figment of his imagination or another cold, unfulfilled dream.

Brown hair and blue eyes filled his vision, and his heart threatened to explode as he struggled to answer. They quirked their lips, tugging at their leather jacket with casual grace. Elliot's gaze was drawn to the leather, and he traced every softened seam that was worn with use and age.

Scrounging up a nod, Elliot set his glass down before he could drop it, holding out his hand instead with condensation still clinging to his fingertips. The man took it with a smirk, his touch lingering. He was shorter than Elliot by half a foot, but his grip was firm and his gaze unwavering. It took everything Elliot had not to look away.

"I'm Shelvin," he said, raising one eyebrow. His brows were a shade darker than his hair, and paired with his scruff, it gave his face an almost rugged look. "What's your name, sweetheart?"

A flush crept up Elliot's neck, there for anyone to see. His tongue was stuck, the silence stretching as he struggled to speak. The music was suddenly too loud with a dark rock song playing that infused a longing to fuck into his blood.

Hunter didn't seem to have any of the same reactions as him, bristling before slamming his drink down and pushing to his feet. "His name is Elliot Lender, and that's my last name, too, I'll have you know. He took it the day I married him."

Oh shit. Elliot crumpled, drawing his hand back to his side, even as he craved to linger in the warm touch. Shelvin's grin only broadened as he spared a glance toward Hunter.

Usually, once someone noticed Hunter, they rarely looked back to Elliot. He was beauty incarnate and could captivate someone with a glance. But Shelvin only lingered for a moment before his gaze pierced straight into Elliot's again.

"Lovely to meet you, Elliot and Mr. Lender. What brings you to this fine establishment? Looking to mix up the love life?" Shelvin leaned between them, waving down the bartender as he let himself sag. The leather pants that he hadn't noticed at first drew Elliot's gaze, the material fitting Shelvin even more firmly than his own and matching his jacket to perfection.

Maybe the warmth of the room was all in his head because Shelvin looked completely comfortable, the zipper of his jacket only partially undone.

"Elliot wanted to come," said Hunter, letting out a huff and flicking his hair over his shoulder. A man across the bar looked Hunter's way, zeroing in on one of the most attractive men in the place. "I still don't know why."

Am I not standing right here? Elliot shuffled his feet, wishing he could plunge his hands into his pant pockets. It wasn't uncommon for Hunter to fill a silence when Elliot sat back to observe, but not usually when there were strangers involved.

Shelvin gave him a nod, taking a swig of his drink before letting out a soft sigh. "It's a great place, even if I'm a little biased. My cousin introduced me to Unkinked a little while ago, and I haven't looked back since. There is something for everyone here — whether you're looking for Dominance, submission, pain or a safe place to broaden your horizons."

Hunter screwed up his face, a retort probably on the tip of his tongue. A few words and he could probably get them both kicked out of the place. They'd be banned for life before Elliot had ever had the chance to appreciate everything that Shelvin was talking about.

That's enough. He wasn't going to let a potential friendship slip by him, especially when it seemed like Shelvin might actually be able to explain some of the things he was wondering about himself. It was one thing to dream about kink, but another to enact his fantasies in a room full of strangers with his husband in tow.

"What do you like?" asked Elliot, biting his lip as Shelvin watched him. That gaze, solely focused on him, was so intense that goosebumps prickled his skin. He swallowed, his mouth dry and his tongue frozen in place.

"I'm a special kind of Dom myself. I thought you were a Dom from the way you were looking at Trick and Nav, but now I'm not so sure. Or are you shy?" Shelvin grabbed a water bottle as it slid his way, offering it to Elliot.

How did he know I'm thirsty? Elliot stared at the bottle, grasping it tight so the plastic crinkled in his hands. Twisting the cap off, he took a long drink, taking more than he thought he would need.

"I'm not shy," said Elliot, using the time to think about his answer. He hadn't been shy since the option had been taken from him. "It's just my first time in a place like this, and I wasn't sure what to expect."

"A place like this," said Shelvin, rolling each word over his tongue as he looked around. "You just walked in the door. You haven't even seen anything, yet."

Before he could stop himself, Elliot glanced over to the last place he'd seen the blond Dom. The booth was occupied by someone else, with the sub that had enthralled him nowhere to be seen.

"You really liked what you saw there." Shelvin let out a whistle. "Trick's my friend, but trust me when I say you don't want to go there. He's all about pushing boundaries that you didn't even know you had, and his sub is just as possessive as he is. You two wouldn't survive him. What about some wax play or a bit of light bondage? You guys into that?"

Hunter gave him an exasperated look, tugging the hem of Elliot's shirt. Elliot pulled away, shuffling down the bar until he was out of reach. It put him closer to Shelvin, his skin prickling at the proximity. "Wax sounds really messy and maybe painful, and I don't think I get the idea of bondage. What's so fun about tying someone up?"

He wasn't trying to sound rude, but from Shelvin's brief crinkle of his forehead, Elliott was worried he had been.

"Sometimes wax is a bit of a chore," said Shelvin, taking another sip of his drink. "But restraint could be handcuffing your lover to the bed and riding them until they came. That sounds fun to me."

That was something they had tried before, with fluffy pink cuffs that Hunter had gotten as a gag gift from a friend one year. They had both been drunk, but Elliot still remembered the dull indifference as he'd snapped the cuffs around Hunter's wrists.

Elliot looked down at his drink, crinkling the plastic in his hands. *Maybe I'm not in the right place.* "What about submission?" He asked so quietly that he wondered if Shelvin would hear him over the music and mass of conversation.

Someone pushed into the small space beside Shelvin, sending him a step closer to Elliot's ear. He seemed to take it in stride, leaning in and lowering his voice. "Do you want to kneel, sweetheart?"

Blood rushed to Elliot's face so quickly that his temples pounded. He grasped the edge of the bar as the water bottle fell from his grip, his knees weak and wobbling. Neither of them made a move to retrieve it as it rolled away into the crowd.

He gave a quick nod before looking back to Hunter, who appeared beyond disgruntled and bored, his empty glass resting on the bar top as he tapped his fingers.

"Can we go now?" Hunter asked, looking over Shelvin's shoulder and letting out a dramatic sigh. "It's hot in here, and more people are coming in."

Am I hot? Elliot couldn't tell anymore, and Shelvin looked so comfortable. His nerves were shot between his flipping stomach and his skin that couldn't seem to make up its mind between clammy and sweating. There could have been a thousand people, but he was only looking at one.

"I want to stay," said Elliot, his voice hollow to his own ears. He swallowed, praying with everything he had. "Please, Hunt. You promised."

Shelvin held up his hands in front of himself in mock surrender. "I don't want to cause any problems or anything, and you can tell me to hit the road, but how about I show you around and point you in the direction of the real action. You guys can take off anytime if you're not interested."

"He's interested," said Hunter, "but I'm not. I'd much rather be on our couch watching Netflix right now."

Shelvin shrugged, looking to the crowd. "Like I said, no pressure. Elliot seems pretty keen, though. I can give him the tour and bring him back to you—hands-off, of course." There were calluses on his palms, his thumb smudged with something gray.

Hunter pursed his lips, seeming to think it over for a moment. "Fine, but if you touch him, I'll kick your ass. And you have to buy me a drink while I'm waiting." He batted his eyelashes, and Elliot had to hold back a snort. His husband was very used to getting exactly what he wanted from everyone he met.

"You drive a hard bargain." Shelvin grinned and waved down the bartender. "Another drink for my friend on me, Maddy."

Maddy sauntered up to them, looking Elliot up and down before he turned his gaze on Shelvin. "Coming right up. You check out back yet, Shelvin? Derreck is showing off his skills tonight." Maddy sent them a beaming wink, filling a glass and sending it their way.

Elliot did a double take as he glanced down, noticing Maddy's bare arms for the first time. Beneath his short-sleeved shirt was a path of crisscrossing marks that covered almost every space. He looked away before he could make a fool of himself again. He'd already been caught staring once.

Shelvin apparently hadn't missed a thing, whispering into his ear as if he could hear everything that Elliot was thinking. "Maddy is into pain and so is his Dom, Derreck. Their tastes are a little too extreme for you, I think, but you haven't seen them in action."

Elliot trembled, reaching for the closest thing to steady himself. It was Shelvin's arm, firm and wiry beneath his tight jacket. "Have you seen them? In action, I mean? What was it like?"

Shelvin chuckled, shaking his head before he glanced to Hunter one last time. "Enjoy your drink, Mr. Lender. I'll bring your husband back in a few minutes."

Threading his elbow through Elliot's, Shelvin dragged him into the crowd, which had grown since Elliot had last looked. The music was dim compared to the conversation, people packing every booth and the small dance floor that seemed to have formed of its own accord. Sweat rolled down his back as he floated, barely feeling his feet as he followed Shelvin.

"To answer your question—no, I haven't seen them in action," said Shelvin, shouting over the noise. "I wish I'd had the privilege, but I'm pretty new to town, and Derreck is a private man when it comes to Maddy. I don't think anyone has had the privilege of seeing one of their scenes yet, but from the way Maddy looks by the time they're done, they must be pretty intense."

Elliot glanced back to the bar, where Maddy was smiling and filling another drink. There was another man behind the bar now, too, piling a tray high before heading out into the crowd.

"He looks okay," said Elliot, his mouth dry. Maddy didn't look any worse for wear as far as he could tell, and his marks had looked old and partially faded.

"You got it all wrong, sweetheart." Shelvin tugged him down as they headed closer to the back of the club and the shadowed edge of the room. "He's not hurt after his scenes... He's peaceful. It's not often that I've seen someone in subspace for so long as him, and it seems to level him out. Derreck, too."

"Oh. I'm not sure..." Elliot trailed off as they approached another curtain. Off to the right was a hallway with a series of doors. They must've been the themed rooms he had heard about. Each one was closed except for the closest one, which was propped wide. There was noise coming from within that he recognized on a visceral level.

A belt against skin made a noise that brought back more than one unpleasant memory.

"You okay?" asked Shelvin, pausing to look at him, his eyes pinched with concern. "I was serious when I said no pressure. I can take you back now."

"No." Elliot turned away from the door, flinching when another slap rang out. Shelvin narrowed his eyes before nodding once and dragging the curtain open. He leaned close as Elliot's breath caught, the world dropping out from under his feet.

"Welcome to paradise."

Chapter Three

Shelvin

He'd been in more bars and clubs like Unkinked than he could count, and every single one of them had left their mark, some more literally than others. When his cousin and owner of Unkinked, Clint, had invited him along to his place nearly a year before, he'd hoped to find a slew of new subs. He hadn't been disappointed, but there had been something missing — something he couldn't put his finger on.

One look from Elliot and he'd known that this time would be different than all the others. He'd never seen a longing so fierce in eyes that were so haunted. The husband Elliot had in tow seemed to be an added bonus...*not.*

The curtain was thick under his hand, the velvet softness of it parting as he pushed it to the side. It was deceptively light but contained a fair share of sounds from within the open play area of the club. Beyond it was another world where alcohol wasn't permitted and looking was as free as speech.

Turning to Elliot, he tightened his grip on his arm, letting the curtain fall shut behind them. "What do you think, sweetheart?"

Elliot was big, beautiful and shy, which happened to be everything he looked for in a sub. It helped that he was smoking hot, with such wide and expressive brown eyes that they threatened to suck Shelvin in. His husband was one lucky guy. *The asshole.* Mr. Lender's type were easy enough to come by and a touch harder to ignore.

Elliot blinked, his lashes long and dark like he'd taken the extra time to put a touch of makeup on before he'd hit the club. He was strong, his biceps thick beneath Shelvin's fingers. Shelvin made a point of touching him as much as he could, kneading the muscles gently as he tugged Elliot farther into the room.

Tall, lovely, but so painfully cautious that Shelvin just wanted to put him on his knees then and there. But then he would be breaking a promise to the very fortunate Mr. Lender.

"It's beautiful," said Elliot, his words soft and deep. His pulse pounded in his neck, surging as he looked around the room. Shelvin could see every thump, watching his eyes widen as he spied different people and scenes.

And there was a lot to watch.

Most of the toys and restraints had been pushed back, making room for chairs that looked up to the main stage. A few couples hadn't been deterred, though, taking advantage of whatever hadn't been put away.

There was so much he could learn about someone, simply by watching them — their tells communicating more than their safewords ever would. Elliot was an open book who was both terrified and turned on by everything around him.

It was the terror that bothered him. Fear didn't have any place in his scenes. There were Doms out there who loved to factor fear play into their dynamic, but Shelvin had never been drawn to it. Surprises — yes, and pumping adrenalin, but not the pounding sweat of distress.

"How long have you been into kink?" asked Shelvin. Elliot was staring at one of the couples, the sub bound to a St. Andrews cross and their Dom spanking their clothed ass with a small paddle. Elliot frowned at the display, turning away.

Impact looked like it was a big no-no on Elliot's checklist. He'd paled at the sound of a belt coming from the *Impact* room, which held more implements than most sadistic Doms could ever ask for. The paddle seemed to have the same response, and Elliot looked like he was a few moments away from being ill.

"Sweetheart, look at me," said Shelvin, doing his best to keep his promise to Hunter and keep his hands off a taken man. *I said 'hands' not 'hand'.* Releasing his arm, he touched Elliot's chin with one fingertip, drawing his attention. "Can we sit down? The presentation is going to start in just a minute."

Even as he said it, the lights flashed twice. Voices dropped into hushed tones and one last slap rang out before the Dom rushed to release his sub from the cross. They hurried to the nearest chair, the sub curling into his Dom's lap with tears tracking down his cheeks. *Fuck, that's hot.*

He didn't have to be into impact to enjoy the sight of a few tears.

Waiting for Elliot's nod, he led them to a set of folding chairs that were right by the other couple—close enough to hear the Dom's whispered words and the sub's quiet sobs. Elliot was rigid beside him as they took their seats, his wandering gaze focused on the couple.

Spreading his legs wide, Shelvin leaned against the back of the seat, subtly watching Elliot as he glanced around. Pulling his jacket from his shoulders, he draped it over the back of his chair. He would have taken it off sooner, but he'd already lost it once in the last week, and it was a classic at this point. It had been with him since graduation.

There were a few others close by that he knew, and a few fresh faces, too—none quite as fresh as Elliot's, though. He was finally starting to remember the names of the regulars, and there were a few subs about who he had scened with. Those had all moved on to other partners. *Not that I encouraged them in that at all.* He bit back a chuckle. He'd warned them that he wasn't a typical Dom.

"I don't understand," said Elliot, his voice low as he stared at the couple. "I would never want to be beaten like that, even if it meant being cherished after." He clenched his jaw, the muscle jumping in his cheek.

Some people *couldn't* get it, no matter how hard they tried to understand. Hunter seemed to be one of those guys, minus the effort of trying. Elliot, though? Shelvin hadn't decided if he was just a newbie off the street looking for a brief whirlwind, or someone who would fall in love with kink as soon as he tried it.

"He was cherished *as* he was beaten," said Shelvin, turning in his chair and crossing his legs so his calf rested against Elliot's knee. *Still not my hands.* "His Dom treasures and respects him for his submission. He must've done something to deserve a punishment—not our place to know what—but look at him now. Look at how fucking peaceful they are."

The sub's face was blissed out as he lay his head on his Dom's shoulder, even as the tracks of his tears dried. His ass had to be smarting, but he didn't look uncomfortable in the least. The Dom turned his head, placing a kiss on his submissive's cheek.

"See? Cherished." He could almost hear Elliot gulp as he lowered his gaze, his cheeks going pink. *So fucking shy.* "Now how about you answer a question, sweetheart. You here for a visit or are you here to stay?"

His voice cut off as the microphone squealed, and Clint stepped onto the stage. His hair was sticking up in a few directions, and Shelvin was pretty sure there was half a beer soaked into the left side of his shirt. It didn't take away from his attractiveness in the least.

Clint was the owner of the club and seemed to do everything to take care of the business, from what Shelvin had heard and seen. Trick had told him how Clint had helped him through the rocky start to his relationship with Nav, and every single member in the club had nothing but praise for him. Even though he was Shelvin's cousin, he was still a fucking enigma. Ex-nurse turned BDSM instructor? Life couldn't get any stranger.

"Thanks for coming tonight, folks. I'm hoping for lots of events and another open house this year on Halloween, so stay tuned about the mandatory dress code for that one. I can't wait to see some Shibari mummies."

There were a few cheers from the gathered crowd, who now occupied every seat. There were people standing, too, clogging the entryway with hushed anticipation. The air was close, sweat lingering, even with the air conditioning blowing from the ceiling vent near Shelvin's chair.

"Tonight I thought we would do something a little different, and have a demonstration of Dominance and submission. Derreck has volunteered his services as a Dom." He motioned to an ominous-looking man who was stepping up to the stage.

He gave the crowd a glower before turning a scowl on Clint. "Maddy volunteered me."

Shelvin chuckled, along with a few others in the crowd who weren't intimidated. He knew Derreck just well enough to know that he was mostly just quiet with a natural frown. It didn't matter to him that Derreck was insanely strong and buried bodies for a living.

"Maddy is his sub—the bartender," he whispered to Elliot, leaning as close as he dared. "He has Derreck wrapped around his little finger."

Elliot scrunched his forehead as he looked to the stage. Another man who Shelvin recognized as Mateo was stepping up the few stairs that led to the stage. He was a new submissive to the scene but was no less dedicated than any regulars Shelvin had met.

"But Maddy's the submissive," said Elliot, his words laced with confusion. "He can't just tell his Dom what to do."

"Not exactly," said Shelvin, wiggling and trying to get a touch more comfortable. He'd spent nearly all week hunched over a desk, and he was paying the price. The stain on his thumb from his pencil hadn't come off with three washes, either. "Derreck would do anything for him, including agreeing to do a demo, even though he hates public speaking and most people in general."

Derreck was one of the most devoted Doms Shelvin had ever seen, and Maddy rarely took advantage of that generosity. It made for a great balance to their dynamic.

Clint set his microphone in its stand, stepping back from the stage. The crowd parted for him as he rushed to the curtain, probably trying to get back to the tower of drink orders Maddy would have ready for him.

Derreck let out a sigh before grabbing the microphone for himself. "I'm not yelling, so I hope you can all hear me." He marched across the stage, barely looking at Mateo, who was trembling near the middle with a downcast gaze. "I'm supposed to let you guys ask us questions." He sent a glare out into the audience who had hushed as soon as he had started to speak.

Shelvin glanced around. *Is everyone seriously that terrified? Let's get this party started.* "Why isn't your submissive kneeling for you?" He shouted the question as loud as he could, waving his hand in the air so people would know who it was coming from. So what if he had a reputation as being a bit of a shit disturber. *I prefer to call myself fun.*

Derreck paused at the edge of the stage with his eyes narrowed before he glanced back to Mateo and growled. "Get on your knees."

Holy shit. Elliot trembled beside him, and Shelvin had to admit that he almost wanted to kneel, even if he was a Dom to his very core. A voice like that would make anyone tremble. Derreck was just that kind of guy, though.

"I don't usually have to ask," said Derreck, circling Mateo once with slow, sure strides. The long cord of the microphone wrapped around Mateo's kneeling form, but he didn't move from his submissive stance, his eyes downcast and locked on the stage.

The cord caught and pulled tight, and Derreck finally stopped. "If someone kneels so easily, is their submission even worth it?"

Shelvin let out a low whistle and whispered to Elliot. "I guess we are getting a side of humiliation and degradation, too."

Elliot shifted, just a tiny movement in his chair that spoke the world to Shelvin. *This can't get any better.* Why was it that all the good ones were already taken?

Derreck tugged the microphone cord lightly and the speaker squealed. Mateo flinched at the sound, quivering as his face flushed bright. His skin looked shiny under the lights of the stage, probably soaked with sweat. The room suddenly felt a whole lot warmer.

"If a submissive kneels before a Dominant who they don't even know, they might just get in the way," said Derreck, drumming his fingers along the base of the microphone. "Besides, kneeling isn't submission for everyone. Next question."

Mateo looked like he was getting close to crying, and Shelvin would have felt bad for him if he hadn't known that that was exactly what Mateo was in to. Derreck must have known it, too, because he was growing colder by the minute.

"Why is he being so mean?" Elliot asked quietly, leaning into Shelvin's side. He was warm and still trembling, sweat prickling on the skin of his arms. Inside his leather pants, he was hard, the impressive outline impossible to look away from.

Shelvin held up one finger, waiting for Derreck to answer the questions that someone else had been brave enough to yell. As soon as there was a lull, Shelvin shouted as loud as he could, his voice projecting in the large space. "What is submission like? That one is for

Mateo, by the way, because I'm sure Derreck can't answer that."

That question caused another glare and a few more chuckles. Shelvin grinned, running a hand through his hair as Elliot looked at him with wide eyes. "Stop provoking him."

"I'm not," Shelvin whispered back. "I'm getting answers to the questions that you're too shy to ask. I'll ask for you, sweetheart, so you don't have to."

Derreck turned to Mateo, passing him the microphone without a word. The wire was still wrapped tight around his kneeling form, but he was able to work one hand in front of him and grasp it. He breathed out, his voice shaky with obvious arousal.

"Submission is like…" Mateo trailed off, chewing his lip. "I really can't describe it perfectly, but it's like having someone take care of your soul. They look after you, nourish and support you, and when you're at your lowest, they bring you back up and make you whole. That's what it's like for me, but I haven't found a Dominant to call my own. I'm sure it's even better for someone like Maddy, who gets Derreck's soul in return."

Derreck swallowed, looking mildly uncomfortable before he took the microphone back and brought it to his lips. "Maddy's submission is the most beautiful thing in the world, and it makes my life complete. Mateo's submission is wonderful, but he won't give me his soul — not tonight." He grinned, with a look that showed off enough teeth to be called predatory. "Next question, and this time Shelvin stays fucking quiet."

"I just have one more." Shelvin waved his hand, barely staying in his seat. Derreck's glower was worth every bit of humiliation. "Why did a big bad Dom like yourself let your little sub rope you into something like this?"

Snickering, he turned to Elliot, raising one brow. He lowered his voice. "Wait for it. This will be a good one."

The grin on Derreck's lips looked like something a lion might have when he realized that he'd finally nabbed an antelope. It was as terrifying as it was appealing, and even Shelvin wasn't immune. The hall went silent, everyone wondering the exact same thing.

"Don't worry. I'll get him back for every minute of it, and trust me… He won't enjoy it nearly as much as I will."

Chapter Four

Elliot

He couldn't stop shaking. Just when he was certain that he'd finally gotten his limbs under control, his leg would start twitching a moment before his hands would begin to tremble. Longing and fear had never been quite so close together for him, but as much as the display on the stage confused him, he wondered what it would have been like to switch places with the sub.

The simple microphone cord was being used like a rope, wrapped tight around his shoulders and chest. Every time he twitched, Derreck would tug a little, sending him back into stillness. Sometimes, Derreck didn't even need to tug, but instead sent a look filled with something that Elliot didn't quite recognize.

"You want to get out of here?" asked Shelvin, leaning close enough to speak right into his ear. His hair brushed against Elliot's cheek, so soft and light in the heavy room.

He tried to tell himself that he'd hardly noticed Shelvin beside him, but he had watched Shelvin more than he'd watched the display on stage. There was something about his casual air that pulled Elliot in, calming him deep inside where he'd been empty for so long.

It's probably nothing.

Swallowing, he nodded, tearing his eyes away from the scene that had spiraled away from a Q and A to something *more*. Derreck couldn't have looked less turned on, but Mateo was flushed and obviously hard as Derreck prowled around him, throwing as many insults as he did praises.

He wanted to watch every moment, but at the same time, he couldn't stand to. They were both so brave and…happy. He couldn't hope to long for the same thing.

Slipping through the curtain was a breath of fresh air, goosebumps prickling on his skin as Shelvin looped their arms together again. Most of the people that had been in the bar before seemed to have moved to the main stage area, leaving one booth open and a couple of stools.

Hunter was on one of the stools, looking as bored as ever as someone next to him tried to grab his attention. Elliot couldn't help the flash of jealousy before he squashed it down. He knew Hunter was faithful, even if his gaze strayed occasionally. Whose didn't?

"So…thoughts?" asked Shelvin, a grin on his lips. His jacket was looped through his free arm, the scent of leather clinging to him. There was a lot of strength beneath his tight shirt and hidden beneath a casual grin. *Not that I noticed.*

"You're a shit stirrer," said Elliot, finally finding his feet a bit as the woozy feeling dissipated. "And that was terrifying, but…" He trailed off. He wasn't exactly sure what to say. Derreck had been scary at first, until Elliot had started to wonder if he was all talk.

But Maddy's marks. No, Derreck was for real. He must've been holding himself back. *But why?*

"Hot, right?" Shelvin sucked his teeth before looking back to the curtain. "If only I were a sub, I would be drooling after Derreck, just like all the other crazy ones, but he's taken. Maddy doesn't look it, but he's a psycho sonofabitch, and I mean that in the most endearing way possible."

He nodded to Maddy as they approached the bar, his hand still on Elliot's arm. The touch burned in the cool air, dragging something from deep within him. How long until Shelvin let go and went back to his own table?

"Maddy, you better watch out," said Shelvin, finally releasing Elliot and slipping onto a stool next to Hunter. "Your man has something planned for you."

Maddy flushed, the drink in his hand steady as his eyes lit up. "I know. Isn't it awesome?" He let out a sigh, closing his eyes as he tilted his head back. "Maybe he'll finally get over himself and mark me like I've been asking him to."

Something wrapped around Elliot's chest, tugging so tight that he could hardly breathe. He reached up, touching the spot, but there was nothing there. There could be something, though — a mark, a *brand* or something better. He'd never even considered it.

"But…" Elliot bit his tongue as he stared at Maddy's arms, not wanting to be rude. If Derreck hadn't marked him…

Maddy winked, turning to deliver another drink before he grasped the edge of his shirt, lifting it to show off a hint of his waist. He was *covered*. "That wasn't Derreck." He sent Elliot another wink.

Shelvin found him with his hand, tugging Elliot until he leaned close to his stool. "Like I said, they are equally fucking crazy. Don't judge, though, or I'll throw you out on your ass myself."

"I wouldn't— I wasn't," Elliot stammered, staring after Maddy. He'd never seen someone with such rich confidence that they couldn't be anything but beautiful. Maddy seemed to know exactly what he wanted and had grasped it with both hands. *If only.*

"It took him a long time to be that comfortable around other people," said Shelvin softly. "We could all be so lucky as to have someone like Derreck to see us through that." He released his grip and Elliot stumbled back, catching himself on the edge of the bar. A gaze burned into him from the other side. *Hunter.*

His husband looked terribly unimpressed, and his eyes were pinched as if he were seconds away from storming out on his own. But he had *stayed* for him. *Because he loves me, you dolt.*

"Can we go?" Hunter asked, shrugging off the attention from the man on his other side who was still trying to talk to him. Elliot was surprised more men hadn't flocked to his side, basking in the breathtaking beauty that belonged to him.

"Yeah." Elliot looked down to the floor that was slightly sticky. His shoe made a terrible noise as he lifted his foot to shuffle uncomfortably. "Thanks, Shelvin, for showing me around."

The words were like bland toast in his mouth and just as unsatisfying. Somehow, he knew that once he stepped out of the door, he was never coming back. If things were different, but… No. It was the last glimpse he would have of something so wonderful.

"No problem, sweetheart," said Shelvin, despite Hunter's renewed glare. He reached into his shirt pocket, plucking something from within and passing it Elliot's way. "You have any more questions, you give me a ring. Don't text me, though. I hate that shit."

"Let's go," Hunter snarled, grabbing Elliot's arm and dragging him a step away from the bar.

A moment before it was out of reach, Elliot grasped the card, bringing it to his chest. It was black with gold lettering, an engraved white building along the right. Shelvin's first name was on it along with three different phone numbers, including his cell.

Elliot's heart fluttered as he tucked it away in his pocket that was almost too tight for his wallet. He didn't want to chance losing the card in his weak grip.

"Come on," said Hunter, pulling him through the curtain and out of the door before Elliot could even look back. He could *feel* Shelvin looking at him, his gaze like ice against the fury of his blush.

"That was ridiculous." Hunter started laughing as soon as the outside door closed behind them. The street was deserted except for one man along the other side of the street who looked their way. "I have never seen so many fucked-up people who are so full of themselves. Un-real." Hunter turned to him, scowling through his laugh. "And did you know that three people had the audacity to come talk to me? Like I would want to have anything to do with them. The last guy wouldn't shut up. I can't believe you left me there while you went exploring. We should have just left."

Cold seized his gut with each of his husband's words, his limbs growing heavier until he could barely lift his feet. *I guess I'm in the group with those fucked-up people.* Was it bad to be proud of that fact? At least he had stood out to one person and maybe even made a new friend.

"What?" asked Hunter his expression morphing into shock as he looked at Elliot's face. "You can't tell me that you enjoyed that."

What does he see?

"No," Elliot said. No, he couldn't tell Hunter that, because there was no way he would understand. *I loved every moment of it…even the ones that were terrifying.*

"Thank God, because I am *not* going back to that place. I feel like I need a shower, or a bath—a long one." Hunter grabbed his keys, unlocking their car with the click of a button. "Maybe you can join me?"

Elliot realized in that moment that he was hard, so very hard and squished in his leather pants that didn't breathe well. Every drop of sweat was crushed against his skin, making him slide with each movement. He had been hard almost the whole time, his cock throbbing to the pulsing beat of the club that had filled him to the brim as if it were alive.

If Hunter noticed, he didn't say a thing.

The drive home was nearly silent, and Elliot stared out of the window, catching snippets of grass that were just starting to turn green again. There were a few clumps of snow that remained where huge parking lots had been plowed into a single spot.

Early in his childhood, he would have been out there with his brothers, climbing the tallest hill and throwing himself down on a homemade crazy carpet that had almost broken his neck once.

The good times had lasted until the moment his parents had passed. After that, everything had changed and had become darker than the heaps of gray slush that were all that remained of winter's chill.

Hunter pulled off his coat as they entered their condo, tossing his key in the bowl before hanging it on his hook. He'd had the cutest ideas when he'd picked the condo out for them, dreaming up a hook for each of their coats with a monogrammed stencil just above it. Elliot had hung them with a grin on his lips, so hopeful of their next steps together as a married couple.

"I'll start the bath for us, baby, and I'll see you in a minute." Hunter disappeared around the corner, the shuffling of fabric following him through their home. When the bathroom door squealed shut, Elliot was plunged into silence.

But it wasn't silent. His heart was beating so loud that his pulse thrummed in his ears, whooshing to the point that he wondered if he was about to pass out. He grabbed his coat hook, clinging to the E as his vision wavered.

Never going back. That had been it—his single journey into the kink world and it had been so short that it felt like it had just lasted minutes. And Hunter had *hated it.* Hunter—his husband and the only person he trusted in the world. Where was he supposed to go from here?

His pants were too tight and damp, his cock almost pruned from all the moisture held against it for so long. The leather was ugly, too, clinging to every unattractive bit on his legs and squashing his junk so it looked as if there was just nothing there. He couldn't even remember how he'd scrounged up the courage to wear the things out of the house.

Ripping his spring jacket from his shoulders, he hung it on his hook, turning away as it slipped to the floor. His shirt was over his head seconds later, followed by his pants and underwear that peeled away from his skin like a piece of melted cellophane. He grabbed the business card from his pants pocket, staring at it for a moment before he tucked it back away, out of sight.

"You coming?" Hunter's voice cut through the condo like a beacon, tugging him back into awareness.

Elliot shivered as he turned back to the hall, his naked skin prickling in the cold. They kept their home cool in the spring, using blankets to try to conserve energy. It felt as if he could almost see his breath if he puffed deep enough.

He stopped, lifting his coat off the ground and rehanging it next to Hunter's, and pausing to fix the sleeve that had flipped the wrong way out. He straightened his shoes next, lining them up and sweeping the bit of gravel that had escaped the tray in his rush. Folding his clothes neatly, he held them against his chest, walking to the kitchen and dumping them straight into the trash.

He tied the bag, walking it back to the door so he could take it out as soon as he'd cleaned up, so Hunter would never see what he'd done. A fresh white bag in the garbage, and it were as if nothing had happened.

"I thought you got lost," said Hunter as Elliot stepped into a cloud of steam that greeted him in the bathroom. Heat prickled against his skin, but it did nothing to actually warm him.

"I did for a little bit, but I'm back now," said Elliot, forcing a grin on his lips. Hunter chuckled as if it were a joke and not the truth. To him, perhaps it was. Hunter had the terrible habit of seeing exactly what he wanted to see, even if it were the best or worst of a person.

Three candles glowed in the bathroom, the oversized tub frothy with bubbles and steaming in the relatively cooler air. The mirror was fogged, and Elliot couldn't have been more grateful. He had no desire to look at himself anytime soon and see the empty stare reflected back at him.

He would just have to find other ways to keep himself fulfilled. Trying new things always did it for a while, and he could suggest mixing up a few things in the bedroom. Or maybe the best route would be to put things in the bedroom on pause until he could get the images out of his head. Hunter deserved better than that.

Slipping into the water, Elliot let out a groan at the temperature. It was like fire against his chilled skin, a flush instantly rising to his cheeks. Hunter sighed, leaning against the little inflatable pillow that he had insisted on buying when he'd had the tub installed.

"Get comfy. I want to snuggle," said Hunter, his eyes barely half-open.

Elliot moved so he was against his own pillow, wincing at the chill of the edge of the tub as it touched him. Hunter was there in moments, leaning against him and giving Elliot the entirety of his weight to catch. He did it with practiced ease, lifting Hunter so his head rested against his shoulder, his face upturned to the ceiling.

"This is so nice. You take such good care of me, baby," said Hunter, letting out a contented sigh. He moved his hands to Elliot's legs, slowly wandering upward.

"Of course." Elliot kissed the top of Hunter's head, the hair sticking to his lips. Wiping his lips with the back of his hand, he grimaced as a few bubbles managed to slip inside his mouth.

He'd been taking care of Hunter for as long as they'd been together, and he loved him with all of his heart. *If only...*

"I could stay like this forever." Hunter rolled in his grip, resting his cheek against Elliot's collar. "Don't let me fall asleep, baby." He let out a yawn that was entirely too cute, one foot peeking out of the bubbles as he stretched.

"I won't," Elliot mumbled. He leaned his head against the pillow, trying to let himself sink into the warmth and contentment that was poking at him like a cattle prod. It was just out of his reach.

"You okay?" Hunter asked, his voice a soft grumble. He moved his hand to Elliot's chest, wet bubbles dripping down his pec.

"Yeah." Elliot glanced to the side at the cavernous bathroom that his friends loved to tease him about. Hunter and himself both had good jobs and a heck of a balance in their bank account, but he had grown up with almost nothing. He'd gone from sharing a bathroom to one large enough to host a party in, and it still rubbed him the wrong way sometimes.

He sniffed, bringing his hand to his cheek when he felt something rolling down it. His dry fingers that he'd rested on the lip of the tub, came away wet. Blinking in confusion, he stared at the moisture for a moment before bringing it to his lips. It was salty and fresh like he'd always imagined the ocean would be.

Wiping both cheeks harshly, he plunged his hands into the tub, washing all evidence and cupping Hunter to him. His husband was asleep, his soft snores like gentle music that would keep him awake in the dark. It was worse when he was on his back, but on his side, it wasn't so bad.

Hunter's dark hair was spread over his chest, each strand like a path in the darkness. He was beautiful and everything that Elliot would ever need. *I'm sure of it.*

He looked to the ceiling fan that was slowly rattling away as the steam started to lessen. The bath cooled until Hunter was the warmest thing in the room. Elliot's core was still cold, though—frozen through with no sign of changing any time soon.

"I'll be fine," he whispered to himself, clutching Hunter closer. "I won't lose you."

Chapter Five

Shelvin

Shelvin glared at the sketch, trying to figure out where the hell he had gone wrong. The structure looked solid and attractive, with more windows than any engineer would strictly approve of, but something was niggling in the back of his mind, telling him that if it was ever built it would last three seconds before it collapsed.

Bringing his pencil to his lips, he chomped down on the eraser, indenting the metal with his teeth. Rubber and aluminum rolled over his tongue, filling his senses along with his freshly shaved wood and thick paper. His fingertips were smudged dark, leaving little traces everywhere he touched.

Ah, there! He scratched in another load-bearing wall, then thought better of it, erasing it and putting in a huge I-beam instead. If he were lucky, he'd find the budget for something more rustic — like a tree trunk's worth of wood — but he'd keep it metal for now.

Scratching at his eyes, he leaned back in his chair, lifting his arms over his head and letting out a back-breaking stretch. He'd been oddly focused on his work for the past week, even if his mind had been tempted to wander to a memory of pretty eyes and sinful lips. If he fixated on every newbie who caught his eye, he'd never get any work done.

His phone chimed with an incoming text, and he grunted with irritation, deleting it without bothering to look at what it said. Clint had texted him twice in the last hour, but he should have known better. Shelvin *hated* texts. There was no feeling to them, no enthusiasm, just blank letters on an empty screen.

Tossing his pencil, he reached for his jacket, locking up his office and trekking to his car. He squinted at the light as he stepped outside, honestly surprised that the sun was still hanging out in the sky. He'd kept the black-out curtains in his office drawn to protect his work from the sun's rays, and he didn't exactly keep steady hours.

Slipping into his car, he started the engine, heading toward the club before the car had warmed. He had three of them, so he wasn't exactly worried about hurting one because there were always two more to replace it.

Honestly, he was growing bored of the shiny gold exterior of his current Audi, anyway. Maybe it was time to mix it up and go for something blue…like one of the newer Jaguars, although, he wasn't exactly in love with the look of them lately.

Traffic was light, and he distantly wondered what day it was as he pulled onto the mostly deserted street that housed Unkinked. The Office Depot across from the club looked like it was just closing down for the day, but it couldn't have been much past noon. Saturday maybe?

He scratched at the stubble on his chin before ducking his head and taking a whiff of his pits. Maybe he should have called instead of showing up to the club with a few days' worth of growth and lacking deodorant.

Shrugging, he pulled up to the curb, parking right in front of the door. There were a dozen or so cars spotted along the street, but that was nothing new. For a fairly exclusive club, it was always hopping. He'd gone through a bunch of hoops before Clint had given him his own set of keys and a pass card to use the private rooms, and they were family.

Not that he had a sub to use them with. There weren't many subs who didn't expect absolute devotion and appreciated Shelvin putting his work ahead of them. *Meh, their loss.*

Unlocking the door with his own key card, he gave the bouncer a wave before ducking through the curtain and heading to the bar. Maddy was mixing drinks and handing them out with a touch of a wince and a definite limp. He smiled when he looked up to see Shelvin. They hadn't known each other for long, but Shelvin counted Maddy among his friends.

"Derreck followed through with his promise?" Shelvin drawled, leaning against the bar. A wave of body odor reached his nose, and he quickly tucked his arms closer. It helped…a little.

Maddy seemed to brighten, his shoulders going straighter and his eyes shining. His grin was so wide that Shelvin could almost see every tooth.

"Yes," said Maddy, giggling a little as he poured another drink and handed it to the last lady waiting at the bar. "Still feeling it, and it's been three days. He's the best." He let out a wistful sigh. "You look like shit, though. I haven't seen you since you got turned down the other night."

"I didn't get turned down." Shelvin rubbed the back of his head, tucking his arm back by his side quickly as he got another whiff. "I've just been working on a project, and I lost track of time." Which was totally reasonable for him, seeing as it happened with almost every project he worked on — except for the boring stuff, because he could do that in his sleep.

"Uh-huh. What day do you think it is this time? I can smell from here that you haven't showered in a few."

Shelvin fought to keep the smirk off his face, leaning against the bar as he threw out his attempt to be presentable.

Maddy must have been put through the wringer to have such a confidence boost. Half the time he was a shy, polite little thing, but when he got in a mood, he could be downright sassy.

"Saturday," Shelvin said with every bit of confidence that he didn't have. "One-hundred-percent sure."

Maddy let out a sigh, shaking his head as he filled a glass with what looked like Sprite. "It's Sunday, Shelvin. This is on the house. Drink up before you pass out from dehydration again."

Okay, now that just isn't fair. He'd only passed out once with Maddy present, and he was pretty sure that had been from heat exhaustion — or maybe regular exhaustion. "Clint was trying to get a hold of me. Where is he at?"

Maddy motioned over his shoulder. "He's in the office grumbling about something he won't tell me about right now. Try to get it out of him so I don't have to sic the Dungeon Masters on him. He looked like he was about to pull his hair out."

Lovely. Shelvin grabbed his drink, knocking it back in three long swallows before ducking around to the office. There was a short hall, then the door, which was shut tight and locked. He tapped once with his knuckles and the grumbling on the other side paused.

Clint looked terrible when he finally opened the door. His hair was standing straight up, and he was in a ripped tank top that exposed a strip of the scars along his belly from an extensive set of burns. The scruff on his cheeks was worse than Shelvin's, too.

But it was his bloodshot eyes that really concerned Shelvin. Either he was finally submitting to exhaustion or Clint had been crying on the other side of the locked door.

Slipping into the office, Shelvin shut the door behind him, flicking on the overhead light instead of trying to see by the lamp alone. He hadn't seen the office in its original state, but he'd heard what Maddy had done to organize the place.

Clint seemed to have had second thoughts, though, with scattered papers on nearly every surface and a few on the floor. Shelvin knelt to grab one, squinting at the tiny lettering. *Ah shit.*

"You're getting fined?" asked Shelvin, flipping the paper the right way when he realized that he was reading upside down. It was on a crisp letterhead that only the government seemed to be able to afford. Shelvin's hackles immediately rose. He'd had his fair share of shitty dealings with city hall.

Clint grabbed the paper from him, tossing it on the desk with a few others before crossing his arms. His lower lip trembled, his eyes suddenly shiny.

Shelvin swallowed, his hands twitching as he fought to keep from reaching out. The last thing Clint needed right now was a hug.

"I-it was the open house. We were overcapacity. I knew that, but I still let everyone in here, knowing how fucking dangerous it could have been. If something had gone wrong—" Clint cleared his throat, cutting himself off.

He didn't need to finish because Shelvin's thoughts had been along the same line. The place had been *packed*, and if something had gone wrong, like a fire, then there was no way that everyone would have made it out okay.

He could imagine the same thoughts going through Clint's mind, only Clint had lived it before.

"You need money for the fine? I can help out with that. And next time we can have Barry count everyone as they come in and make them wait outside once we're full," said Shelvin. That's how they'd done it back home.

"Yeah, like I'm going to have someone stand outside in a leather thong and pasties. We never should have started the open houses in the first place, but I don't have the heart to just cancel the next one, either. So many people have found us, and they've fit right in like they've always been here." Clint rubbed the back of his head, his hair standing even straighter.

"Like me," said Shelvin with a shrug. He'd had an in, but it still hadn't been easy to get a membership. Being Clint's cousin hadn't made the background check any easier.

"Or like Nav and Maddy, or half a dozen others out there that are like family to me now. I don't think Unkinked would be what it is today without Maddy."

It was a rock and had been for a long time for a lot of people.

"I've already heard a few loud whispers from around town, too. The more public we get, the more people don't like the idea of us being here." Clint leaned against the desk, squashing a few of the papers that had been leaning over the edge. "Sorry, Shelvin. I didn't mean to vent. I try not to let it get to me, but with this fine, and how fucking reckless I've been... Sorry."

Shelvin shrugged, grabbing the nearest chair and sliding into it. "Vent all you want. I've never seen you pissed off before, and it's actually kind of fun. If I poke you a little, will I get to see the dragon?" In this case, he didn't mean Clint's cock, although he'd heard it was a nice one. Clint was hot and built with a mysterious edge that only one had managed to crack. Too bad he was Shelvin's cousin.

Clint chuckled, a grin finally tugging at his lips. "You should have seen Derreck get to work a few days ago if you wanted to see a dragon. He hasn't scened in public for years, and *fuck* was it good. I have a whole new respect for Maddy."

Aww dammit.

"Anyway, thanks for coming. Did you read my text?" asked Clint.

Shelvin shot him a glare that hopefully conveyed exactly how he felt about the damn texts. Text messages should have been reserved for anyone under thirty, which was not him.

"Of course you didn't," said Clint, apologetically. "Sorry... I always forget you're a one-hundred-year-old man trapped in a forty-year-old body." He winked, scratching at his chest where one of the rips in his shirt was. "I need you to build me something."

"Uh." Shelvin blinked, rubbing his fingers together where they were still stained from the pencil. "Like build-build or design-build? Cause I can barely use a hammer anymore. Your nursing skills will be required."

The last time he'd tried to build something, it had been a DIY desk with simple instructions that he couldn't have possibly messed up. Three hours later and with a broken finger, he'd given up and called up a friend. They'd had it up in twenty minutes, and they hadn't nearly chopped their hand off with the circular saw, either.

"I'm thinking something big…like *epic* big," said Clint, holding his arms wide. "I'm imagining like a mansion with different themed wings and a swimming pool out back for nice days in the summer. I've already got the land that I inherited when Ross' parents passed, and it's just sitting empty. We could do outdoor activities there, and so much more. It would be awesome."

What the hell is he talking about? "I can design you a house like that easy peasy, but it's not going to be cheap. I'm not building it, though. Leave that for the real experts. How many bedrooms do you want?" He should have brought a notepad with him. He grabbed a paper off the ground instead and a pen off the desk, scribbling a few notes on the blank back.

"Don't need any bedrooms—or maybe just one. I guess I could give up my old condo and move in there. It would make things a lot easier." Clint tapped his chin, seemingly rolling something over. "Or we could have a few so there is a safe place for couples to wind down after a scene."

"You want people sceneing in your house?" Shelvin scribbled a few more notes, pausing as the pen stopped working. "To each their own and all that, but that seems a little out there, even for you. Do you want me to design a floating bed for the pool so people can fuck in there, too?" He chuckled before he realized that that was actually a pretty neat idea.

How the hell would I keep people from tipping over, though? Bedrails? He scribbled the pen until it started working again before sketching a quick mock-up.

Clint let out a groan, rubbing his face vigorously. "I don't want a house, Shelvin. I want you to build me a new place for Unkinked...one that's not in the middle of town. I want a place where people can actually go outside and still feel like themselves. I want to have more than just a few playrooms, an open play area and a bar that's sticky, no matter how many times I mop. I want a home away from home for my friends and family—people like you and people that I'm just getting to know."

The pen stuttered to a dotted halt, and Shelvin jerked his head up.

"You're going to close down Unkinked, aren't you?" His stomach dropped as Clint's face turned ashen. *Fuck no.* "Clint, this is one of the coolest kink clubs around, and I've seen them all over the world. This place is perfection—or as close as someone can hope to get to it." It wasn't just the rooms or the setup, but the community itself.

"Then I'll cut off new memberships instead, and open houses will be a thing of the past. No more newbies unless someone gives up their membership." Clint pursed his lips before dragging a hand through his hair, his eyes suddenly looking shiny again.

And that was shit, too, especially when a pair of beautiful brown eyes were still doing their best to haunt Shelvin. No newbies meant no one like Elliot for Doms like himself. And if someone really needed Unkinked as a second home, they would be shit out of luck until someone else fell out of the lifestyle.

"I don't have a choice." Clint dropped his voice into a whisper. "The guy who owns the building won't renew my lease. He was okay with it when it was a smaller group of us, but things are getting bigger. And now with this fine…" He let out a sigh. "I build a new place or I shut things down…permanently."

No wonder he'd been crying. Unkinked was Clint's dream and probably one of the last things he had that he and his husband had built together. Losing it would mean losing everything.

"Well, fuck, why didn't you say that in the first place?" Shelvin retrieved the paper that he'd dropped, double-checking to make sure his pen was still working. "Let me finish up the project I'm working on now, then you'll be next in line. It's gonna be expensive, Clint. We're talking in the millions for what you described." He waited for the cringe, but Clint only nodded slowly.

"I know. Don't worry about the cost. I'll use every penny I've got to make sure that my kinksters always have a safe place to go."

Shelvin let out a breath, rubbing his eye where his lashes were clinging together. He couldn't do this emotional shit when he was so tired. When was the last time he'd even slept? *Meh, there are worse things out there.*

"On a lighter note, did you see that newbie I picked out the other night?" asked Shelvin, tucking the few notes that he had in his pocket. He'd ask for more details once they'd both had time to rest.

Clint grinned, his eyes sparkling again for the first time. "Brown eyes, dark hair and an accessory named Hunter? Yeah, I saw and heard. You are hopeless, Shelvin."

Shelvin sighed, throwing his arms out dramatically. "But perfect otherwise, right? Damn. All the good ones are taken. Well, except you, Clint, of course."

Clint snorted, crumpling the closest paper and tossing it at Shelvin's head. "Uh-huh. You know I'm taken. Unkinked is my bitch and my baby."

"Yeah," Shelvin grinned right back, dropping his voice into a growl. "But when's the last time it made you beg?"

The grin dropped from Clint's face faster than Shelvin could blink. *Thought so.* Clint had barely scened since his husband had passed, and he was treading on thin ice.

Tossing the pen back toward the desk, Shelvin pushed his way out of his chair. His bones creaked as he stood, and he let out a wince as his hip gave a pang. Thirty-nine had been great, but forty was apparently the limit for his joints.

"Take care of yourself, Clint. I'll call you when I'm ready to start the design."

He slipped out of the door, shutting it softly behind him. Maddy poked his head into the hallway, raising one eyebrow in question. Shelvin could have hugged him. Without Maddy, Clint would have sunk months before. Shelvin would have offered his own assistance, but he had to sleep *sometime.*

"Nothing to worry about, Maddy. Clint's just pouting that nobody wants to see his dragon." He sent him a wink as he pushed his way toward the door. The first stop was his shower, then food. As hungry as he was, he wasn't sure if he could stand his stink for another moment. That, and he wasn't quite sure when he'd eaten last, so it probably couldn't wait.

Chapter Six

Elliot

He slammed the door, wincing when the picture frame on the wall jumped. Grabbing it before it could fall, he closed his eyes, taking a deep breath. Energy bubbled under his skin, even after a full work week and four nearly sleepless nights. He had to struggle to keep from tossing the picture frame out of the fucking door.

The jacket hook stared back at him, the cursive 'E' ugly and tacky compared to the rest of the condo. Maybe he'd grab his drill and take care of it, too. Just another thing to throw in the trash.

The 'E' was worse than the cream-colored walls and the accent piece next to the kitchen that was built of glass shards twisted into the shape of a unicorn. Every time he walked by it, he would catch a thousand glimpses of himself, and they were just as ugly as the damned beast.

Even now, his image stared back at him, broken and shattered as he kept his breathing calm. *In and out.* The black bags under his eyes, that his coworkers had been commenting on throughout the week, looked even darker than they had in the morning. He'd started to carry eyedrops to cover up the endless tracks of red lines against his sclera, but it looked like it was time for another dose.

"Hey, baby, I'm in the office finishing up. I'll be out soon."

Elliot turned toward his husband's voice. Hunter's tone was so chipper that it nearly yanked him straight out of his mood. The vase of daisies on the table did the rest to send him off-kilter, leaving him emptier than ever. The little flowers were his favorite, and Hunter loved surprising him with them. Any other time, he'd grab one and bring it to his nose, breathing in the scent of freshness and freedom.

But not today.

He looked down at his hands, his keys still clutched in his fingers. He'd forgotten to put them in the small bowl that Hunter kept by the front door. It was an accent piece, too — a blue glass dolphin with a dip near its head that was just large enough for two sets of keys. He couldn't remember where they'd gotten it.

Do I even care?

"How was your day?" Hunter asked, his voice still a distant shout from the office. Even though Elliot rarely worked from home, they still had separate offices for the times when inspiration inexplicably struck — or when a problem was too pressing to wait.

Hunter had organized his like a picture, each book and paper having its space. Elliot could imagine him sitting on his soft leather chair, his feet propped up on the little exercise machine that he kept underneath his desk.

"Fine," Elliot mumbled, tossing his keys on the kitchen table. The newspaper was folded open on his spot, his favorite page marked for him. He grabbed it, glancing at the real estate section that he loved to browse. He had no intention of moving any time soon, but he enjoyed looking at other people's work.

Today the black-and-white images didn't hold his interest. *Too cheap. Too small. Too ugly.*

"Hey." Hunter was standing in the doorway, his long hair free around his shoulders. His loose T-shirt slunk below his collar, displaying a fine dusting of chest hair that was only a touch thicker than the hair on his arms. "I didn't hear you answer. Your day was okay?"

Elliot nodded, dropping the paper and numbly moving to the cupboard. His day had been the same as every other day for the past two weeks as he'd tried to avoid his husband without looking like he was.

He'd never been hornier in his life, but as he'd made love to Hunter after their bath together two weeks before, he'd realized something. His cock had shriveled inside the tight heat that he'd always loved, and he'd turned away, giving Hunter one last kiss before he'd retreated.

He couldn't do it. As much as he'd promised himself and Hunter that he would, he'd hit a wall that took every remaining ounce of determination from him. He couldn't pretend to be someone he wasn't anymore.

His hands trembled as he looked at them. They felt like they belonged to someone else — someone who knew what the hell was happening in their life.

He hadn't gone so long without coming since before puberty, and it only seemed to make things worse.

Even now he had a semi, and he had no fucking clue as to why.

Hunter sidled up behind him, wrapping his arms around his chest and placing a kiss on Elliot's shoulder. Elliot fought down the flinch, gripping the edge of the countertop to steel his nerves. *It's just a kiss. I love kisses.*

"I just need a glass of water," said Elliot, relaxing the moment Hunter withdrew. He hadn't even realized how tense he was, until suddenly he went lax, like pulling a plug from an overfilled sink.

"Okay," Hunter said quietly. "I thought maybe we could go out for dinner tonight on a date. It's been so long since we've done something romantic, and I wanted to treat you. Dinner, a back rub, then let me take care of you tonight. You seem so stressed, baby."

Well, that plan failed. He'd tried so fucking hard to act normally, and he'd blown that, too. Elliot filled the glass, bringing it to his lips to avoid turning around and answering. He wasn't even thirsty, but he topped it up a second time, bringing it back to his lips. Hunter was still there. He could feel him, just beyond his reach, and hear the hushed sounds of his breaths.

"Unless you want to stay home?" asked Hunter, even quieter. There was something else in his tone — something so terribly sad that Elliot *had* to look.

Hunter was chewing his lower lip, his eyes downcast and shiny with unshed tears. There were bags under his eyes, too, probably partially hidden beneath a layer or two of concealer. Elliot loved him in a bit of makeup that enhanced his masculine looks but added a softer edge that brought out the beauty of his soul.

"I love you," said Elliot, setting the glass down and dropping his hands to his sides. He couldn't even hold his husband. He wanted him so badly, but he wasn't sure what was real and what was a figment of his imagination anymore.

Guilt flooded him a second later. Hunter was *enough*. He just needed to convince himself of that fact. Everything else was just an extra.

Hunter blinked, the first tear rolling down his cheek. He was beautiful, even when he cried, his cheeks remaining pale and his makeup staying exactly where he'd placed it.

"Is there someone else?" asked Hunter softly, clutching his hands together and staring down at them. There was a hangnail on his thumb that he must've torn, the skin still red and raw. Usually they were manicured without so much as a cuticle out of place.

"No." It was flat, even to his own ears. There wasn't someone else, but sometimes he wished there was. The little thoughts that weren't halted by guilt snuck in and whispered terrible things to him when he was on the verge of sleep. They made him wonder what it would be like if there was someone who could give him everything that Hunter couldn't.

"Okay." Hunter sniffed, rubbing his nose with the back of his hand. "Is there anything I can do? I love you so much, but I feel like I'm losing you." He leaned against the table, his breath rushing out of him as if he could barely keep upright. "It's been so long since you've been yourself, but lately you're a completely different person. You don't sleep, you barely eat and you can't bear to touch me. Tell me what to do, *please*. I can fix this—fix us."

And that's the problem, isn't it? Elliot pursed his lips, nearly shaking with the anger that simmered just under his skin. He'd tried to tell Hunter what he needed, but he'd been dragged through the dirt instead. He couldn't tell Hunter what to do anymore. In fact, there wasn't a single thing that he was willing to dictate at the moment. The entirety of their relationship rested on Hunter's shoulders.

Which just wasn't fair.

"I…" Elliot looked to the crisp tiles that chilled his feet even through his socks. They'd always been cold, and he wondered how long he could press his bare skin to them before he had to pull away. How uncomfortable would they be against his knees?

"Fuck, just tell me, Elliot. This silent treatment has gone on long enough." His voice caught on the edge of a sob. Hunter *never* cried, and he rarely swore, either. Elliot had pushed him to the edge of his control, apparently.

"I can't do this anymore," said Elliot, clutching the counter as his knees trembled. He was going to fall, but he needed to hang on for just a moment longer. Hunter crumpled before his eyes, grabbing at his chest as tears rolled down his cheeks. "I can't keep pretending to be somebody that I'm not. I've tried for years, but it's dragging me down, and I think I'm at my breaking point." Elliot grasped his hair, tugging a few strands free. He was probably beyond his breaking point. The best thing he could do for both of them was come clean. "Hunter, I'm a bottom." There it was, his second secret that he'd discovered shortly after his first coming out. "More than that, though. I'm submissive, too. Being on top and even making decisions in the bedroom is really hard for me."

"But…" Hunter swallowed, wiping his cheeks with the back of his hand, "I don't understand. I thought you were cheating on me, but you just don't want to fuck me anymore?"

Fuck, he doesn't understand at all. Elliot rubbed his chest where it ached the most. Nothing helped lately.

"It's not just the sex," said Elliot quietly. "I could fuck you, but only if you told me to—*ordered* me to. I want you to put me on my knees and make me submit to you, get rough with me, tell me what to do, then take care of me." He was shaking, his teeth chattering as everything came pouring out.

"So you want someone else? Someone that treats you different than I do?" The tears were back, only this time they weren't quite as pretty. "I love you so much, baby."

Fuck. It was now or never. He could bury his needs again and see how long he could last until he snapped. The only alternative was to end his relationship with the man who he loved more than anything in the world.

"I want to go back to Unkinked." He crossed his arms, wondering if he could somehow hide behind them. A tiny bit of hope flared in his belly—the last strand that he had left.

Hunter squinted, his lips turning into a frown and his nose scrunching up. He didn't have to say a thing for Elliot to know his answer.

"Why would you want to go back to that place? It's disgusting! I don't understand—"

"Then maybe we should talk to someone who understands." Elliot cut him off, his rage boiling over. He grabbed at his half-empty glass, dumping the rest into the sink and tossing it into the dishwasher. It *thunk*ed off the back of the machine, probably cracking from the force. "Shelvin understood me. I talked to him for two minutes and he already knew exactly what I needed, and you sat there the whole time bitching and complaining about how *disgusting* I am."

He let out a shuddering breath, scrubbing his face before pushing past Hunter. His husband flinched. Grabbing his keys from the table, Elliot stormed toward the front door. "I'm going back to work. My phone is dead, so don't bother calling."

He'd drained it looking through pictures. It was the same thing all over again. He tried to catch little snippets of a life he'd never have, longing and breaking at the same time.

"Elliot." Hunter called out to him. "Elliot, stop right now. You are *not* walking out on me. Sit down and we'll talk this through like adults."

Elliot whirled on him, Grabbing the wall when the room spun. Exhaustion weighed on his limbs until it felt like he was breathing through molasses. He couldn't recall ever being so tired. "You don't want to listen, Hunter. Be honest. You just want me to go back to being the way I was and ignore every problem between us, hoping they will just disappear on their own."

"Sit down." Hunter patted one of the kitchen chairs, taking a seat himself. His voice was low and calm, his tears all but dried. Elliot had never understood how he could control his emotions so well when the smallest things would send his own mind into a spiral.

It was probably the only order Hunter would ever give him. Swallowing, he gave in to the fight that he wasn't strong enough to make. He dragged himself into the chair, sitting down heavily. His hands trembled, the keys jingling as he dropped them back on the tabletop.

"How long have you felt like this?" asked Hunter softly, folding his hands in front of him. His gaze was steady, only a bit of redness and moisture on his cheeks the evidence of his tears. It was the same kind of look he would get in a meeting, staring at his computer screen as he got ready to make his stand.

Sighing, Elliot glared at the daisies, wondering if the flowers held the answers. There was a time in his life when he'd asked himself the same thing. When was he going to find that piece that always seemed to be missing? Then, he'd met Hunter, and it hadn't seemed to matter as much. *Until it did.*

"As long as I can remember. Maybe even before I knew I was gay," he answered just as quietly. His rage was gone, leaving an empty shell behind. Hunter let out a small sound beside him, his shock evident.

"I wish you would have told me, but now we can work together to find a solution."

Always the problem solver. Elliot both loved and hated him for it.

"We can't. You can't just pretend to be something you're not, Hunter." He scratched at the table, his bitten nails dull against the smooth surface.

"You did." Hunter reached for him, lacing their fingers together. "But that's not what I meant. Talk to me and help me understand what you need. I'll do everything in my power to give it to you."

Elliot looked from the marble countertop to the stark white cupboards and the shiny backsplash. Hunter had picked out every bit of it and he had just smiled and nodded. Maybe there was hope for them yet.

Decorating a condo is a far cry from being a Dom.

"It's hard to explain." Elliot scratched his cheek as he flushed. It was almost impossible for him to put into words what Shelvin had seemed to *know.* "Make me submit."

"I don't know what that means. Just with sex?" Hunter traced his thumb over the back of Elliot's hand, sending a shiver over his skin. Elliot shook his head, biting his lip. "How?"

"Just..." He trailed off. It had seemed so easy when he'd pictured it in his head, but now he wasn't so sure. It wasn't something that he could plan ahead and follow through with. And how did he know that Hunter's helpful tone wouldn't become ignorant dismissal as soon as he said it? "I don't know. I'm sorry, Hunt."

"It's okay." Hunter raised their hands, placing a kiss on Elliot's. "This is new for both of us, and maybe you're right. Maybe we should give that guy a call, and he could help us with this — help explain it so I can be there for you in every way you need. You kept his card. I saw it in your wallet the other day."

Elliot nodded. Of course he'd kept it. It went right next to his social insurance number and his health card. Even if he never planned on calling the number, there was no way he was throwing it out.

"Then call him."

Chapter Seven

Shelvin

Pulling up to the curb, Shelvin cut the engine on his Porsche Boxter, glancing up at the building and double-checking the address. It was a nice part of town, with high-rise condos that he remembered being advertised a few years before. He hadn't been in town at that time, but he had colleagues all over who kept him informed of the new builds all around the province.

The base price had been half a million, if he recalled, and the view would have to be fantastic from the sheer glass windows that overlooked the city. It was a little plain, though.

His shy boy was better off than he'd thought. His first impression of the cheap leather pants and basic black T-shirt had been that Elliot was a nine-to-five kind of guy who was scraping through for a measly pension and a bank account under ten grand.

Apparently, he'd been wrong. *Very* wrong.

Ducking out of his car, he strolled up to the building, pausing just outside the door to let the air wash over him and take the last of the dust from his office away.

The spring air was still crisp, especially so early on a Saturday morning. Frost clung to the small grassy area in front of the building that was decorated with a few empty flower beds and a concrete sculpture that looked something like a bird. Shelvin paused to snap a picture of it. He was always looking for inspiration.

After more than two weeks, he hadn't thought he would hear from Elliot again, but just as he'd given up, he'd gotten the call. Elliot wanted to see him again, but not *just* Elliot. His piece-of-work husband did, too.

Shelvin scoffed at his dim memory of Hunter. He'd met a few guys on the scene that were high and mighty before, and it got old real fast. But somehow, he'd still dragged his ass out of bed early on Saturday and hauled himself to the far side of town.

Elliot's eyes still haunted him. The longing in them made him ache at the memory. *If only.*

He pushed the intercom for Elliot's condo, humming under his breath as it buzzed, and the door snapped open. He ducked through it before it could relock, heading straight for the elevator. There was no way he was walking twelve flights of stairs, especially when he had no idea what he was getting into.

For all he knew, Hunter was looking to scowl some more.

I shouldn't do this to myself. He'd sworn off newbies for a long time, until Trick had nagged on him and practically pushed him into Elliot's path. Some newbies were just curious about the lifestyle, while others promised they were devoted, only to back out the first time a punishment was in order. He'd had a few subs walk out on him before their contracts were up, and it pissed him off more with each time it happened.

It was one of the reasons he hadn't had a contract in years.

Kink wasn't a passing phase for him that he'd forget when he found something new and shiny. It was part of his life and his soul. He knew that he'd never grow out of being a Dom. It was who he was on so many levels.

The air was thick with chlorine from the pool that was no doubt on the ground floor. He spied a sign for the gym down the hall from the elevators, too. With marble and slick granite everywhere in sight, it looked to be one of the higher-end condos in town. *It's still plain.*

Taking the elevator to Elliot's floor, he peered down the hall, counting the number of doors. It looked like there were only a few, making the condos more spacious than he'd initially thought. The floors on this level weren't marble but covered by a pale carpet that was surprisingly free of stains.

After checking to make sure he had the right number, he tapped on Elliot's door, tugging his jacket so it hung straight. He usually didn't give a shit about his appearance, but for some strange reason, he wanted to impress Elliot. He'd even showered, doubling up on his deodorant before he could get distracted.

There was a shuffle on the other side of the door followed by the sound of a deadbolt turning before the door was pulled inward.

He'd expected Hunter to be standing on the other end, but there was Elliot, looking so much better than he remembered. He was big, beautiful and muscled, probably from frequent trips to the main-floor gym.

With his dark hair and strong chin, he looked like an unlikely type to be a sub to the inexperienced eye.

Shelvin had seen *all* types. From the petite Domme with a bear sub, to the pack of muscled men who declared themselves switches. Looks were never right. Shelvin had never fit in a mold either — too short and easily distracted for some men's ideals of the perfect Dom.

But the way Elliot blushed, his gaze dropping to the floor, was more telling than anything else. *Fuck he's adorable.*

Cuteness aside, it should have been Hunter at the door. And Hunter should have been the one to call him, too. If he was supposed to be mentoring the prick in being a Dom, then he had his work cut out for him. A Dom should have been the one to greet him. He shouldn't have sent his sub to do his dirty work.

"Thank you for coming," said Elliot, the tips of his ears going pink. "I wasn't sure if you would even remember me when I called. I'm surprised you did."

Shelvin peered past his shoulder and into the apartment. There were a lot of beige walls and a white couch beyond a little hallway, with no Hunter in sight. *Is he even here?* Adultery was not his cup of tea.

"Don't be so hard on yourself, sweetheart," Shelvin drawled, shoving his hands into his pockets. Leather engulfed him, the same material he wore almost year-round when he could get away with it. "It would be impossible to forget you."

Elliot flushed deeper before beckoning Shelvin inside. "Can I get you something to drink? I just made a fresh pot of coffee, or I have tea, too. Here, let me take your coat."

Raising one eyebrow, Shelvin tugged his jacket off, handing it to Elliot. *Somebody's a service sub...or really excited.* Elliot's hands were shaking as he hung it on a hook by another jacket, a twisted *E* set above the hook. Another hook beside it with an *H* was also occupied. It was minimalist and a touch ugly, if he had to admit it.

"Coffee is fine," said Shelvin, drying his hands on his pants when Elliot looked away. His gut was tight, with the edge of nervousness that he hadn't felt in a while. Usually, he kept to the club for the safety of himself and his sub when he was playing with someone new.

"Let me show you around, or maybe...how do we do this?" Elliot seemed to lose himself, faltering just past the hallway.

That's a good fucking question. "Where's your husband? I'm assuming he's in on this, too, unless he hasn't done a one-eighty since we last met." *Or he doesn't know at all.* Shelvin pursed his lips. Of what little he knew about Elliot, he didn't seem distrustful.

"He's in the office. I'll go get him."

Elliot disappeared around a corner, and Shelvin looked back at the door, shaking his head. He still had time to get the fuck out. He never should have agreed to the whole thing, but who was he kidding? Elliot was cute—adorable even. Any chance to dominate him was worth a bit of awkwardness.

He lounged on the couch as he waited for them to appear, glancing around the well-kept living room. It was modern, if not a bit stark, but the art on the walls more than made up for that—that, and one of the biggest televisions he'd ever seen.

Hunter and Elliot appeared at the crest of the hall. The former had his lips pressed into a line, his hands clenched at his sides. He wasn't that much shorter than Elliot, but he was skinny and pale, the only thing in shape about him his flat belly. His long hair gave him an almost feminine look, accentuated by his soft lips and eyes. He could have been a model, if he ever learned how to smile.

Elliot was a step behind, hovering awkwardly as Hunter slowed to a stop before letting out a huff and moving to sit in an armchair next to the couch. He crossed his arms, chewing on his lower lip.

Teetering at the edge of the room, Elliot made no move to sit, clasping his hands behind his back. The light that had been in his eyes when he'd answered the door had dimmed in Hunter's presence and that riled Shelvin up more than anything.

"So, let's get the giant fucking elephant out of the room first," said Shelvin, cracking his knuckles on the armrest. It was plush and soft, dipping under the weight of his hand. "You asked me to come here for some kind of one-on-one session, so if either of you has a problem with me, you might as well get it off your chest. I won't be disrespected."

He shot a glare at Hunter, who seemed to wilt a touch. Elliot stayed silent, his gaze dropping to the white rug that was softer than chinchilla fur. Hopefully, it wasn't made of a hundred of the poor creatures.

"Okay, then. You want an arrangement, so let's talk limits. Since it's your first time, I'll jump in." Shelvin grabbed his phone where he kept a detailed list of his limits, so he didn't forget any. For most, it was second nature, but he had a wandering mind and sometimes he forgot things. He'd drafted up an extensive list the night before.

"I'm going to set a soft limit at impact play until I get to know you better," said Shelvin. He remembered the way Elliot had paled and flinched at the sound of a belt. *And so Hunter doesn't freak out.* He looked like the type to freak. "Knives, blood and all that fun stuff will be a hard limit, along with scat and piss play. I'm not into age play, and don't call me Daddy. You can address me as 'Sir' or 'Master', but we'll get into that later. What are your limits?"

He looked to Elliot first, who had started squirming at the first mention of impact play. A flash of fear had sparked over his face almost too fast for Shelvin to see.

"My hard limits are impact play, breath play and really pain in any form. No bodily fluids, either." His words were quiet, a flush intensifying on his cheeks as he spoke.

"Are you including spanking with impact?" asked Shelvin. "An open-palm slap on your ass... Would that be a hard limit, too? Or just with implements like a belt or flog." At the word *belt*, Elliot paled a few shades, his stance wavering.

"An open-handed slap is okay, but n-no implements." Elliot adjusted his hands, bringing them in front of him and picking at a hangnail. His jaw was tight, a strain to his face that Shelvin hated.

"Did you want to sit, Elliot? I want you to be comfortable." Shelvin patted the seat beside him, but Elliot shook his head. "Okay. Those limits are really good. Thank you for telling me. Anything else?"

"Don't call me 'boy' in a scene."

Interesting. Shelvin tapped out a note in his phone, so he didn't accidentally slip up mid-scene. "So, slut, slave, cumdumpster? Those would all be okay?"

"Yeah." Elliot nodded, looking a bit dazed. It was certainly an improvement from his reaction to discussing implements.

Shelvin bit back a chuckle before glancing at Hunter. His blood threatened to boil when he saw the look on Hunter's face. When Elliot looked over to his husband, he visibly wilted.

"Problem, Hunter? You look like the elephant I mentioned earlier just crawled up your ass and died." Shelvin couldn't keep the edge of anger from his voice. A look like that—full of judgment and disgust—could break a sub before he ever learned to trust. He barely knew Elliot, but he certainly didn't deserve that. *I have my work cut out for me.*

"I just don't get it," said Hunter, shaking his head. His hair whipped around him like a curtain caught in the wind, each strand brushed to perfection. *Maybe spend less time on yourself and more time on your fucking education.* "Why would you want to be called a slave? It's so demeaning."

Oh, this will be fun. Shelvin clenched his fist. He'd punched fuckers before when they got on his nerves, but respect went both ways. He wouldn't be the first to lash out where Hunter was involved, because he would lose Elliot's trust.

"Ah, so you think that my slave would be demeaned and degraded?" asked Shelvin, crossing his arms to keep his fists to himself. "Then you are probably right. One of my biggest turn-ons is degradation, with a side of heavy humiliation. But you're missing the point. I would love my slave and cherish them more than anything in the world. Every moment they submit to me would only strengthen our relationship. I would covet him, protecting him from everything in the world that could ever hurt him. Every time I broke him down to nothing, I would build him right back up and cherish him until he knows he's whole again — until he knows *he's* my world."

Elliot shuddered, taking a step back to lean against the wall. His shoulder touched the edge of a painting, sending the frame askew. Hope and bliss were written in his features, and it was heartbreaking to watch.

Hunter looked down, his gaze focused on his naked feet. His toenails were as manicured as his hair, only shinier and polished with a sparkly blue glow. "Can you teach me? I want to give Elliot those things. I want him to know that he's cherished."

Maybe this was the Hunter Elliot saw, but Shelvin wasn't sure which one to believe.

"No." Shelvin shifted on the couch, wishing he had stayed on his feet so he could pace. Pacing always found him the answer he needed the most. "I can't teach someone to be a Dom, just like I can't teach someone to be a sub. You either are or you aren't."

Mentoring was another thing altogether but trying to teach Hunter to be a Dom would be the same as convincing a knife that it was a head of lettuce.

Hunter let out a sigh, slumping his shoulders. Elliot looked close to tears, despite the tent in his jeans, his hope starting to waver. *Don't give up yet, sweetheart.*

"But," Shelving scratched the stubble on his chin, "*I* can be the Dom that Elliot needs."

Hunter snapped his head up, his eyes wide. He morphed from surprise to rage in the blink of an eye, red mottling his cheeks with unhinged fury. A man so quick to anger, with seemingly no control, would never make a good Dom.

"Hunter—" Elliot cut in, snapping his mouth shut when his husband sent him a glare.

This was such a big mistake. Shelvin was going to have a headache from all this later and at least one sleepless night. It would take him a long time to forget Elliot's shattered expression.

"Fine," Hunter growled, his voice low for his thin frame. "But I have conditions." He narrowed his eyes, standing and strolling the few steps to Shelvin.

"If you are trying to intimidate me, you're doing a piss-poor job," said Shelvin, shrugging as Hunter's glare turned murderous. "What's your condition? No fucking? Fair enough. Your hubby has to be home by nine at night? You can go pound salt."

Hunter turned to Elliot, every ounce of hostility draining away in an instant. He lowered himself to one knee, clasping Elliot's hands in his own. "My condition is that he can't make you come...not ever. He can have sex with you and demean you, and you can get everything else you need from him, but *that* belongs to me."

Maybe there's a baby Dom in there after all. Either way, Shelvin wasn't complaining. He didn't have to make someone come to send them into subspace, although it did help sometimes.

"I can agree to that," said Shelvin, slipping his arm over the back of the couch. "Let's make it a limit. As long as Elliot is all for it?" Elliot's nod was all he needed. "Well, guys, I gotta thank you in advance. This is going to be fun."

Chapter Eight

Elliot

"Where would you be most comfortable for our first scene?" asked Shelvin, clasping his hands together. He looked like the picture of calm, even when he'd faced the full force of Hunter's fury.

Elliot was trembling, inside and out. The only reason he was still standing was because he was clutching at the wall, his sweaty hands sticking to the flat surface. For a moment, he'd wondered if Shelvin was going to leave. Christ, he was still wondering if he hadn't actually woken up that morning and was caught in some sort of nightmare.

And Shelvin wanted to know where he would be comfortable? *Fuck.* They were really doing this. He wasn't going to have to pretend anymore. No more lies and no more secrets. He could go back to loving Hunter the way he should have been all along and not resenting him for something he couldn't control.

Thank you, Thank you. There would never be enough thank yous for Hunter. Elliot owed him *everything.*

"Anywhere but here," said Elliot, balking when Hunter shot him a look. He'd thought it was a good idea. Hunter obviously didn't fully approve, and it would keep Shelvin out of his line of sight. Unless he wanted to watch...

"I can leave, you know," Hunter grumbled, standing from the couch where he had taken a seat again after rhyming off his one and only condition.

"I don't want you to leave," said Elliot. "I want to go, knowing that when I come back here, everything will be the same between us." He didn't want Hunter to see or hear what they did because deep down he knew the resentment would be there. This way, it would be the same as when Elliot left for a work meeting or to visit a job site. And he'd be just as sweaty upon his return...hopefully.

"Sounds good." Shelvin cut in, slapping the arm of the couch. "Let's go to the club and I'll see if Clint has a spare room for us. It's still early, so it shouldn't be too busy."

Elliot took a deep breath, sending Hunter one final look. Everything was shifting so quickly, changing his life in a whirlwind of movement and sound. Hunter didn't meet his gaze, retreating to his office as they headed to the door.

* * * *

Shelvin had been right. When they arrived at the club, there were only three other cars out front, the rest of the street desolate and private. Elliot strode to the door just a half a step behind, pulling his jacket closer as cool air swept over him.

He was trembling, but he doubted that it was because of the weather. An energy had injected into his limbs as soon as he'd first seen Shelvin standing outside his door with an air of confidence that seemed almost permanent.

The feeling settled in his belly, filling him until he had the sudden urge to hum under his breath. He couldn't remember the last time he'd felt so brimming and confident, his urge to cower slipping away.

"I'm going to set some protocols between us," said Shelvin, tapping his white key card against the lock. "Call them rules, if you will." He pulled the door open a crack before pausing. "If I hold a door open for you, you're welcome to come inside. If not, well, enjoy yourself while you wait."

Elliot shuddered. The idea was so humiliating that he was hooked in moments. To be barred entrance somewhere simply because Shelvin wanted him to wait, probably assuming that he would be thinking about him the entire time and wondering if he was ever going to be let in, was exhilarating.

Thank goodness that he'd put an extra layer of boxers on to try to hide his inevitable reactions from Hunter when he'd prepared for their meeting. Hunter just wouldn't understand that in the same way a lot of things seemed beyond his comprehension. But away from his apartment, his boxers were too tight, his junk squashed and strangled as he responded to Shelvin's low murmur.

It was probably a good thing, because he wouldn't be coming any time soon.

"Do you understand, sweetheart?" Shelvin looked over his shoulder. "Always answer when I ask you a direct question."

"Y-yeah." Elliot swallowed. His tongue stuck to the roof of his mouth. "Are we going to talk about safewords, too? We didn't get to that earlier."

"Of course." Shelvin nodded, pulling his hand back from the door. The lock *thunk*ed home again as the system timed out. "I usually go by the traffic light system. Green means everything is good and please continue. Yellow, we pause and talk about things and maybe switch up what we're doing. Red is a full stop — the scene ends, and we go straight to aftercare."

"Okay." Elliot glared at the sidewalk. Somehow, he'd forgotten about the aftercare part. Maybe he'd thought that Hunter would take of it. He wasn't sure how he felt about the sheer vulnerability he would face with someone who was almost a complete stranger.

But if he trusted Shelvin enough to be his Dom, he would have to trust him for aftercare, too.

"Good." Shelvin shot him a wink, tapping his key card again before slipping through the door, leaving only enough space for himself. It eased shut after him, the lock engaging as soon as it sealed.

Elliot stared at the blank surface, inexplicably throbbing as he was left alone on the street. The wind kicked up a bit of dust, sending it his way in a flurry. Another couple was walking his way, their hands clasped together as they approached.

"Excuse me," one of them said. He didn't recognize them from the other night, not that he could remember more than a few faces. His only real memories were of Shelvin.

He ducked to the side, pressing his back to the brick to stay out of their way. Leaving wasn't an option...only waiting. Surely, Shelvin wouldn't forget about him so soon. Or maybe it was all part of his play — to wind Elliot up and see how far he could push him before he left on his own.

Maybe he didn't think Elliot was cut out for kink — or that he wasn't strong enough to handle the weight of his sadism.

But Elliot *was* strong. As much as he wanted to give in, he wouldn't that easy. He'd been strong enough to pretend with Hunter for years. Being left on the street alone was *nothing* compared to that.

He looked around as the couple moved through the door, leaning against the hard brick and peering up to the sky. Storm clouds were rolling in, the sunshine from the morning already starting to fade. He didn't care if it started to rain. Hell, it could pour and soak him to the bone until he was freezing, but he wasn't going to move.

Why? He hadn't quite figured that part out yet.

Closing his eyes, he drifted, listening to the cars come and go and a few voices pass him. Some went into the club, while others walked by. There was a siren in the distance, which wasn't an uncommon sound in the city. With so many people jammed into one place, there was bound to be conflict.

A cold hand on his chin shocked him into awareness, his eyes flying open as he started. He blinked at Shelvin's dazzling smile that met him, looking down at the Dom who already seemed to hold so much power over him.

"Hey, sweetheart. I'm ready for you to come in now, unless you need more time out here? You looked content." Shelvin moved his hand as he spoke, tracing Elliot's chin before dipping down his neck to the collar of his jacket.

"I'm ready." Elliot cleared his throat when his voice came out strangled and sleepy. His limbs were sluggish as he pushed away from the wall, ducking through the door as Shelvin held it open for him.

Every move Shelvin made echoed through him as if it were his own. He was hyperaware of the way Shelvin's hand twitched before he reached for the curtain, and the smirk that spread across his lips as he winked at the bouncer.

Something surged in Elliot's gut. *Jealousy, maybe?* He wasn't sure about anything except how he wanted Shelvin's gaze solely on him.

"What are we doing today?" asked Elliot, his voice like an echo. He'd been dreaming about this moment, but with everything they'd discussed, he still had no idea what it would entail.

Shelvin chuckled, threading his and Elliot's hands together. "I can't give away all my secrets, can I? You don't have to be worried, though. We're just going to get to know each other today."

"Oh." Elliot slumped his shoulders. He couldn't help but be a touch disappointed. He'd waited so long that all he could think about was jumping straight in and getting to the good part.

Shelvin led them to a booth, one of many that were unoccupied at the moment. The bar was nearly empty, with only a few couples milling about and some individuals seated on the stools by the bar.

He couldn't imagine that the club had been open for long, and only Clint was behind the bar, with Maddy nowhere to be seen. Elliot had hoped to see Maddy again, if only to bask in the confidence that the man seemed to reek of.

"Have a seat." Shelvin waved at the booth, easing onto one of the benches with a sigh. He spread his legs wide, leaning one elbow on the table.

Elliot took one step toward the opposite seat before he paused, frozen with indecision. He *could* take the seat opposite to Shelvin, but that was the last place he wanted to be. He didn't want to be his equal anymore.

But…Derreck's question and answer demonstration floated through his mind. He couldn't kneel, either. He couldn't give in so easily that his submission was worthless and ready for any Dom who came by.

No, he'd made his choice. Shelvin was his Dom. He just didn't know how to make that clear to both of them as well as any onlookers.

"Did you need a pillow? I didn't ask if you had bad knees or anything," said Shelvin, pointing to the floor next to his bench. "But now that I'm asking, anything I should know about?"

Swallowing, Elliot stared at the floor. "I injured my rotator cuff a few years ago." He rolled his right shoulder. It still ached when it rained sometimes or if he spent too long in the gym. "My knees are fine, though."

There was a moment of pure panic when Shelvin let out a soft sigh, tapping his foot with what had to be impatience.

I ruined it already. Between his indecision and wandering thoughts, Shelvin must've been fed up with him. But it was too late to sit on the hardwood, or kneel, or whatever he was supposed to be doing. He just stood, staring down at the spot by Shelvin's feet with wide-eyed fear.

"If I kneel so easily, is my submission even worth it?" he asked softly, blinking back the tears that caught him off guard. He didn't know what to do. He wouldn't make a decision — no, he couldn't. One more choice and he was going to break.

"Sweetheart." Shelvin, touched his hand, before bringing it to his lips. He kissed Elliot's palm before tugging him a step closer. "Kneel. I know how much you want to, and trust me when I tell you how happy it would make me."

Elliot stumbled one step before his legs gave out and he dropped to the floor with an *oompf*. His knees met the hardwood with a sound that told him he was going to be nursing bruises for days. He couldn't bring himself to care. He'd wear the brands with pride.

Slowly, Shelvin stripped Elliot of his coat, then his shirt, leaving him naked from the waist up. A shudder racked Elliot's body before he closed his eyes, his strength sapping from him in a single gush.

Shelvin guided Elliot's head to his thigh, stroking his hair with tender touches. "Better?"

Elliot nodded, letting out a shaky breath. Every part of him was brimming, suddenly full of so many emotions that he wasn't sure if he wanted to laugh or cry. A haze rushed over him, stealing all his thoughts except for the ones that were focused on Shelvin.

He could feel the touch against his scalp and the drag of Shelvin's nails that only made him sink deeper in his crouch. His knees were aching, but it was better than any orgasm he could recall. His nose was filled with Shelvin and the leather of his coat, along with a mild cologne that reminded him of a spa dipped in lavender.

"Are you comfortable?" asked Shelvin, moving only to pull his own coat off his shoulders. Then his hand was back, petting Elliot and sinking deep within him while only skimming the surface.

"Yes." His voice was slurred and slow, and Elliot blinked, trying to make sense of what was going on. It was almost as if he were drunk, only it was Shelvin on his tongue and not a two-hundred-dollar bottle of wine.

"Fuck, sweetheart." Shelvin let out a chuckle, digging his nails deep until Elliot let out a gasp. "You are so fucking perfect. Ten people watching us, but you still slip into subspace like the perfect toy. Feel what you did."

Shelvin grabbed his hand, placing it over his own groin. It took Elliot almost a full minute before he understood what he was touching. Beneath the fitted jeans was molten steel, so hard and hot under his hand that it must've been painful. His own cock ached in sympathy.

"I'm not allowed to come," said Elliot, wondering through the fog whether that was his own rule or someone else's. It didn't matter. His own ache was secondary to the heat against his palm. He squeezed, biting his lip as Shelvin let out a gasp.

"That's right. You aren't allowed to come, sweetheart. But I can come as many times as I want. I could fuck you raw, then lick my taste from your ass without breaking your husband's limits. We are going to have so much fun together, baby."

Elliot twitched—a whole-bodied thing that had him sinking lower into the fog. "Yes, I want that." *I want it all.*

Chapter Nine

Shelvin

A bit of light kneeling and his sub slipped into subspace like he was desperate for it. He'd obviously underestimated Elliot's simple need to submit. That, or he'd put it off for so long that his exhaustion was taking over.

Either way, it was fucking beautiful to watch.

His cock throbbed against Elliot's palm, the sight of his glazed eyes and even breaths better than cocaine and way more addictive. It couldn't have been more perfect, and they were just getting started. He couldn't push too far — not with his sub already floating — and their relationship was new. Exploring each other was the best damn part.

"You can safeword at any time, sweetheart. What's your color right now?" Shelvin tangled his fingers in Elliot's hair, the smooth strands so soft that he wanted to bury his face into them.

"Green," said Elliot after he seemed to ponder it for a second. "I feel weird, though. Floaty."

Chuckling, Shelvin spread his leg wider, guiding Elliot between them. He had to talk to Clint about getting some swiveling chairs in the main area in the new place. Not that it was typically a place for sceneing. Shelvin usually kept that for the open play areas and rooms. But after a quick conversation with both Clint and the door guy, Shelvin had convinced them to let him work his new sub in a more public setting.

The bar was barely open, so it should be slow for the next bit. He'd gotten the permission of every couple already there, and the door guy would give any newcomers a heads up. It was a fucking kink club, after all. Sometimes he wondered why Clint was so damn strict.

Consent is everything. As far as Shelvin was concerned, by walking in the door he was consenting to see naked ass and cock. That was the *idea.*

He could recall walking into a BDSM club once, coming face to ass with a fisting scene. With no privacy curtain at that club, the scene was visible to anyone who had cared to look every time the door had opened to the street.

He was into humiliation, but he wondered if that had pushed it a touch far, even for a sadistic bastard like himself. Either way, no one outside the club was seeing Elliot's ass except Hunter.

Fucking Hunter. He had to do something about that guy, but he wasn't sure what yet. He dreaded taking Elliot home, only to have his husband look down on him. But he couldn't exactly keep him. *Right? No.* Kidnapping was still against the law.

Shelvin shifted, reaching for the button on his jeans. He'd gone commando underneath, in the very hopes that they would end up in this exact position. The Elliot in his memory had blushed with desire when he'd mentioned the word *kneel*, but he'd had no idea how the reality would live up.

With a quick zip, he had his fly down and his cock exposed to the warm air of the club. He did the button back up, encasing his groin with denim while leaving his shaft exposed. He would have to try to stay still so the zipper's teeth didn't slip and dig into him.

He looked for the simple tells, watching as Elliot blinked and licked his lips. His pupils were blown, sweat gathering on his temple as he squirmed. He had to have been hard in his pants, but there was nothing Shelvin could do about that.

"Suck me off and swallow. I don't want you to spill a drop."

Elliot flushed, pulling back for just a moment to look at the bar behind him. A few more people had entered since they'd arrived, but no one was looking their way. That probably wouldn't be the case for long. Everyone loved a good show, and Shelvin was more than happy to give it to them.

"What's the problem, slut?" asked Shelvin, letting his voice drop into a lazy drawl. Guys usually loved it when he rolled his r's, and from Elliot's flush, he seemed to be in the same boat.

They'd already spoken about test results after Hunter's *conditions*, so Elliot had nothing to worry about there, unless he was about to safeword.

"Here?" asked Elliot, some of his haze appearing to clear. He shivered, clutching himself as he turned to stare at Shelvin's cock again. *One more push.*

"Yes. I want to show off how good that mouth of yours is. It's awful pretty, but it would look a lot better with something in it. Suck me or safeword." Shelvin gripped the table, keeping his hands to himself. It was Elliot's decision if he wanted to go deeper into subspace and their relationship or call it a day.

One moment Elliot was licking his lips, and the next, his nose was pressed against the denim at Shelvin's groin. Shelvin bit back a gasp, doing his best to act unaffected while Elliot's throat milked him like a champ.

He'd grossly underestimated his sub's skills. Hunter had no fucking clue how lucky he was.

"Good," said Shelvin, his voice steady despite his racing heart. "Not too fast, though. I want your jaw to ache tomorrow. Take it slow."

Elliot eased back, nursing the head of Shelvin's cock and flicking his tongue along the edge of his foreskin. The guy had fucking *skills*, and after only a minute or so, Shelvin was barely hanging on.

"It's passable," he said, throbbing as Elliot flushed brighter, his eyes losing focus again. "Show me how deep you can go. Choke yourself on it."

He grabbed Elliot by the hair, slowing his movements as he moved to rapidly plunge down. Giving his hair a quick jerk, he let go, tapping one finger to Elliot's cheek.

"That's one. I said *slow*."

Elliot nodded, blinking back tears as he swallowed and slowly started to bob his head up and down. His face was flushed, sweat trickling from his temples while his shirt stuck to his body. It wasn't hot in the club, though. On the contrary. If not for the heat at his groin and his effort of holding himself back, Shelvin would have been chilly.

"They're watching you," said Shelvin, glancing to the bar with a smirk. One man had turned in his bar stool, watching them with zero shame. *Perfect.* "I wonder who they want to switch places with — me or you?"

Elliot grumbled in his throat, his teeth scraping the underside of Shelvin's cock for the first time. *Fuck.*

Letting out a hiss, he tapped two fingers against Elliot's cheek. "That's two. Would you like to know what happens when you get to three? I'll give you a hint. You won't like it."

Tears glistened in Elliot's eyes as he jerked back, staring at Shelvin as he panted. He poked his pink tongue out, licking the moisture from his lower lip. "I'm sorry. I just..." He looked away, biting his lip.

Now that just won't do. Seizing Elliot's chin, he dragged him back, forcing their gazes to meet. "You just what? I can't read your mind, sweetheart."

"They don't get to be me," said Elliot, the first hint of a growl in his voice. His chest was rising and falling rapidly, the flush on his cheeks spreading down his neck.

Awww. Shelvin smirked. "My sweetheart is a little bit jealous, I think. That's fair. As much as they get to look, no one is touching your ass but me."

Elliot's grin was dazzling, especially with the tears rolling down his cheeks. Fuck, he was beautiful.

"Make me come, and I'll let you keep me warm. I have a few people I want to talk to, and I don't want my cock getting chilly."

Elliot lunged at Shelvin's groin, pausing when he engulfed the tip as he seemed to remember himself. He worked himself down leisurely, taking bit by bit and swirling his tongue along the way. There was no sign of his teeth that were gently tucked behind his lips.

It didn't take more than a few minutes for Shelvin to come down his throat, holding himself deep until he started to soften. To his credit, Elliot never choked once, swallowing it all down with his throat bobbing as he struggled to breathe. The only thing giving away his struggles were the fresh tears that gathered in his eyes. He didn't pull back, though, not even when Shelvin went fully soft.

His jaw had to be aching. No one who put that much effort in wouldn't feel it.

"Don't suck me. Just hold me in your mouth and keep me warm. Don't try to swallow, either. I want to watch you make a mess of yourself. If you need a break, tap my thigh twice." He let out a lazy smirk, settling against the booth as much as he could.

Elliot didn't respond, his eyes distant and unfocused. There was no wet stain on the front of his pants, which was a blessing, and the fabric was still tented. He was obviously floating, the shallow rise and fall of his breaths barely there.

"Make sure to breathe, or I'll be upset."

Elliot took a deep breath through his nose, shutting his eyes as if he couldn't hold them open. Shelvin wasn't sure if he'd ever seen a sub fall quite so deep so quickly. He would have to keep an extra eye on him and track his breathing, just to make sure he didn't hurt himself accidentally.

The curtain swished to the side as someone new entered, and Shelvin caught their eye before flagging them down. *Now for the real test.*

* * * *

Elliot

He was hardly doing anything except holding Shelvin's cock in his mouth and trying not to let it slip away. There seemed to be an art to it. Too much pressure with his lips, and it started to slip away. But if he applied any suction to get it back where it belonged, Shelvin would tap his cheek and give him a quick shake of his head.

Then there was the drool. It poured past his lips, soaking his chin and the denim pressed against his mouth. It was damp and warm to the touch — and increasingly uncomfortable.

His knees were the worst, though, along with his neck and thighs. At first, he'd sat heavily on his feet, leaning back to ease the tension of his legs, but soon his feet went numb and his knees started to ache, giving him no option but to shift forward. His thighs trembled, his neck aching from the awkward position that was so close to being comfortable.

But through it all, he'd never been more content. His mind was completely empty, everything around him like a sluggish version of itself. Even his breathing felt slower than normal, each inhale more delayed than the last.

A tap on his cheek made him blink. Shelvin looked at him, his face stoic except for the heat in his eyes. He was rugged, even with his short stature, his hands stronger than Elliot had given him credit for.

"Breathe, sweetheart."

Elliot sucked in a deep breath through his nose. It was so much easier when Shelvin said it. Otherwise, it seemed to slip to the edge of his mind.

There was someone else at the table just on the edge of Elliot's vision. He wasn't sure how long they'd been there, and he hadn't decided if he actually cared. The people behind him were nothing to the cock in his mouth and the simple balance of keeping it inside.

"You thinking of a contract?" The person asked Shelvin, shifting their foot so it entered Elliot's vision. It was a dress shoe, shiny and polished like a fresh Mercedes. Their pant leg was a suit, a bit of dark hair peeking out where the ankle had ridden up.

"That's up to him," said Shelvin, his hand suddenly in Elliot's hair again. Elliot relaxed into the touch, humming in contentment. Things seemed to be getting clearer again, the world coming into focus like he'd been asleep and had just woken from the most wonderful dream. Elliot tried to cling to it, but it slipped through his grasp, wilting away to nothing.

What would Hunter say if he saw me now?

Struggling to swallow, Elliot tilted his head back just a bit, blinking at the man above him. Shelvin shot him a smile that eased every bit of worry that had started to build. This was about him and Shelvin, not Hunter. He loved Hunter with all his heart, but there were some things that his husband would never understand.

"You back with me, sweetheart?" asked Shelvin, cupping Elliot's cheek and guiding him away from his cock.

The move sent an ache through his entire body, his knees throbbing and every muscle protesting. He was in shape, but he wondered how long he'd been sitting there without moving—long enough that his stomach grumbled angrily from his missed lunch.

"Where would I go?" asked Elliot, flushing when Shelvin wiped his chin for him with a cloth that he'd had by his side. A moment later, his cock was tucked away, looking a lot firmer than Elliot remembered. It must've filled slowly as he held it, going deeper so gradually that he hadn't noticed in his state.

"Did you want to go somewhere private for aftercare? There is a lounge by the open play area where no one will bother us." Shelvin turned to the man across from him. "Shoot me an email, Thomas, and I'll add you to my waitlist. I've got a few priorities ahead of you, but I'll let you know a timeline once I get more details."

The man was dressed in a prim suit, his long hair braided so it fell to one side. With plucked eyebrows and lip gloss, he looked nearly as polished as his shoes, only far more handsome.

"Will do. Look after your boy, and I'll get the details to you," said Thomas, grasping his drink.

Elliot flinched at the endearment. It brought back too many memories that he wanted to stay buried forever. Shelvin reached for him, resting one hand on his shoulder.

"He prefers 'sweetheart', but don't worry. I'll take good care of him. Come on." Shelvin coaxed him to his feet, catching Elliot when he almost fell right down again. Everything was asleep below his waist, and he wasn't sure if he could even support his own weight.

Tucking himself against Shelvin the best he could, Elliot held on for dear life as he was led away from the booth to the lounge area just outside the open play area. There were a few sounds that made it through the curtain, but they were muted enough that Elliot was able to ignore them.

He collapsed into one of the chairs as soon as they reached it, the strength draining from his limbs. It was almost as if he had run ten miles while trying to break his own speed record with how shaky he was.

"Sorry about Thomas, sweetheart. He should have asked before he called you that. I'm sorry if he triggered you." Shelvin slid next to him, wrapping one arm around Elliot's waist.

The chair was big enough for them to sit side by side with space to spare, and the armrests were padded and soft. There was a stack of fresh towels on a table nearby, along with a basket filled with what looked like lube and condoms. A gentle beat sounded above them, softer than it had been in the bar.

"It's okay." Elliot looked to his hands that were trembling before his eyes. His stomach felt strange, and he couldn't decide whether he was going to throw up or eat three sandwiches.

"No, it's not," said Shelvin, stroking his back. "If I said it, it wouldn't be okay, either. The last thing I want to do is trigger you or push your limits further than what you're comfortable with. Do you feel okay? Is there anything I can get you? You're probably thirsty."

"I don't know." He clutched his hands together to try to get them to stop shaking. His leg bounced instead, full of nervous energy. "I feel strange and really sore. I'm not really sure what happened. I've read about subspace, but I didn't think it would be like that."

The peace and calm had been wholly unexpected. He had been looking forward to a rush of endorphins that would slate his hunger, but instead, he'd almost fallen into a trance.

"It's different for everyone, just like dreaming," said Shelvin. "You were very good for me, and hot as fuck.

You're even more beautiful when you're floating. I didn't even think that was possible."

"It was perfect." Elliot closed his eyes, reliving every moment of the scene in the blink of an eye. Every muscle movement and sigh were ingrained for him to revisit later — hopefully many times.

"Good." Shelvin chuckled, pulling Elliot into a quick hug. "I was going to wait a bit, but I want you to think about a contract. You would promise to become my submissive for a year, and I'll make sure you see subspace again as often as you need it. I can't promise it every day, because I work a lot, but I'll do whatever I can to give you what you need."

A contract? Elliot had never dreamed of actually getting to experience kink, let alone a contract. Butterflies burst in his stomach as his jittery energy peaked. He should have asked Hunter. They were married, after all. A marriage contract was probably more important than one with a Dominant.

But Elliot hadn't been this nervous on his wedding day. He'd *never* been more content or more fulfilled. He needed to see Shelvin again, and the thought that he wouldn't made the ache in his legs almost unbearable.

"Okay." He let out a breath. He didn't have to think. *I'm free.*

Chapter Ten

Elliot

Elliot started as his phone rang. The chime wasn't all that loud, but he'd been lost inside his head for the last hour and staring at the blank screen of his computer when he should have been working.

His work schedule varied and included time in the office, at home and on job sites with clients when he was needed. He loved it, too, but for the last week, he'd been drifting in and out of reality.

A contract. They'd talked about so much more than just the kneeling and aftercare in the days since their first scene. Their dynamic wasn't as hands on as Shelvin said it was with some other couples, but to Elliot, it seemed perfect.

He bit his lip, grabbing his phone and accepting the call. He knew exactly why his mind was wandering, but he was hopeless in his attempts to stop it. Shelvin had been haunting every minute of his thoughts, the 'what-ifs' piling high.

What if I had been allowed to come? What if I have another scene? What if Hunter finds out I signed that contract? What if I wasn't married at all?

Every thought just dug him deeper, making him ache and want to cry at the same time. If Shelvin were there, he would know exactly what to do and say to make it better. Every day at ten in the morning, Elliot called him like they'd discussed, but he'd never managed to muster up the courage to ask any of his questions.

He hadn't seen Shelvin since he'd driven him home, but his face was still vivid in his memory, his voice a daily reminder. Shelvin had offered to escort Elliot upstairs, but Elliot had passed, his heart racing as he'd stared at his condo building.

When he'd arrived back in the condo, Hunter had acted as if he'd never left in the first place. The local paper hadn't moved from his spot, and there had been fresh flowers on the table. The smell of bleach had hung in the air, which meant that Hunter had probably passed the time by cleaning. It was something he often did between lulls at work.

Elliot had played along with the ruse, trying to understand himself and Hunter's reactions at the same time. Hunter hadn't asked him a single thing, and Elliot hadn't wanted to imagine his husband's face if he did fess up. *I sucked another man's cock, but I didn't come, so that makes it okay.* Fuck, he was pathetic.

"Hello?" He answered the call, grabbing a pen and paper as he tried to focus. He *had* to focus. He loved his job, and he'd worked his ass off to get it. He wasn't going to let anything interfere with that, not even Shelvin.

"I've got a project for you, Elliot," said his boss with zero prelude. Sillib Manchester was a single father of four, but still managed to put more hours in at the office than he did at home. His kids were mostly grown, which helped, and one of them was more often than not sitting in on one of the meetings. One day, she'd take over the company, and Elliot would relish knocking her down a few pegs.

"I'm already working on the apartments downtown," said Elliot, tapping his pen against the paper. It wasn't a massive project, with only twenty-four apartments on three floors. The city had already given them a few issues, though, so he was guarding the project closely.

When he'd graduated, he'd never imagined how far his engineering career would come. Now he could drive around and see his touches and influences everywhere on homes and buildings in the city.

"What's the timeline?" He could juggle two projects at once, but it made for sleepless nights and a craving for binge watching a few series once he was finished. The last time he'd juggled three, he'd gained fifteen pounds from stress eating extra buttery popcorn.

"It's with some fancy hotshot architect who thinks he can get this done in a few months. The project is way out of his scope, and I need someone to shut him down before it gets out of hand. I've never worked with him before, but he's got a reputation for being an asshole."

Elliot let out a sigh. *My specialty.* Sillib loved to send the assholes his way, because once Elliot put his foot down, no one was changing his mind. "What are we talking?"

"Private residence, but the land is a freaking swamp," said Sillib, not pulling any punches. "It's going to take a miracle to even get the permits approved."

"Then why the hell are we even involved in it?" asked Elliot, letting out a huff as he scrawled out a few angry scribbles. He didn't have time for this shit. The last thing he needed was a rich tire kicker, and Sillib knew it.

"Your bonus will match your yearly salary if you get it done in three months."

Elliot dropped his pen. It snapped against the ground, two pieces of it rolling under different edges of his desk. He did salary and bonuses with each contract, but one that big would probably set him up for an early retirement.

"When do I start?" asked Elliot, gulping before grabbing a new pen and scribbling out the address. He had some contacts with the city, and he could pull strings and beg for favors…if he could find a place on the land to build that wouldn't turn into a sinkhole in the next few years.

"This guy has some kind of home office, and he wants to meet there to talk specifics. He said he already has the schematics drawn up."

Elliot rolled his eyes. If there was one thing that seemed to be true for all architects he'd dealt with, it was that their schematics were closer to something out of a fantasy novel than what would actually be erected in the real world.

"Let's do something entirely of glass. I'm talking windows, doors, walls…everything." Elliot remembered having that conversation while trying to explain that some glass had the same insulation value as a piece of sandpaper—freezing in the winter and a virtual greenhouse in the summer.

It might look *cool,* but there was a reason that greenhouses were made of glass. And had they ever heard of that little thing called privacy? Not to mention, hiding duct work and electrical in a see-through nightmare was impossible. *Let's hope it's not like that again.*

"You'll have your work cut out for you, Elliot. You're the best guy for the job, and if anyone can do it, you can."

Elliot hung up with a click, jumping from his chair before running straight to the front door. If he was going to get it done in three months, he didn't have a second to waste.

He bypassed Hunter, who blinked at him from where he was seated at the table and lost in a novel.

"I'm meeting with a client, Hunt. I might be late." He grabbed his coat from the hook, shuffling back down the hall when Hunter didn't answer him.

Hunter had set his book on the table, the pages bent wide to hold his place upside down. He delicately stroked the table with one hand, his other resting in his lap. His lips were pursed, his eyes downcast.

"What's wrong? You should be happy for me. This contract is *huge.*" Elliot scratched his chin. "We could take that trip to England that we've been talking about. A month of you and me in every castle we've ever seen in a magazine."

Hunter let out a huff, hunching his shoulders before he leaned on the table. "You don't have to lie, Elliot. If you're going to see *him* again, then you can just say it. It's been a while, so I totally understand if you wanted to. We've hardly been intimate at all lately, even after…"

Hunter looked away, blinking as his eyes turned glassy.

"What?" Elliot strode to the table before dropping to one knee, even with the clock ticking in the back of his mind. He grasped Hunter's hands in his, kissing his knuckles. His hands were chilly and pale, the knuckles dry. It was so unlike him.

Have I been ignoring him? It certainly hadn't been on purpose, but looking back, maybe he had. He'd attempted to pour himself into his work with renewed energy, only for his mind to wander to the moments in the club. There hadn't been much time for Hunter in between.

"I'll bring back butter chicken," said Elliot, squeezing Hunter's hands one last time before he retreated to the living room. He returned a moment later, tossing a thick blanket over Hunter's shoulders. The light blue plaid was vibrant against his pale skin.

"This client is on the other side of town, but they're working with a hotshot architect." Elliot shrugged. The first hint of a smile appeared on Hunter's lips. Hunter seemed to hate architects as much as Elliot did, for some reason.

"Who knows how long that will be, then," said Hunter, pulling the blanket tighter before reaching for his book again. "I'll probably be able to hear the arguing from here."

"Maybe." Elliot grinned. The funniest part was that he'd debated for years if he'd wanted to go to school for architecture or engineering, and ultimately engineering had won out. Two things that had been very similar in his mind had formed a drift that would probably never be repaired.

"Love you." He placed a kiss on Hunter's forehead before he pulled his coat on, heading for the door again. Hunter's echoed reply had him brimming, his hands shaking as he jogged to his car.

There was so much that he could do with that bonus, but only if he could convince Mr. Architect that he was insane for that timeline. It didn't matter if it was a house or an apartment, materials had delays, and sometimes city hall dragged their heels on permits. Plus, if it really was a swamp like his boss had implied, they'd probably have the Ministry of Natural Resources on their case, too.

With so many endangered species, it was hard to know where nesting grounds were anymore. The last thing Elliot wanted to do was disturb a cute pair of owls.

Slipping into his car, Elliot sped across town, nearly blowing through two red lights in his haste. Money wasn't everything, but time was. The bonus meant that he could spend more time with Hunter and work through the few things he was comfortable bringing up.

They could take off a whole month together and travel to different parts of the world. It would give them some much-needed time to reconnect. Lazy days on a beach somewhere or sweet sunsets behind frosted glass would be perfect.

His eagerness slipped the tiniest bit as he pulled up to the address. The building was a beautiful beast of a monstrosity, but there was no way it was practical in any form. There were more angles than he could count on the roof, and every window was obviously a custom. It was almost a mix of imperial and colonial, with enough confusion in the middle that it left him baffled and intrigued.

He thanked his infrequent trips to this side of town for not noticing it before. He didn't have any builds that he'd worked on close by, either, most of them being uptown and in the extensive subdivisions.

Seriously? A sandbox? Instead of flower boxes, there were large sand gardens with shimmering rocks inside. The sand was swirled in a pattern that was probably supposed to be Zen, with one stray cigarette at the very corner. It turned the otherwise beautiful display into a disgusting mess.

The doors were the most intriguing. Somehow, there was water inside them, cascading down in an endless flow of colorful light. It was one of the most beautiful doors he'd ever seen but an engineering nightmare.

Honestly, how do you even replace the water pumps once they fry? The real answer was that you couldn't. The whole door and system would have to be replaced. He wasn't even sure what could be done if they filled with limescale.

But they were pretty. *Passable, I guess.*

Hotshot, indeed. Anyone who had managed to build something so beautiful that actually *worked* had his respect, even if he begrudged the fact. If he would have been on the project, he could guarantee that he would have thrown the plans out with one glance.

He snuck a look at the paper in his hand with the address. His writing was barely legible from his earlier excitement.

The building looked to be made up of apartments, which wasn't exactly what he'd expected. From the way his boss had made it sound, the guy was full enough of himself to have an entire building erected in his honor. But maybe he'd just leeched one of the condos as part of his bonus.

Apartment six. He pushed his way through the doors, which surprisingly enough, weren't locked. There was a small lobby, with no sign of mailboxes, just a few other doors that were locked and an elevator that looked to require a key card to activate.

Elliot peered around, looking for some type of security. Inset in the walls, were a few glass globes that could have been decorative or hidden cameras with the way they fit the décor so well. There were plants here, too—lush ones that made up for the sterile sand of the exterior. The lights overhead shone on them with what looked to be specialty lightbulbs that would echo the sun's rays.

The centerpiece of the room was a massive fountain that reached almost to the fifteen-foot ceiling. The water didn't so much squirt over the top as it did flow over a series of outcroppings, each a different color that shimmered with hidden lights. Coins gathered in the pool below, with a few outdated pennies mixed in with the bunch.

"Can I help you?"

Elliot peered around the fountain, blinking at the security guard who had appeared through one of the doors. A lock sounded behind him as the door relatched. He was built, with a few inches on Elliot and arms thicker than tree trunks. And was that a taser at his hip?

I grossly underestimated the security here. In his own building, he'd always been happy with their level of safety. Now he was wondering if he'd just had his head in the sand.

"I'm looking for Mr. Mainstay." Elliot glanced at the paper again. The name was completely unfamiliar, which wasn't a good sign. He knew everybody who was somebody in the business. "We have an appointment."

The guard seemed to relax, moving his hand away from the black handle at his waist. He gave Elliot a quick smile before beckoning him forward.

"You're lucky. He just got back with coffee. I hope he brought one for you the same as he did for me," said the guard, striding to one of the doors and unlocking it with a card that was strung on a cord at his hip.

As he pushed it open, Elliot caught sight of hardwood floors and walls made of thick rustic beams with rich green paint in between. It looked like he'd stepped out of the jungle and into a goddamned forest.

What the hell is this place? Granted, he rarely came to this side of town, but he was surprised he'd missed something so unique. He begrudgingly raised his opinion of the guy by a few notches.

"He's door number six. Knock loudly, as he usually has some music playing. Any problems, just give me a shout. You'll need me to let you back out if you are alone, but this whole place is wired for sound. I'll hear you if you scream." The security guard touched something at his other hip that looked an awful lot like a baton.

Is that even legal to carry? Elliot swallowed as he passed him by, resisting the urge to drop his gaze. The guy screamed *Dom* in every sense, and Elliot had no doubts that he knew how to use that nightstick...*or a whip.* He shuddered at the thought, pulling his jacket tighter.

"Have a pleasant evening."

"Thank you," Elliot shot back, just as the door slid shut behind him, locking with an automatic *thunk*. So maybe he had underestimated security, but what about fire safety? If the power cut, he didn't want to be locked in the place for hours with no sign of rescue. *Fucking architects, putting design over safety.*

He moved along the hall, raising one eyebrow as he passed the first door. The numbers were Japanese Kanji, which were almost impossible for him to comprehend. How the hell was he supposed to know what the number six looked like?

Glancing over his shoulder, he counted the doors as he passed, pressing his ear to the sixth one along the hall. True to what the guard had said, he caught the distant hum of music through the thick wood.

Smacking his knuckles against the door, he tapped out a pattern of growing impatience when there was no answer. His knuckles throbbed, probably bruised, but there was no doorbell to speak of. He let out a sigh before kicking the door with his shoe instead, the whole thing trembling from the force of the hit when he smacked it too hard.

Oh, that smarted. He reached for his foot as the awkward hit made something in his foot twinge. Half bent over, he heard the first sounds of the lock and the doorknob shifting before the door was pulled open.

Elliot looked up, his mouth going dry. His heart raced and he was trapped between the decision to drop the rest of the way down or straighten. A wicked smirk looked back at him, blue eyes sparkling in earnest.

"Well, hello, sweetheart. I wondered when you would come crawling back to me."

Fuck. It was Shelvin.

Chapter Eleven

Shelvin

He was only two coffees in of his three for himself from the café when a knock sounded at the door. Shelvin rolled his eyes, taking another sip before sketching out a line on his schematic. *Probably that fucking engineer.*

The problem was that Clint needed this build ASAP, and he needed it to be the best of the best. Three months would be impossible for him to tackle on his own and he had called for backup during a weak moment. He'd asked around, chatting with a few friends on recommendations seeing as he was still fairly new to the area. They had all told him the same company.

It was a big one at that, with enough guys on staff that he could fire the first three that he didn't like. But they got shit done, which was the only thing he needed from them. Their opinions and *observations*, they could keep to themselves.

If he wanted to have a debate about stresses and beam layout, then he would talk to the construction team, not some asshole with less schooling than him but twice the entitlement.

The knock came again, this time loud enough to shake the frame of his door — his very expensive *custom* door. The company that had made it didn't even exist anymore, so it would be a bitch to replace if anything happened to it — something Shelvin hadn't *exactly* planned for. It was pretty, and that's what mattered.

He pulled the door open, ready to chew the guy a new asshole. It was too late in the day to deal with this shit.

His gut clenched tight, his palms instantly going sweaty. *Elliot.*

Elliot was in a half-kneel, holding his toe, which wasn't punishment enough for kicking his door, in Shelvin's opinion. He looked good, though, his muscles loose and his eyes bright like they had been the last time they'd met.

How long had it been? He wasn't sure of the exact date at the moment. If it hadn't been for Elliot's daily calls, Shelvin would have wondered if he'd already moved on because of Shelvin's lack of attention.

He had warned Elliot of that, but he couldn't help but feel a bit bad. His submission had been honest and absolute, something that any Dom would wish for. And Shelvin had barely had to lift a finger, which wasn't exactly fun, but maybe expected from someone so desperate.

"Well, hello, sweetheart. I wondered when you would come crawling back to me." His card that he'd given Elliot originally had had his first name and phone numbers on it, but not his address. Still, it wouldn't have taken much to track him down.

A flush burst over Elliot's cheeks, and his gaze dropped to the floor as he chewed his lip. Shelvin wondered how low that flush went...all the way to his nipples or farther south to his cock? He hadn't got to see everything that his sub was made of, but there was no time like the present.

"I'm here for work, actually," said Elliot, sounding grieved over the fact.

Wait...what?

Shelvin struggled to keep his face calm while his brain took a temporary vacation. *Work?* Shelvin was only expecting one person and...*oh.* Elliot was the engineer...because of course he was.

Things just got a hell of a lot more complicated, and Shelvin was almost ready to tap out.

His work was the furthest thing away from his BDSM life, and he'd never worked with one of his subs before, not that many ran in his field. The few that did, he avoided the best he could.

It wasn't that he didn't trust them or thought less of their skills in any way, quite the contrary...but he didn't want to accidentally take advantage of them or keep them from speaking up if they noticed an issue.

"Well, fuck." Shelvin slammed his mouth shut before offering Elliot his hand and pulling him the rest of the way to his feet. He could roll with this for now, if only to see Elliot again. He tried not to let his hand linger longer that what would be considered professional.

"Welcome to my humble office, then. I didn't realize you were the one working on the house project. I didn't even know you were an engineer, actually."

Elliot scratched the back of his head as he walked past Shelvin and into the office. He still looked out of sorts, which just wouldn't do. If there was one thing Shelvin refused to fuck up, it was his work.

"I don't think we *should* be working together, now that I know it's you," said Shelvin softly. Elliot didn't seem to hear him.

Elliot moved around the single desk in the room, flicking the light on over the sketch that Shelvin had been working on for the last few days. It was still a work in progress, but fuck he was proud of it. He couldn't wait to present it to Clint and get his thoughts.

"These footings aren't going to work," said Elliot, tapping near the bottom of the page. "If it's a swampy area, we'll have to use more than a hundred truckloads of fill, and on our timeline, that's not going to fly. This here is wrong, too." He tapped along the base of one of the many peaks in the roof. "Not only is this going to be a nightmare in the winter with ice dams and the like, but the load will be too great on this beam. It looks like you want it exposed, but we can't do a wooden one there with that kind of load, and an I-beam will look like shit in the middle of the ceiling."

Holy fuck. Was it possible to be pissed off and turned on at the same time? Shelvin had always known that he had a competence kink a mile wide, but that hadn't worked out for him so far. He'd never seen it coming.

The worst part was that Elliot was *right*. As soon as he'd pointed it out, the niggling voice in the back of his head finally went silent, as if it had been trying to tell him the same thing all along.

"It's not finished," said Shelvin defensively, gathering himself and grabbing his pencil. "I planned to have a load-bearing wall here and here, and I was considering doing a tiled metal roof look, which will do a better job than straight shingles."

"You'll need a wall here as well, if that's your plan. And is that supposed to be some kind of turret? This is a house, not a castle." Elliot tapped the circular room that Shelvin had worked on for hours.

Shelvin gritted his teeth. *Don't get pissy already.*

"The medieval design is deliberate. I thought that could be the impact room, with the flogs on the walls and a cross bolted right into the stone wall. Or the sub could be handcuffed in the middle of the room and blindfolded. With the echo, they would never know where their Dom was coming from."

Elliot blinked, sending Shelvin a confused look. "Impact room? What are you talking about?"

So maybe his sub didn't know everything. Shelvin kept his glee to himself. "The house is for Clint — or rather, for Unkinked. This section here will be where he lives and the rest will be set up like the club, only bigger better and way kinkier. See? Here's the *Wet* room." Elliot tapped his pencil against his plans for the room that was all tile with extra venting and four showers within. "Here's *Spoil,* with the bed and fluffy couches. I've got a whole section for 'littles' with games, candy dispensers and a chalkboard wall that they can draw on."

Shelvin trailed off, glancing to Elliot. His jaw was tight, his forehead furrowed as realization seemed to dawn.

"You had no idea."

"I had no idea." Elliot echoed. "It makes the project a lot more interesting, though. I thought it was just another pushy rich guy with a big bonus, but I'd like to help Clint on this one. You've got a good start here, and

I think with some extra hours, we might just be able to pull it off with more than a three-month timeline. I'd need to see the land to really know."

A smile tugged at Shelvin's lips, and he couldn't help but grin. He'd given the short timeline to try to help Clint out—and to separate the men from the boys. Despite Elliot's critique, he was actually looking forward to working with him now that he knew his skill level.

"Come with me to my car, and I'll take you to the spot."

Grabbing his coat, he held the door for Elliot, ushering him outside after unlocking the outside door and waving to Markus the security guard. Markus really was a great guy, if not a little overprotective.

It wasn't until they were in the car and Elliot's cologne wrapped around him, that he finally understood what he was getting himself in to. He was never one for self-control, and Elliot was gorgeous and willing in every way. Keeping on task would be the hardest part.

"Does your husband know you're here?" Shelvin asked softly as he pulled out of the driveway. The sun was getting low, so he egged the car on a little faster, hoping they'd make it to the spot before dark.

"Uh…kind of?" Elliot flickered his gaze to him in a flash before it was gone. "He knows I'm meeting with a client, but he doesn't know it's you. In my defense, I didn't know, either."

"Do you think it would piss him off?" He chose his words carefully as he merged onto the highway. Flicking down his visor, he reached for his sunglasses before the evening sun could blind him. His Mercedes purred on, his hand steady on the wheel.

Elliot shrugged after a long minute. "He knows that you can give me something that he can't, and I think that upsets him. He loves me enough that he tries to understand, though. I know you don't know him that well and he sometimes gives off the wrong vibes, but he really is a good man — the best."

Shelvin didn't have to know much about Hunter to know he was a dick. But he wasn't going to say shit about it. He wasn't planning on being Hunter's replacement. That had never been his dynamic.

"Good. So, after you look at the site, he won't mind if I put you on your knees and give you what you need? After the work is done, of course." It had been the main thing circling Shelvin's thoughts since he'd seen Elliot on the other side of his door. Self-control was overrated anyway.

Elliot sucked in a breath before giving him the slightest of nods.

"Oh, come on, sweetheart. That's not good enough. Tell me what you want and what you need. Say it out loud and humiliate yourself for me." *This is me officially crossing a line.*

The funniest part was, he had his go bag in the back seat, but Elliot had no way of knowing that. He'd gone shopping after Elliot had signed their contract, and he'd kept his supplies close, not knowing when he would need them. He'd been totally prepared to drive straight from work to meet Elliot at the club at a moment's notice.

"I want…" Eliot looked at his clasped hands. "I want you to show me my place and tell me what to do. No matter how hard I beg, I don't want you to listen because you know what's best for me. Take care of me, Shelvin. *Please.*"

His cock throbbed to life, pushing at the zipper of his jeans. Shelvin squashed it with his fist, keeping his mouth shut until he knew he wasn't just going to offer that they pull over and take care of the kink part first. "I'll think about it."

"After work, though." Elliot took another sharp breath after he said it. "I refuse to mess up this build."

Shelvin nodded, suddenly serious. "Even if you tried, I won't let you. You're in good hands, sweetheart."

* * * *

It was dusk by the time they pulled up to the lot, only a few pinkish rays of light clinging to the horizon. Once the trees loomed closer, most of the daylight was cut off, leaving them in a semi-darkness that would probably be ripe with mosquitoes once the weather warmed.

Shelvin left the car running, turning his high beams on to illuminate the area. The entrance, if you could call it that, was thick with trees and natural bushy shrubs, but the spot he planned for the house was a grassy clearing that could do with a bit of weed whacking. Of course, there was a small stream running right through it, but he'd planned for that, too.

"This is insane," said Elliot as soon as he stepped out of the car. The toe of his expensive shoe sank a few inches into the muck, and he shot Shelvin a scowl. "We are not putting the house here. You think this is bad? It has hardly rained at all this spring. Just wait until there is an actual flood."

"But a water feature," said Shelvin, framing up the stream with his hands. "Imagine a bridge between

Clint's quarters and the rest of the club. This little stream would be a beautiful thing to wake up to."

"And in the summer, it will smell like a swampy pigsty." Elliot crossed his arms. "Where else? This plot is a few acres, so give me your backups. And please tell me you *do* have backups."

"Let me get my phone for the flashlight." Shelvin grabbed it from his seat, turning on the app with a shake of his wrist. The forest was instantly brighter, the muck not nearly as foreboding between the close trees.

"Neat trick to turn your flashlight on, but I prefer this one." Elliot brought his phone close to his mouth before whispering "Lumos". The phone illuminated like one-hundred flameless candles.

Shelvin melted inside. A big, beautiful sub *and* he was a geek at heart? Maybe Shelvin could show him his collection of *Final Fantasy* figurines, and Elliot would actually appreciate them — unlike the last person he'd shown.

"I still read the *Harry Potter* books sometimes," said Shelvin as they stepped through the trees to the back of the property. They could probably find a path large enough for a driveway in the daylight, but not at night. "The movies, I'm not as big of a fan of. They had the opportunity to make a smoking hot cast of teachers to live up to my fantasies, but every last one of them was a dud, except maybe Severus."

"There are Harry Potter books?" asked Elliot, snickering a moment later when Shelvin turned on him with a look of utter betrayal. "Just kidding. I was at the release parties for the last two books. It was midnight at the bookstore, and I was there dressed as Lucius Malfoy to get my own copy."

"I loved those release parties. I was in New York at the time, and it was *insane*. I thought I was going to get *Avada Kedavra*'d if I cut the line." *Those were the days.* "This is the spot here."

He brought his phone up, instantly sobering. He'd have to downsize his sprawling plan to make it work and the pool would be out, but the earth was more stable than by the creek. Elliot toed the ground with his ruined shoes, nodding once.

"If we get the permits by the end of next week, then we can start cutting these few trees down. How long will it take you to finish up the schematics? I want to look over them first before we submit them." Elliot circled the area once before tapping one of the larger trees near the center. It was an old oak, its branches stretching far out of sight. "Shame to cut this baby down. How about a tree feature instead of a water feature? It would be great until the first windstorm."

Shelvin snorted. Even *he* wasn't cocky enough to fuck with trees.

"If I pull an all-nighter or two, then I would have everything drawn up by Thursday. As soon as we get back, I'll make the changes we talked about."

"Good. Then I think this will work." Elliot turned away, making it one step before Shelvin reached for him, clutching his elbow tight.

"Where do you think you're going, sweetheart?" Shelvin took a step closer before dropping his hand. He didn't need to manhandle his sub to get what he wanted. In fact, in a fight, he would stand no chance against Elliot.

"D-didn't you want to get started?" asked Elliot, his voice losing every bit of confidence that he'd shown in his work. His uncertainty was like a fucking drug.

"Get on your knees and wait for me here. I'm going to grab something from my car and you're going to kneel patiently." Shelvin took the first step to the car before he changed his mind and looked back. "And, sweetheart? Get naked."

Chapter Twelve

Elliot

It was cold. No, not just cold. It was absolutely freezing. With the sun completely gone, the temperature had dropped enough that he wondered if he needed his jacket that he'd left in the car. His breath misted in the light from his phone, a shiver working its way along his skin.

His phone shone a narrow beam so he couldn't see more than a few feet at a time. It had been fine in the semi-darkness to scope out basic terrain and trees, but alone, it wasn't nearly enough — especially not when he was working his way steadily to the freezing point and his clothes were piled…somewhere.

Shivering, he wrapped his arms around himself as he went to his knees. Despite the temperature, the peace was almost immediate. Even with Shelvin trekking to the car and the quiet night around him, he didn't feel alone. Shelvin would be back to take care of him.

Like I deserve. He'd tried saying it over and over until it sank in, but he still struggled sometimes. When he was on his knees, it seemed easier because things were finally perfect.

The sparse grass and moss were spongy beneath him, coating his naked shins in a thin film of earth. It had nothing on the swampy area, but it did leech the remaining warmth from his skin, leaving his flesh chilled. With proper drainage, it would be a perfect spot for a house.

Leave work behind... He didn't want to be thinking about schematics or drainage with calmness taking over the edge of his thoughts.

A flash on his periphery caught his eye, and he lowered his gaze to the ground, trying to make out the shape of the scraggly leaves that clumped together from the previous fall. He'd set his phone to the side, the light shooting straight up into the speckled sky and illuminating a narrow space around him with bleak whiteness.

A few twigs snapped as Shelvin moved closer, as if there were a bear in the bush and not a man. Something fluttered in the undergrowth behind him, but he didn't dare look. There were no bears about, but he wouldn't put it past a raccoon to interrupt their scene.

Shelvin will take care of me.

"You are so beautiful, sweetheart," said Shelvin as he approached, setting his phone on the ground next to Elliot's, but using a rock so the beam shone Elliot's way. He blinked in the sudden onslaught of light.

"I'm glad I planned ahead. I should have warned you that I'm prepared as fuck, and the more public we get, the more I get off."

A moment later, bright yellow light flooded the area and Elliot closed his eyes tight, turning away. *Too bright.* A flush rose to the surface of his skin when he realized that Shelvin had lit some kind of lantern to better see him by.

It was easy to be exposed in the darkness, but so much harder with the light. Every flaw and every twitch would be there for Shelvin's perusal. He wasn't sure if that was a good or bad thing, but it did make him burn hotter.

Now he was too warm and wishing he had another layer he could peel back.

"Much better." Shelvin dimmed the light until it was bearable. A moth fluttered close, tapping against the plastic surface. "How are you feeling? Comfortable? I brought a robe if you get too chilly."

No way. He was not putting clothes on, even if it rained.

"I'm green," said Elliot, dropping his hands to his knees and straightening his posture. If Shelvin was going to look, he was going to give him something nice to look at. "Thank you."

Shelvin crouched in front of him, cupping his chin and forcing his gaze up. "Okay. Starting now, I don't want you to speak unless it's your safeword. If you need a break, you say yellow right away. If you get cold or need to stop, go straight to red. I don't want you to get sick. Nod if you understand."

Elliot nodded like a bobble head, gripping his knees as he prepared for whatever Shelvin had to give him. He'd been looking forward to another scene as soon as the last one had ended, and his heart was pounding in anticipation—not to mention, his cock.

He tried to close his legs, crushing his cock between them, but it was no use. It popped up, dripping against his belly. The head was already red, and the slit was starting to leak like it did when he was close. *How embarrassing.*

"I've been trying to think of ways to push the rules as far as I can," said Shelvin as he circled around him and disappeared from view. Elliot struggled not to crane his head to the side to try to find him again.

"I really just want to torture the fuck out of you, to be honest." Shelvin let out a sigh, something jingling as he moved. "No orgasm for you is some hefty fucking torture, and I'm going to enjoy every second of it."

Please. Please. Elliot knew he wasn't getting a release from the scene, but that didn't stop him from wanting every moment of the buildup.

Shelvin's breath brushed against the back of Elliot's neck, and he went stiff, shifting as much as he dared. Blinking his eyes against the light, Elliot let himself sink that much further.

"But I can't trust you." It was barely a whisper.

The jingle came again as Shelvin touched his shoulder. "I know you *want* to be good, but I can't expect you to be able to stop yourself from coming. Only the most experienced subs can do that. So I got something to help you. It might be cold, but that will help too."

Kneeling between Elliot's legs, Shelvin brought something into the light. At the first glance, Elliot didn't even recognize what it was. Something flashed across his brain, everything going hot as he finally understood.

It was so small and unassuming, just a few metal wires twisted into a shape that pointed down with a slight curve. It wasn't insanely small, but enough for an average cock to sit in comfortably when soft. A cage to house him so he wouldn't get hard.

But he already was hard, and the sight of the cage hadn't helped. He throbbed and leaked, dripping down his shaft and to the earth beneath him. He would *never* fit.

"You like it. That kind of defeats the purpose, sweetheart." Shelvin shot him a wink before reaching for him.

The first touch of warm hands on his cock, and Elliot had to bite his lip to keep from groaning aloud and thrusting. Shelvin's hands were coarse and callused, his fingers long and delicate. There was no intentional heat at the touch, only the sure movements, and Elliot's uncontrollable reactions.

Elliot spread his legs wide to give Shelvin better access, submitting to the examination of his most intimate places. He knew he was a good size, and Hunter had never complained, but no one had ever looked at him quite so closely.

Lifting a metal ring that was separate from the cage, Shelvin clicked it open, forcing it wide and wrapping it around the base of Elliot's balls and cock all in one go before he snapped it shut. It was snug, not budging when Shelvin gave it an experimental tug.

He didn't *not* like the sensation, but he wasn't sure how the ring would do anything to help. It was way too loose to act as a cock ring, and he'd come despite the silicone ones before.

"Here comes the fun part," said Shelvin, his voice drawing Elliot in just like the moth that still fluttered against the lantern. He was lost already, but he wanted to be present for the scene this time. He didn't want to drift away and let time roll over him. Not yet, anyway.

"You can think of something gross, or I can force you in there. It will hurt either way." He slicked Elliot's cock as he spoke, lube glistening in his hand. His touch was soft and just enough to guide the head of Elliot's cock into the cage. It was a tight fit, and there was so much still to go.

How? Elliot shuddered, trying to think of the grossest thing possible. The cage already felt so tight, and he was barely inside it. The lube was easing the way, but lube could only do so much.

"If you can't do it, I could always try crushing your balls. That should get you soft quick." Shelvin tilted his head, keeping his hands still. "Or maybe you want that, too?"

Ghosts. A grandma in a bikini. My first cat dying. The latter almost brought tears to his eyes as he thought about it. It seemed to work, though, because before he could shudder, there was a click and the cage locked into place.

"I have the key here," said Shelvin, showing off the tiny silver piece before placing it in the pocket of his shirt. "Let's hope I don't lose it in the bush."

Elliot sucked in a breath, rocking his hips to try to get used to the feeling between his legs. It was heavy, pulling his cock and balls down to the earth uncomfortably at the same time it kept him restrictedly uplifted. The original ring that Shelvin had put on first, held it all in place, meaning that even if he did get hard, there would be nowhere for his cock to go.

The bars around him were the worst. Now that he was looking at it, he could barely hold off his groan from the pressure. It fucking *hurt*.

"Looks good. What do you think?" Shelvin moved beyond the ring of light, shuffling through something in the darkness. "And now you won't break your rule. You should thank me."

Elliot shivered, clutching the grass to try to focus on anything but the ache of his cock. He wasn't supposed to say a thing, of that he was certain. A stray drop of sweat dripped down his spine, the chill all but forgotten.

"I should leave that on you when you go home so you can never come again. Eventually it will shrink your cock, you know," said Shelvin, tugging a duffle bag into the light before dipping his hands inside. There was a jingling of different metals inside along with other things that Elliot's imagination could barely comprehend. "All you'll have left is two useless inches. You don't need it, baby. I have cock enough for both of us."

He's not even exaggerating. Dick size had never been a high priority for Elliot, but Shelvin was graced in that department. His cock throbbed against the cage as he thought about never coming again, trapped in between and on the edge for the rest of his life.

He stared at the cage, unable to look away. There was a small hole at the tip of it that looked familiar to some of the videos he'd endlessly searched online. It looked like something could be screwed into it and locked into place. A thrill went through him as his gut went tight.

"Yellow?" He had to ask. The question burned straight through him, leaving him gasping.

"What's up, baby? What do you need?" Shelvin was suddenly there, kneeling before him. He didn't look concerned, only attentive and patient.

"Did my cage come with a sound?" Elliot asked softly, unable to tear his gaze away from Shelvin's flickering one. A urethral sound is what they'd been called online—a solid piece that could slide into his tightest place. "I would like one."

He'd dreamed about what a sound would feel like gliding into his cock and plugging him tight. With the cage holding him on all sides, he imagined the pressure would only be more intense.

"You like that?" Shelvin grinned, scratching at the scruffy growth on his chin. "Not today, sweetheart, but I'll give it to you when you deserve a reward. I'd want to be really clean for that, and you're fucking filthy. I have something else, though, if you are okay to continue."

"Green." He couldn't hide his disappointment. But the offer of a reward would give him something to work toward...something that wasn't just reliving every moment with Shelvin. He loved a good goal.

"You say that now, but you won't in five minutes — maybe even less than that. I know you're strong, so prove me wrong." Shelvin's grin was back, his body rippling beneath his tight shirt. Elliot couldn't remember when Shelvin had taken off his leather jacket.

Something swelled in his chest, and Elliot couldn't help but puff out a bit. He'd never considered that he was strong. Physically, yes, but when it came to having a spine, he only had one when he was working.

Shelvin knelt behind him, spreading his cheeks wide. Elliot flushed with humiliation before he threw the last of his reservations out of the window. Tipping forward, he rested his cheek on the soft earth, tilting his ass so he could put it on display. Shelvin grumbled his approval, running a finger along his exposed seam.

"It's shit like this that gets you rewards." Shelvin popped the lube open again before Elliot felt the cool dampness against his skin. He shuddered as it dripped past his hole to his trapped balls that throbbed fiercely.

Something pressed against his hole that wasn't a finger. He shifted, trying to get a feel for what it was by rocking back a bit. It was blunt and cold — so much colder than Shelvin's hands. It was slippery, too, and presumably coated with lube.

"How long has it been for you?" asked Shelvin as he eased it harder against Elliot's entrance with slow, even pressure. It didn't feel all that large, but it was hard to tell from just the tip.

A long fucking time. Hunter wasn't a top in any sense of the word, and Elliot was usually too embarrassed to use toys when he was alone, not that he had the opportunity often. Hunter worked from home and sometimes followed Elliot around the house like a shadow when he was there.

The tip of the toy popped past his entrance, and Elliot let out a hiss, arching his back to try to escape some of the pressure. He wasn't a virgin, but penetration without any prep still hurt when he wasn't fully ready for it. The ache spread from his hole to the base of his spine, and he let out a gasp.

How big is it? Shelvin kept pushing and it sank deeper and deeper, somehow growing wider with each passing inch. Elliot sucked in a breath, grabbing a fistful of earth. *I can do this. I'm strong.*

The pain tapered off to a burn as he pushed out and let himself relax, leaning against the toy and taking the rest of it inside without a fuss. It sank to the base, suddenly going thin as it snapped inside. *A plug.* The narrow neck was a dead giveaway.

He wasn't sure how Shelvin managed to have all these toys at his disposal when they were in the middle of nowhere…fresh off the job, too. Did he drive around town with a bag of plugs and cages in the trunk?

"So fucking good. Another reward for taking that so well. You look tight, but not for long. I'm going to break your fucking ass, and you're going to let me."

Elliot nodded, pressing his cheek into the dirt and closing his eyes. The only sound was the distant hum of the lantern and their mingled breaths. He couldn't even feel the cold anymore except when Shelvin lifted his hands away.

"Scream for me, sweetheart."

Something clicked and Elliot jolted, a gurgle pushing through his lips as he scrambled to his hands. The plug had come alive, but not with vibrations. It was almost like a static shock, only directly against his prostate. The sensation went straight to his balls, until he was sure he was seconds from coming.

No, no, no. It couldn't be over. Not so soon.

"Yellow." He couldn't come. If he did, everything would end — and not just their scene. He couldn't let Hunter down.

"What do you need, sweetheart?" Shelvin asked softly, the shocks ceasing immediately. Elliot went limp, letting out a breath that he hadn't realized he'd been holding.

"I'm going to come. I'm going to ruin everything." Elliot cried out, tears on his cheeks. He wasn't exactly sure when the tears had started, but now that they were there, he had no way of stopping them.

"No, you won't," said Shelvin, placing a soothing palm on Elliot's hip. Elliot leaned into the touch as he sobbed. "I won't let you."

The shock came again, a pulsing surge that made his body twitch in pleasured agony. It was nothing like he'd ever imagined it would be, slamming him to the edge of orgasm over and over and nailing his prostate head-on. He was certain that he was leaking, the ground probably wet with his cum.

When the familiar build started and his balls went tight, everything stopped in its tracks. He was right there on the edge, his cock ready to shoot, but his orgasm dangled out of reach, the rhythmic pulses matching his heart.

His balls ached as it went on, the pulses seeming to get stronger. Shelvin was talking to him, but Elliot couldn't make out the words through his own noises, which were getting progressively louder. He bit his lip, doing everything he could to stay silent. *I'm strong.*

"You got this, sweetheart. You're doing so fucking good. Don't try to hold back. I've got you."

Without conscious thought, he did just that. The scruffy grass and leaves slipped through his fingers as he relaxed all at once, holding onto just enough energy to stay on his hands and knees. Everything throbbed, his orgasm teasing him over and over before Shelvin tore it away from him.

"Good."

The lantern light blurred, his breaths coming slower as Shelvin tugged the plug from him. He was only empty for a moment before there was something new there and Shelvin's groin was pressed against his ass.

Elliot let out a low hum, sobbing as he was fucked for the first time in *years*. Shelvin snapped his hips, driving into his oversensitive prostate with brutal accuracy. His knees scraped over the ground until he was sure that he was absolutely filthy, just like Shelvin had wanted.

Maybe they should have done it in the mud, so every inch of him would have been drenched. Shelvin would have stayed spotless behind him, only his cock exposed.

Shelvin slammed deep, and Elliot wondered if he was about to break. The cage was stifling, the pressure more intense that any case of blue balls in his life. His cock tried to get hard with every thrust, but the cage stopped him, feeling like it was shrinking it was so tight.

"Hurts." He clawed at the ground, rocking back to meet each thrust at the same time. Sweat crawled over his skin, leaving itchy trails everywhere.

He'd never thought he would like physical pain, especially something so intense and pinpointed at his groin, but he'd been so wrong. The ache was like a drug, each moment of dissatisfaction better than the last.

"Good." Shelvin pounded harder, grabbing Elliot's hair and forcing him to arch his back. His muscles burned, the angle of Shelvin's thrusts changing until he was pounding Elliot's prostate into absolute submission. "Don't talk, sweetheart, just fucking take it."

"Ah." Something unraveled and snapped, settling over him like a distant dream. Shelvin thrust deep one last time, releasing his grip on Elliot's hair as he started to shoot.

With his only tether gone, Elliot smacked face-first into the ground, his body going limp against his will.

Shelvin followed him all the way down, not letting them separate by an inch.

The cage ached as it dragged against the ground, pinning his cock at an awkward angle, but Elliot never wanted to move again. He shivered against the sudden chill, so calm that he wondered if he would float away.

"Here, Sweetheart. Come here."

Shelvin touched him, his hand the only warm thing in his world made of damp grass and yellow light. Elliot used every ounce of power to follow that source of heat, turning and wrapping his arms around Shelvin's neck before hugging him tight. Something deliciously soft and warm blanketed him a moment later, like fire against his oversensitive skin.

"I'm going to take you home with me to bring you down. Just let me grab our stuff, then I can lead you back to the car. Do you think you can walk?"

Elliot nodded. He would do anything for Shelvin, including walking or freezing to death on the forest floor. Struggling to his feet, he gripped his Dom's hand, refusing to let go, even as Shelvin attempted to gather everything around them.

The forest faded, his feet squishing into the top layer of soil that became softer with every step. The sliver in his heel didn't matter, nor did the few rocks that poked his soles as they neared the car.

Shelvin opened the door for him, helping him into the seat and buckling him tight. Arranging the housecoat tighter, he produced a blanket, tossing that over Elliot and tucking in the sides. Elliot snuggled deeper, despite the sweat clinging to his skin, missing the warmth of Shelvin's touch already. His feet stuck to the mat, dirt and grime smearing on the once-spotless interior.

"Did you like our scene?" asked Shelvin softly as he pulled out of the lot and onto the highway, his high beams lighting up a small path on the ragged earth.

The tires spun on the gravel for a moment before they caught the concrete of the main road, the car lurching into motion. As soon as they were up to speed, he snuck his hand across the center console, gripping Elliot's palm in his own.

"Yeah." Fuck, he sounded terrible. He hadn't even realized that he was thirsty as all hell either. Shelvin somehow seemed to read his mind, grabbing a bottle of water for him and passing it over before he clutched his hand again.

"It was exposed, but not." Elliot scratched at his cage through the blankets, the metal still tight and unyielding against his cock. The jostling movement seemed to make it even worse.

"It was maybe a bit too chilly for keeping you naked for so long, but I really wanted to try it," said Shelvin, turning as they reached the first exit. "I couldn't ask for a better sub than you to experience that with. You were amazing."

Elliot flushed, ducking his head and closing his eyes. He was still buzzing, a sleepy heaviness over his limbs and mind. He let his head loll against the window, chuckling for no reason at all. The ache in his unfulfilled cock meant nothing.

The next time he opened his eyes, they were at Shelvin's office building—the artistic details lost on him in his haze. Shelvin led him inside, slipping his shoes on and wrapping another blanket around him and somehow avoiding any other people in the condo complex. When the door closed behind him, Shelvin took him into his arms, leading him to the shower before rinsing the mud and dirt from his skin.

It was only after he was clean and dry that Shelvin took him to bed, stretching him out beneath the covers and holding him tight. Elliot hummed under his breath, shifting closer until Shelvin's head was tucked under his chin with his Dom lying on his chest.

It was perfect.

Chapter Thirteen

Shelvin

Shelvin glared at the sketched plans before him, scratching his chin as an alarm rang in his head. Something was off, but he couldn't figure out what the hell it was. The supports were in place, according to Elliot, and all the fine and massive details had been argued over and attended to.

Then what?

He looked up at the crunch of gravel as another truck rolled into the lane, the company's logo plastered on the filthy side. With the foundation laid and the timber starting to rise, things were moving way faster than expected. City hall had approved the permits with hardly any struggle at all, which was just strange. Shelvin was sure that one of them was probably a kinky fucker who owed Clint a huge favor.

Something's wrong. He grumbled at the drawing, tracing every line with the tip of his finger. If it had been one of his originals, his finger would have come away smudged with graphite, but the one in his hand now was a printed version, every line long since dried.

Looking away from the schematics, he touched his phone, grimacing as he noticed the time. He had the fucking thing on full blast, but he still hadn't caught the sound of his ringtone and it was ten-thirty in the morning. He'd even checked for texts, much to his chagrin.

Nothing.

Maybe it wasn't the best idea to dwell on it, but the fact that he'd seen Elliot three times since their scene in the woods, and they'd been strictly for professional business, irked him something fierce. Elliot always made his calls in the morning on time, but it was the only time that they seemed to speak without any other purpose between them. This was the third time he'd missed one. Three days in a row of no contact.

Shelvin ran a hand through his hair. He'd been too lenient, setting protocols and not sticking to them enough. Well, that was about to change. He knew when he was being avoided, and he was not fucking cool with it. Impact play was a hard limit, but that didn't mean that he couldn't use his *imagination* to think of a punishment.

This silent treatment had to end. The house was coming along better than expected, even with Clint nipping at their heels with his unparalleled enthusiasm. He'd kept far away from the site, though, not wanting to *distract* any of the sexy construction workers.

Shelvin grunted as he looked around to the few men and one lady close by. The only person he wanted to see was working hard in his office, ordering some custom flooring that was stylish and waterproof.

I can afford a day off to reconnect. If he left it any longer, he'd never get Elliot on his knees again and back on track. It was his fault for letting it slide. It was the same reason that his kinky relationships seemed to expire quickly, too.

He nodded at one of the workers as they walked over to him, slipping his hard hat off and tucking it under his arm. The wind was surprisingly brisk, and the damn thing had blown off three times already. Thank God there hadn't been a camera aimed his way when he'd chased the fucking thing across the site.

"Hey, Shelvin, we've got an issue." The lead hand, Samson, shuffled to a stop, crossing his arms. His T-shirt was frayed and stained, his work boots worn to the extent that the leather was probably one of the most comfortable things on the planet. He was a good guy, though, so Shelvin let the fashion sense slide. Plus, he was a big hunk of eye candy when Shelvin got bored.

"What's up?" Shelvin rolled the plans back up, resigning himself to figuring out the issue at another time. *Soon.*

"Our supplier that we wanted to order the tile from went bust, and the closest competitor wants double. Even with twice the pay, he won't have it here until the end of the month." Samson let out a sigh before scuffing his boot against the gravel and kicking up a few loose stones. They were freshly laid and still soft beneath their boots.

Shelvin tried to suppress his eye twitch as a flash of anger rushed through him. It was so unlike him to be quick to anger, his unsettled business with Elliot irking him more than he cared to admit.

He clamped down on the feeling as fast as he could. Samson was a fellow kinkster, and Shelvin had seen him in a few scenes before. There was no use getting riled in front of him, especially when he was doing his best.

Shelvin tried to push the thoughts of sceneing from his mind, the plans crunching as he clenched his fist.

"Well, fuck. Just when I thought everything was going well. If they went bust, maybe the bank wants to sell us some of their assets. If we're lucky, our order will be in that pile. I'll make a few phone calls." Shelvin gripped the schematics tighter, knowing that the plan was probably doomed. He didn't have that kind of pull when he was fairly new to the area, and he was fresh out of favors.

"Thanks, man..."

The rest of what he said was completely lost on Shelvin as he looked over Samson's shoulder to the newest vehicle pulling in the lane. With an emerald exterior and an engine that could purr like a drunken walrus, the BMW pushed every one of his buttons. The real treat was the driver, though.

"Thanks, Samson. I'll get out of your way so your guys can get to work. They don't need me looming over their shoulders. I'll bring the coffee tomorrow morning first thing." He nearly dropped his hard hat as Elliot stepped out, his hair catching the breeze in a flash of ebony light.

He couldn't look away, warmth rising in his chest as he took in every detail. No one should be that perfect or striking. At first he'd thought Hunter was the looker between the two of them, but the more he looked at Elliot, the more attractive he seemed to become.

"It's Friday, man. Bring them Monday and we'll call it even," said Samson, apparently not noticing that Shelvin's attention had strayed to much firmer ground.

How could he ever be expected to get anything done with a man like Elliot in their midst? Working together was such a terrible idea. *Fuck,* he loved it.

What had Samson said? *Friday?* Friday meant club night, whether he was alone or not. He barely saw Samson as he turned away, solely focused on Elliot as he approached.

He was wearing a leather jacket today, with aviator sunglasses and jeans so tight that Shelvin could see the outline of his cock. It was almost a shame that Shelvin had removed his cage before sending him home, because he would have looked so much better with it on, tenting the fabric and letting everyone know that he was not in short supply downstairs.

But *Jesus,* the way the sun caught his hair as it ruffled in the breeze, his feet kicking up a bit of dust that swirled around him, made his mouth go dry. *Fuck, I've gone soft.*

Shelvin shook his head, pushing every romantic notion from his thoughts. Elliot was his sub, but that was as far as it would ever go. The guy had a devotion to his husband that was just unreal. That, and Shelvin was not the vanilla relationship type. *No, Sir.*

Elliot hadn't even looked his way, headed straight for the build, and so completely focused that he'd probably missed Shelvin gawking. *Thank goodness for the little things.*

"Elliot," Shelvin called out, squaring his shoulders and dropping his voice into Dom mode. It wasn't a conscious thing on his part, but subs had told him about it in the past. "Get your ass over here."

Elliot turned, hesitating for a split second before he walked over, his gaze dropping to the rolled papers in

Shelvin's hand. His lower lip was red, an impression of his teeth still fresh.

Had he been nervous to trek out to the build? Shelvin fought off the guilt that threatened to surface. Maybe this was a bad idea, especially when there was punishment on his mind. Elliot was so new and fragile. He didn't want to break him.

"Oh, perfect. I need to see those. I think I figured something out," said Elliot, reaching for the plans. His fingers brushed Shelvin's, the touch like a shock.

Shelvin passed the papers off, turning his hand and grasping Elliot's wrist before he could pull away. It was now or never. "I'm taking you to the club tonight. I can pick you up at eight."

Elliot blinked, taking a half-step back as he stared at Shelvin's hand. A flush rose to his cheeks, highlighting the dark streaks under his eyes. There was something on his face that didn't belong. "I can't."

Elliot looked around, lowering his voice. There were a few workers close by, not to mention Samson. Elliot probably had no idea that Samson was in the lifestyle right along with them. The signs were hard to miss, if you knew what to look for.

"Plans?" Shelvin pressed, dropping his hand at Elliot's wince. *What the hell?* He was not in the mood to fuck around right now. Seeing the state that Elliot was in, only had him more on edge.

"Cancel them, sweetheart. You've been avoiding me, and you have to get over it. We fucked in a forest… It was awesome and you were amazing. Why the hesitation now?" Shelvin spoke normally, waiting for Elliot to shush him. He never did, his eyes going watery behind his glasses instead.

"I can't." Elliot lowered his voice, dipping his chin. "I'm so sorry." His posture was rigid, and Shelvin thought he could see a tremble to his lower lip. *Baby, don't cry.* He wasn't going anywhere near a punishment anymore or he'd risk how far they'd come together.

"Are you really going to fight me when you want it so bad?" asked Shelvin. "I can see it every time you move. Every time you look at me, all you can think about is how my cock felt in your mouth and in your ass. You dream about being caged again, and you can't wait for your reward. You've been *good*, sweetheart and you deserve it, but not if you are going to avoid what you *really* need. You haven't called me in three days."

There it was — the little twitch under Elliot's eye that gave him away, even with the protection of his sunglasses. He was barely hanging on. The only thing Shelvin wasn't sure of was why, but he could guess. Hunter was becoming a *big* problem.

"Go to your knees for me, sweetheart. I've got you. You don't need to be so strong when I'm here for you. I'll always catch you." Shelvin grasped the rolled plans before Elliot could drop them, tucking them under his own arm so they'd be out of the way.

Elliot looked over his shoulder and back to the build where a few guys were still in view. Samson glanced at them, scratching his head under his hard hat with a look of concern on his face. The poor guy probably thought that Elliot was upset about their supplier.

"They're watching," said Elliot, his voice trembling. There were dark shadows under his eyes and more growth than usual on his chin. *When's the last time you ate? When's the last time you slept?*

"So?" Shelvin smirked to keep the concern off his face, raising one eyebrow. "You think it will be

147

humiliating? Sweetheart, they *all* know. You're like a cute little puppy when you follow me around this job site. They're waiting for me to teach you how to sit."

Elliot went to one knee, his breath rushing out of him in an instant. He wasn't looking over his shoulder anymore, only at Shelvin.

Shelvin was enthralled in an instant, threading his fingers through Elliot's hair and tugging him until his head rested against Shelvin's belly. He fit perfectly at just the right height.

"I don't want to make them uncomfortable," said Elliot, turning his head and squishing his face directly into Shelvin's tummy. His little bit of padding dipped, and he tightened his core to keep Elliot from noticing. He already had a touch of a size complex, and he didn't need Elliot noticing that he didn't exactly have the most defined abs.

"Don't go tense. I like that you're squishy," said Elliot, letting out a huff as he started to relax. His glasses must've been digging into his nose, but he didn't seem perturbed.

Throwing back his head, Shelvin let out a laugh, Elliot's head bouncing against him with each chuckle. He tightened his grip, tilting Elliot's face to the sun and flicking his glasses off with his finger. They crashed to the ground, the lenses probably okay on the dirt.

His eyes were bloodshot and tired, looking so much worse without the lenses in the way. *Oh, baby. Why didn't you ask sooner when you obviously need it?*

"Talk to me, baby," said Shelvin, placing a kiss on Elliot's forehead. Elliot closed his eyes, leaning into the touch and humming. "Tell me why you didn't call me or ask for another scene, and I'll try to be a bit nicer when I punish you. No guarantees if you don't fess up."

Sweet, sweet punishment. He had to go with his gut. If Elliot was testing him, he had to show him that he would correct him.

Elliot's pupils blew wide, even in the daylight. He licked his lips, his pink tongue so fucking suckable that Shelvin had to hold himself back from leaning down for a kiss.

"I forgot about Hunter," said Elliot, the heat leaving his gaze in an instant. "The last time we were together, I told Hunter that I was meeting with a client, and I'd bring him home dinner. But then it was you and we scened, and I didn't get home until after midnight. He *knew* I'd been with you, but he didn't say anything when I got home. He just sat at the table looking sad."

Like a pouting fucking puppy is my bet. The kind that piddled on the floor when you went away, not the one that greeted you with kisses.

"Oh, sweetheart. Come up here." Shelvin wrapped his arms around him as soon as he stood, and Elliot shivered beneath his touch. "Cry if you need to. You don't have to hold on to something like that all by yourself. Let me take care of you, and give me your guilt. I won't ever let you forget that you need this." *Even if I have to set a fucking alarm.*

"I just…" Elliot sniffed, the saltiness of tears hitting the air. "You don't have to do this. You're my Dom, but I can't rely on you for *everything.*"

"Who says?" Shelvin leaned back even though he wanted to hold Elliot close and never fucking let him go again. "I'm your Dom, and I'll look after you in any way that I see fit. If I think it's in your best interest to send you home early from a job and ask you to get a few hours sleep, then that's what I'll do. If I want to hold doors open for you and push your chair in or treat you like you're made of glass, then nothing's going to stop me. You're mine, baby."

Elliot turned his watery eyes on him. Fuck, he looked tired, the weight of the world on his strong shoulders. Shelvin should have been carrying that weight, though, and he was happy to—if only Elliot would let him.

"But...Hunter."

"Is your husband. He may love you, but sometimes he doesn't know what's best for you. That's why you're mine, right? And if you ever doubt that, call me. We can talk to Hunter together if you'd like, but never keep us from him. He's doing this for you, too. Remember that."

"Okay." Elliot dropped back to his knees, almost dragging Shelvin down with him when he didn't let go right away. His back let out a twinge, and Shelvin winced. He loved having a big sub, but he was a twink at heart. Unless twinks had an age limit...

"Good." Shelvin patted his head, twisting the strands through his fingers. "I need you to go home and have a nap, because that's what's best for you right now. I'll pick you up at eight o'clock, and I want you to be ready inside and out. Don't wear anything you like, because it won't last long. And, baby? Never miss a call again."

Chapter Fourteen

Elliot

Shelvin hadn't been kidding. Three steps into the club and he'd been ordered to strip everything except for his boxers...only he'd hadn't worn boxers exactly. His face had warmed to the surface temperature of the sun when Shelvin had taken his first look at the lacy pink G-string that Elliot had worn.

Elliot had put them on as a test of sorts. He hadn't been sure what Shelvin's reaction would be when he'd slid them up his legs, but he'd longed to know.

"I'm surprised you didn't go with leather," said Shelvin, tracing his fingers over the scratchy frills. He circled behind Elliot, tugging at the G-sting until it was rubbing between his cheeks. Elliot had to fight with himself not to squirm.

"You said not to wear something I liked," said Elliot, looking down at himself. His package bulged obscenely, tenting the lace until it hardly touched anything except the head of his cock. "I found these on sale online, but they never really fit me right."

It was probably the boldest thing he'd ever done. He'd grabbed them because he'd known Shelvin would ask him to strip, and he'd known people would be watching. The rush of their eyes on him was like a drug.

Shelvin gave him a wink, and his heart thudded as he noticed how *many* people were watching them. They weren't even in the open play area yet, but Shelvin was strutting his stuff like he didn't even care. Their scene had begun before they'd even stepped foot inside. *It's not like I'm the only naked one.* There were two others in view that had less on than him.

"I think it's perfect." Shelvin hooked one finger in the tented fabric at the front, tugging it to the side so Elliot's cock sprang free. He released it with a snap, a grin on his lips. "I was wrong. *Now* it's perfect. Come on. I want a drink."

Elliot reached for himself automatically. He was big, but he could mostly shield himself with his hands if he tried. It was nearly impossible when he was so hard, but he couldn't just walk around with it sticking out like that. What if he bumped into someone?

"Are you hiding yourself from me?" asked Shelvin, giving him a sharp look that was threatening on so many levels. He clicked his tongue. "I guess your punishment won't be so nice after all."

Dropping his hands to his sides, Elliot took a humiliated breath. "I'm sorry." There were probably about twenty strangers that now knew how big his dick was and that he wasn't circumcised. Maybe he should have just added a piercing to the head to give them something better to look at. *Ouch.*

"Go get me an iced tea, slave." With that, Shelvin turned away, heading for one of the occupied tables and starting up a conversation with someone who looked vaguely familiar.

Fire and ice battled in his gut, sweat sparkling on his skin even as he shuddered. It took a conscious effort to keep his hands off himself and to not adjust the little triangle that would have offered him that smidgeon of modesty. The few looks of interest spurred him on, and he straightened his spine, marching to the bar with renewed purpose.

"I wasn't sure if I'd see you in here again," said the bartender Maddy, shooting him a quick smile. "I'm glad you came back, though. What'll you have?"

Oh God. His tongue was suddenly stuck as he stared like a deer in the headlights. What had Shelvin asked for? What would happen if he came back with the wrong thing? He glanced over his shoulder to where Shelvin was waiting for him. He was gesturing and laughing as he spoke with someone, looking like he was already high on adrenaline.

"I don't remember," said Elliot, biting his lip. *I am the worst sub ever if I can't even remember a stupid drink order.* He crumpled a bit, sagging his shoulders. A stray hand came a little too close to his naked cock and he shied away from it.

"Shelvin likes to mix it up," said Maddy, giving the owner of the stray hand a glare before he continued. "He likes things interesting…like you. I can make him something that will blow his mind, and I'll make it a virgin so he can blow yours."

The drink came out pink and sparkling with a rim of blue that smelled sweet. Elliot took a small sip of it, licking his lips and humming at the taste.

"Will that do?" Maddy cocked one brow.

"It's perfect. Thank you so much, Maddy." Retreating to the table where Shelvin stood, Elliot presented the drink, wilting a little when Shelvin squinted and looked at it with a tilted head.

"That's two," said Shelvin, grasping the drink and taking a sip. "It is good, though." He set it on the table, turning back to the two others seated there. "What was I saying, Trick? Oh, yeah. How can I torture the fuck out of someone without hitting them? I know you're an impact guy, but you have one hell of an imagination."

The blond sat straighter as he looked to his sub who was seated beside him. Elliot sucked in a breath as he had a sudden realization. Trick was the one he had been watching all those nights ago when Shelvin had seen him across the bar. Only now his sub was sitting next to him and curled into Trick's side and not on his knees. His gaze was distant and peaceful, his entire body relaxed.

"You ever think about CNC?" asked Trick, pulling his sub closer and placing a kiss on his head. "That's the biggest mind-fuck out there for me, but it might be a hard limit for some."

CNC? What the hell is that? Elliot chewed his lip, trying to stay quiet, even as a million questions burned. Were they talking about him? Shelvin was doing a pretty good job pretending to ignore him. He seemed to really like doing that.

Well, two could play at that game, especially if he was getting punished anyway. The reaction he'd gotten from the panties didn't live up to his expectations, anyway. *Does Shelvin even want me here?*

Elliot shifted one step to the left, until his exposed cock came precariously close to Shelvin's arm. Shelvin didn't notice from his seated position, continuing his conversation with Trick without even glancing his way.

Biting his lip, Elliot tried and failed to squash his budding irritation. *Everyone* was looking at him except for the one person he wanted to.

With Shelvin's hand on the table and his T-shirt sleeves cut short, it left a naked strip of skin at the perfect height. *This is going to suck.*

With a small jerk to the side, Elliot slapped his cock against Shelvin's arm just hard enough that the *thud* went all the way to his balls. Shelvin paused mid-sentence, his mouth still open as he turned to him with one raised brow.

Even Trick looked surprised, a smirk stretching across his face before he hid it behind his hand. His sub was still gone, floating in a place that Elliot wanted nothing more than to be in.

"That's three," said Shelvin, his voice surprisingly calm as he tapped three fingers against the same spot that Elliot's cock had left a small smear. Are you really going down the brat road tonight?"

Elliot flushed, straightening his spine as he refused to back down. He knew what he wanted, but it wasn't what he was getting. That was the fucking problem. Shelvin had *promised.*

It was bliss to be ordered to do the basic things like shower and rest after their last scene, and he'd basked in it as if it were the sun. He wanted more. He wanted every bit of Shelvin's attention on him for the night. *I deserve it.*

"Come on, brat. You want to act like one, and I'll treat you like one. Come by later if you're up to it, Trick." Shelvin grabbed Elliott's cock, squeezing hard as he stood from the table.

"Ow. Ow." He tried to gently tug free, but Shelvin was surprisingly strong, and Elliot didn't want to lose that part of himself in a tug-o-war.

"I can't believe you slapped me with your dick," said Shelvin, his voice so soft that Elliot had to struggle to hear it. "It'd be hilarious if it wasn't so disrespectful." His grip went even tighter, until Eliot was sure his cock was going to be strangled, before Shelvin let go all at once.

He sagged his shoulders, gulping in a breath as his cock throbbed, harder than ever. Shelvin was already walking toward the back where all the rooms were hidden. Scurrying after him, Elliot tried to catch his breath, his legs bowed as he continued to throb with each step.

Pausing at the door labeled *Feel,* Shelvin sent him a look that brooked no questions. "Get inside."

Elliot scrambled through the door, trying to remember what his co-worker had told him about the room. He thought it was about sensation play or something of the like, but with his heart pounding, he could barely focus.

Why the hell did I do that? Shelvin didn't look pissed, but that was more worrisome. What if he was disappointed in Elliot? That was so much worse than anger.

Shelvin propped the door all the way open, the music and conversation from the bar floating clearly though. Was it staying open? God, he hoped so.

Shelvin's distraction with the door gave him a few moments to look around, not sure what he was seeing. *A feather?* It was long and purple, sitting on a shelf next to dozens of things that Elliot didn't recognize. One of those things looked like a glove, only it was covered in metal spikes. Another was a purple case full of things that looked a bit like oversized dental tools. He couldn't recall what they were called. *Violet somethings?*

"I'm going to restrain you," said Shelvin, stepping to the middle of the room and reaching for a pair of manacles hanging from the ceiling. He wrapped Elliot's wrists in them as soon as he approached, the soft leather much more comfortable than he'd expected.

With a clink of chains and a few adjustments, Elliot's arms were pulled just above his head with enough slack that he could take a step in any direction and not twist his shoulders too hard.

"Is that okay on your shoulder? I don't want it to hurt you," said Shelvin, touching Elliot's right shoulder exactly where his old rotator cuff injury was. It was a spot that ached constantly, but the position was giving him no more discomfort than usual.

"I think I should be fine," said Elliot, tugging at the chain to test it. The position was actually quite comfortable, taking the weight of his arm and some of the strain along with it. He licked his lips as he throbbed in time with the distant beat. How could he be so close when Shelvin had barely touched him?

"I didn't ask you for your fucking opinion, slave. What's your color?" Shelvin's voice was steady, but his words were sharp, cutting through any of his remaining defenses.

I guess the punishment has officially started. Was it bad if he kind of liked it? Elliot took a shaky breath, spreading his legs wide as a bit of regret seeped in. Maybe he'd gone too far with the dick thing. "Green."

"Tell me as soon as that changes."

"Yes, Master." It was so automatic that Elliot didn't even realize he'd said it until Shelvin was smiling. He was in a different mindset already, slipping under a veil that belonged only to Shelvin.

But could he go there? What would Hunter think of him, loving being called a slave with cuffs around his wrists, his cock poking out of a pair of lacy panties? Hunter would never understand.

Elliot shook his head, but the memory of Hunter's increasingly frequent frowns refused to leave his sinking thoughts.

"That won't save you now," said Shelvin, going to a cupboard that Elliot hadn't noticed. The bag that Shelvin had had with him when they'd first arrived was lying on the couch, the unknown mysteries within leaving the first dew drops of sweat on Elliot's skin.

"Let's take care of that pesky cock first. I even got you a present, not that you deserve it." With no preamble, Shelvin lubed him up with a few precise strokes, snapping the cock cage into place once Elliot finally managed to go soft. It took longer than last time, the sensation battling with his will.

It felt tighter than the previous one, squeezing him, even though his cock had fully softened. If he got hard, he was certain it would be agony. There was more than just the even pressure from last time, though. Along the inner tube were raised bumps pressed to his flesh, like pebbles in the bottom of his shoe that would strike his sole with each meandering step.

Elliot glanced at it, trying to get a good look as his cock flopped down from the weight. It *was* smaller but somehow heavier.

"That one fits better, I think, and you'll love the little nubs on the inside. They're smooth, but I'm sure they'll feel like spikes in no time at all." Shelvin snapped a pair of white latex gloves on while he spoke, dabbing the head of Elliot's caged cock with a small, damp square.

"This baby has some bumps too that I'm sure you'll love." From a small black case, Shelvin pulled a silver sound. It glinted in the overhead light, the metallic sheen matching that of the cage. It was slightly thinner than a pencil at the tip with small bumps along the shaft and a larger bulb at the end. It was only a few inches long, but so was Elliot's cock at the moment.

Fuck. Fuck. Elliot had dreamed of this moment—and being filled in all of his tightest places and completely under Shelvin's control. This wasn't a punishment. It was torture. *The best kind.*

"Take a breath, slave."

Shelvin pressed the tip of the sound to Elliot's cock, squirting a drop of lube down the metallic shaft before he slowly started to ease it into a hole that had never been touched by anything.

The first inch was pure stretch and a violation that Elliot had no way of stopping. It was as terrifying as it was thrilling, dragging him in as the pressure turned into a slight burn as the first bump pressed against his tip. The heaviness of it pushed his cock into the nubs of the cage as it slid deeper, breaking him from the inside and out.

It was different than he imagined.

"Fuck, I can't." Elliot bucked, jerking away as the sound went impossibly farther. No matter how hard he wiggled, Shelvin moved along with him, holding the sound steady with even pressure. His cock tried to harden, but the cage clamped down on it with an agonizing force.

Maybe it was a punishment. Everything hurt worse than when Shelvin had grabbed him by the cock, and his balls were aching with the need to come. Only, he wouldn't be coming — not now and not ever.

Swallowing down his regret, Elliot breathed through the sensations, closing his eyes against the threatening tears. *I want to. Please.*

"Not your decision to make," said Shelvin, still calm as ever as he sank the last inch inside and twisted the sound, locking it in place.

He wouldn't be coming any time soon.

A tear rolled down his cheek as he let out a ragged breath. He didn't deserve to come.

Chapter Fifteen

Shelvin

Feel had always been one of his favorite rooms, but he'd never had a sub quite like Elliot in it. Every time they were together, it was as if Shelvin peeled a new layer back, exposing Elliot for who he really was. And just when he thought he'd finally figured Elliot out, he got slapped with a dick.

The tears seemed right on par with the size of cage and sound he'd picked. He'd tried the same combo out before, and it had brought tears to his eyes, too. *In a good way.*

But a brat? He hadn't been expecting that. It had taken everything in him to not burst out laughing when Elliot had slapped him. There were a few things he'd been on the fence about, not sure if Elliot was ready or not, but now they were *on.* If Elliot was comfortable enough to brat, then he was comfortable enough for a public punishment.

Elliot's mostly naked ass longed for a slap, but Shelvin held back, respecting his sub's limits. No impact took a lot off the table, but after he was through, his sub would think twice about disrespecting him again. And even though Elliot had said slaps were fine, he didn't want to go there for a punishment.

"So, I'll start slow and go from there. If you're good, then I might decide to let you have some fun." This was about *fun*, after all. They weren't in a twenty-four-seven dynamic, so he was fine with mixing a little reward and punishment in the same shot. And he'd never been much of a stickler for the rules — another flaw of his.

Strolling to the wall, he plucked a pair of vampire gloves from their package, making a note to give Clint a tip for them. Some of their play items and sex toys just couldn't be cleaned one-hundred-percent, and something like the gloves wouldn't be reused for another sub. But Clint always managed to keep things well stocked with quality items.

Shelvin made a mental note to try to double the storage area he had prepped in the new place, too. With so many rooms, Clint would need that much more in the supply department.

The gloves fit snuggly, the little spikes on the fingers glistening in the low light. They were sharp enough that they'd draw blood if he landed a slap or squeezed too hard, but not too sharp to cause any permanent damage. They really worked best with a blindfold as well, but he wanted to see Elliot's reaction to his humiliation.

He wanted to cross the lines and mix the pain that Elliot hated with the thing he seemed to love most. Then, when he was at his breaking point, he would take every whispered ache away, leaving only pleasure behind.

I am so bad at punishments. Still, it was a great fucking plan. Hopefully this one actually worked out.

Right on time. He caught movement out of the corner of his eye as someone shuffled inside and seated themselves on the couch. Elliot stiffened, snapping his spine straight as he let out the first sound of protest when he must've realized what the open door meant.

It's all fun and games until you get put in your place in front of a crowd. Shelvin didn't waste another moment to let the reality sink in. Reaching for Elliot's ass, he dragged the glove over the pale globe, each spike scratching its own path and leaving pink marks behind.

Elliot gasped, bucking away and jerking to look over his shoulder as he tensed his ass. "That hurts."

He seemed so surprised.

Shelvin put on a show of rolling his eyes while adjusting the glove from where it had slipped a bit. *One size fits all, my ass.* "Really? I had no fucking idea."

He reached for Elliot's other cheek, scraping the prongs a touch harder until he was almost breaking skin. He knew what it felt like — a thousand needles dragging across flesh and piercing the outermost layer — but it was about to get worse.

Cupping as much as he could of Elliot's quivering ass, he *squeezed.*

"Ah!" Elliot twisted in his chains, the slack going tight with a metallic jingle. Ripping out of Shelvin's hold, he danced as the manacles pulled tight and threw his weight off. "That fucking *hurts.*"

Shelvin licked his lips, making a show of grabbing his groin with his uncovered hand. "I know." Elliot's eyes went wide, and Shelvin watched the veil of subspace drop over his sub, consuming every thought as his adrenalin faded to pure endorphins.

Hopefully Elliot would realize soon that this wasn't a punishment at all, but just another level to what was developing between them. Shelvin wanted to see every part of his sub, even the bratty side that preferred cock slapping to words.

"What a pretty sight." He reached for Elliot's other cheek, squeezing until the tiniest drops of blood bloomed. This time, Elliot stayed put, gasping when Shelvin didn't release him. His caged cock jumped, trying and failing to get hard. It had to ache something fierce, but Shelvin couldn't summon an ounce of sympathy, not when Elliot was sucking up every moment of attention until he practically glowed.

Over and over he scraped and squeezed, pushing until Elliot's ass was a scratchy mess of reddened skin with a few drops of blood. Then he teased over his balls with much gentler strokes, making sure they got their own type of torture as well. Only when Elliot was moaning and begging did he turn for the case of violet wands.

The crowd had grown, three people on the couch and another four against the wall. Two subs were seated, watching the scene with wide eyes. Their presence was probably a warning more than anything, although one looked interested. Shelvin honestly didn't give a shit. None of it was for *them*.

It took a few minutes to set everything up before he circled around his sub, pausing before him. Elliot was still with him, even if he did look a bit dazed. He was so beautiful in his calm, every strong inch at Shelvin's whim. It was a fucking rush to say the least.

"I think you liked that," said Shelvin, scratching his chin as he waited for Elliot to respond. His sub blinked, giving him a subtle shake of his head before hanging it low and staring at the ground. His cock was red in its cage, squeezed so tight that it must've been agony.

"You certainly didn't hate it," said Shelvin, flicking the cage and grinning at Elliot's flinch. "But you weren't *supposed* to like it. It was your punishment." Maybe Trick was right about the mindfuck thing. Watching Elliot war with himself was beautiful.

Elliot mumbled something too low for him to hear, shuffling his feet as Shelvin cupped his chin and tilted his face up. His pupils were blown, and Shelvin had an inkling that he couldn't push much further until it was too much. Subspace did funny things to people's minds, and he didn't want Elliot to regret a single second of their time together.

"Speak up, sweetheart, and be honest. Did you like it?"

"I liked that *you* liked it," said Elliot, his voice a tad breathless.

And if that wasn't the hottest thing that Shelvin had ever heard, he wasn't sure what was. He knew a few soft tops that got off on pleasuring their sub, and who didn't have a sadistic bone in their body. It wasn't nearly as common for subs. Subs usually loved pleasing their Master, but they didn't usually get high just from their Master's pleasure.

"I think you need a reward, sweetheart." Shelvin turned to the couch, grabbing one of his toys from his bag and a bit of lube. A few people had stayed, while others had moved on now that the punishment was over. He motioned to the rest to get out, shutting the door behind them as they left. *The rest is just for me.*

Circling back to Elliot, he parted his cheeks, lifting the G-string to the side before squirting a dollop of lube on his hole. He didn't bother with any stretching before he pushed the small toy inside, turning it until Elliot let out the telltale gasp as it settled against his prostate.

A prostate massager wasn't usually his go-to toy, but Shelvin had bought it for Elliot on a whim. The shade of blue matched a few of the other things he'd bought just for his sub. It was nice being able to spoil someone again.

He set the massager to its lowest setting, sending a hum against his sub's prostate that was no doubt much softer than the shocks he'd experienced in the woods. Elliot moaned, jerking his hips as his cock probably tried to get hard in its metal cage. Shelvin came around just to watch his caged cock twitch and flail, the tiniest pearl of fluid making it past the sound and gleaming at the tip.

Elliot was breathing hard, a flush all the way down his chest with his eyes rolled back in his head. The veins on his arms stood out as he tugged against his restraints. It probably wasn't a conscious move on his part.

"Relax, sweetheart," said Shelvin, resting his hand on Elliot's chest. His skin was slick, his heart pounding beneath Shelvin's palm. "Could you take just a little bit more for me?"

Elliot's nod was almost frantic. He was so close to his limit that for a moment, Shelvin doubted himself. The last thing he wanted to do was push Elliot too far. But there seemed to be no safeword in sight.

Grabbing the violet wand where he'd left it, he double-checked that it was at the mildest intensity. A humming buzz filled the air with an ominous sound as soon as he turned it on.

Elliot snapped his head up, his eyes widening.

"What is that?" asked Elliot, the chains jingling above his head as he flinched when Shelvin snapped it against his own finger. There was a mild tingle, but nothing nearly as dramatic as the sound.

Sure, it probably sounded intimidating as hell, but Shelvin had grabbed one of the lower-intensity models that gave out pleasant tingles and not full-blown shocks. It still sounded like something out of a Frankenstein movie, though. But that was part of the fun.

"Sweetheart." Shelvin shot him a grin despite the uncertainty starting to build in his gut. Taking a chance, he cranked the intensity so the buzzing strengthened. "Don't you trust me?" He tried to sound teasing, but he'd never been more serious. They were walking on dangerous ground, and something was telling him that it was about to crack.

Elliot had always been down for anything and aimed to please, even when he'd been buck naked in a forest. Shelvin hadn't caught a single glimpse of that person today.

Shelvin let out a breath as Elliot nodded without hesitation. *Good.* He'd wondered if it was time to call it. Maybe he'd just pushed too much for one day, but Elliot seemed game.

"Sorry, Master." Elliot flushed, looking downright bashful. "I'm just scared. I didn't mean to question you."

That won't do. Questions were part of the game, especially when they were still getting to know each other.

Shelvin flicked the wand off, setting it back in its case. "Tell me what's wrong, Elliot. I need to know if I call it or if it's safe to keep going. You aren't yourself today, and I don't want either of us getting hurt."

Elliot bit his lip as he looked away, shifting between flushed and pale quickly before he gripped the chains above his bindings. "I-I." He looked to the violet wand, his eyes going wider. "Not that?"

"Okay. Thank you for telling me." Shelvin flicked the vibrator off before he reached for the bindings, freeing Elliot's wrists a moment later. They fell away with a clink and Elliot immediately looked at his wrists, which were only slightly reddened.

"Let's have a chat, okay? This one is person to person. This is a relationship for our mutual satisfaction, and I need all the cards on the table." He glanced to the cage before thinking better of taking it off. Last time, Elliot had almost begged him to leave it on. It seemed almost comforting to him.

He led Elliot to the couch, twisting the cap off an unopened bottle of water before passing it to his sub. Elliot's skin stuck to the pleather as he sat stiffly, rubbing his wrists and staring at the bindings that were still swaying from the ceiling.

"I really don't want to talk about it," said Elliot, his face going even paler before he ducked his head. Shelvin grabbed the robe from his bag, tossing it over Elliot's shoulders when he noticed his trembling.

"Okay," said Shelvin, keeping his voice soothing. *Shit.* "But I can't scene with you until you tell me what's going on. I know it's something personal, but I can't risk triggering you inside a scene. I refuse to hurt you like that."

Elliot went rigid, rubbing at his cock cage as the bottle crinkled in his other hand. "What? So you're dumping me? I don't want to get electrocuted, and you call it quits?" He glared at the open case for the violet wand.

"No, not at all." Shelvin tried to stay calm, even as his sub started to lose his composure. The guilt was already eating away at him, dropping his high and reminding him of what a shitty Dom he could be. He *never* put his subs first, and maybe that was the problem. Maybe that was why nothing ever worked out for him.

"I just want to fucking kneel, okay?" Elliot growled, crossing his arms and leaning against the backrest. The bottle fell from his hand, splashing to the ground, but he made no move to retrieve it. It glugged three times, liquid spreading and turning the floor slippery and dark.

"I don't need all this other stuff. I just want to kneel and for you to use me how you want. I don't want to make a decision, and I don't want you to give me a choice about it. I thought you understood that, but I guess not."

Ah fuck. "So when something goes wrong, it's all my fault." Shelvin let out a sigh, running a hand through his hair. He should have seen the signs, but Elliot had been so fucking eager and beautiful that maybe he'd swept them under the rug a bit. Who could blame him, though?

It made sense. Elliot's limit list was pretty short, and he'd been so fucking *desperate*. But Shelvin didn't want to make a mistake and have Elliot pin the blame on him for not being able to magically read his mind. He was already damaged enough without adding a pile of guilt to that bag.

The worst part was that Elliot wasn't denying it. That was *exactly* what he wanted.

Grabbing the key from his pocket, Shelvin bent down to unlock the cock cage, pulling the sound out a moment later and tossing everything into his bag to be cleaned later. Elliot gripped his thighs, his fingers digging hard into the muscle as he let out a whimper.

"Can I take the toy out?" asked Shelvin when Elliot stayed silent. He carefully wiped the lube from Elliot's cock with a damp cloth, watching the tears gather on his sub's lashes.

I fucked up. Huge.

"Just leave it." Elliot stood and grabbed his clothes from where Shelvin had stashed them in the bag. His lips were pressed in a thin line, his face shuttered and his mind apparently made up.

"Can I at least give you aftercare before you storm off?" asked Shelvin as his gut plunged. He really didn't want to fuck up so badly. Elliot was something special, and someone to be treasured, but he'd ruined it like every other contract. "I'm sorry, Elliot. I'm sorry I can't give you what you need, but please don't storm out. *I* need you to stay. *Please.*"

Elliot paused, his lower lip trembling as his eyes went glassy. A full-bodied shudder ran through him as he dropped his head into his hands, his clothes falling to the floor in a haphazard pile. The edge of his shirt landed in the puddle of water, the fabric blooming dark.

Fuck. Is he crying? Ah, shit, he is. A couple of tears were one thing, but this was downright sobbing.

Shelvin was off the couch in moments. Wrapping his arms around Elliot, he pulled him close, shushing him as tears flowed down his cheeks. "Breathe, baby, just breathe. I'm here for you. Let it all out and give it to me. I'll take care of you."

"Fuck." Elliot tried to jerk away, but Shelvin held fast. His sub was strong, but Shelvin was a stubborn bastard when he needed to be. "I told myself I wasn't going to do this. You're just so…perfect. I don't even know why you'd want me as your sub. I can't do anything right, and Hunter hates me, too — and I just don't know what to do."

Aw shit. He thought he'd put the Hunter issue to rest already, but apparently, he'd neglected that, too. He had a few visits to make if that were the case. If Hunter was shaming Elliot in any way, he was going to get his ass kicked. That, or Shelvin would have to make Elliot his in *every* way. But he'd rather not be the homewrecker.

"Not sure why you think I wouldn't want you. You are beautiful, Elliot, inside and out. You're the best sub I've ever had, and I wouldn't change anything about you…except maybe the dick slapping thing, because that was not cool." Shelvin chuckled as Elliot gave him a soft laugh.

"Sorry about that." Elliot hugged him back, his warmth like an inferno.

"Don't worry about it. It's shit like dick slapping that makes kink fun. Hell, if you just kneeled at my feet all day, every day, I'd probably fall asleep. No Dom will ever admit it, but they want their sub to challenge them every now and again. It tests the strength of our relationship and balances everything out." Shelvin pulled him tighter, delaying letting go as long as he could.

"When we leave today, I'm going to take care of a few things and give you some time to think things over," said Shelvin, cupping Elliot's chin and holding his gaze. "I am here for you whenever you're ready, and no amount of time in the world will ever be too long. If it takes a year, then that's what it takes. If you need me, I'm only a phone call away. I will *never* abandon you."

Elliot collapsed against him, and Shelvin took his weight with a grunt, his legs shaking from the extra load. He wasn't exactly out of shape, but he needed to make some time for the gym.

"Thank you."

Crisis fucking averted.

Chapter Sixteen

Elliot

Everything was coming together so well with the house that Elliot was afraid to say something out loud and jinx it. The joists were complete, and the outside of the hefty build was covered in Typar and awaiting brick. They'd had to go with their second choice of brick due to some astronomical costs, but the rest was set.

And as much as he hated to admit it, it was fucking beautiful. The peaks that he'd thought would be a bulky array of nonsense instead gave it more character than he'd imagined. It looked like mix between a castle and one of the fancy condo buildings with glass from floor to ceiling and chandeliers in the loft. Only, instead of a chandelier, maybe a sub would be dangling, wrapped in rope.

"I'm heading out, guys!" Elliot lifted his bump cap, scrubbing his hair to relieve the itch that always built under the thing. Even if the days weren't hot yet, he'd still managed to work up a sweat.

"See you Wednesday," said Samson, pausing his examination of some electrical before looking his way. "Don't forget that it's your turn for breakfast. Allan can't have cheese—"

"Or peppers." Elliot grinned at Samson. "Don't worry, I remember. That shit's serious, and I don't want any of the crew getting hurt or sick."

He couldn't remember the last time he'd had so much fun at a build site. Sure, most crews were easy to get along with, but for the most part, they did their thing and Elliot complained that they were doing it wrong. He'd gotten a few threats early on in his career when he'd tried to tell the old boys how to do their jobs, and he'd figured out after some time how to get along with most construction workers.

Still…they weren't usually so welcoming and open, communicating the little details so they could work as a team instead of two sides fighting for the same coin.

"I have to ask you something before you go, Elliot." Samson jogged the few paces down the temporary steps that they'd erected near the middle of the build. Permanent ones would come later in a different spot all together.

"What's up?" Elliot took a quick glance at his watch, relaxing when he realized he was more than an hour ahead of schedule. Maybe he'd be able to surprise Hunter and be home early for once.

Samson shot a look over his shoulder, shuffling closer when he saw that one of his guys was near the top of the steps. "You and Shelvin…is there something going on there?"

Elliot clenched his jaw, cracking his knuckles on one hand. *Good question.* After his mild breakdown, they'd barely spoken except for their daily check-ins. He *knew* things were good between them, but he still felt off. There was a gaping hole in his life every time he thought of moving on without Shelvin and pounding fear when he imagined them together.

"I don't mean to pry, and really its none of my business, but I don't want anything to affect the job here." Samson held his hands up as if offering his pre-emptive surrender. "My crew saw you kneeling, and I shut down any grumbling right away. I'm in the lifestyle myself, but a lot of my guys aren't, so I keep my builds professional. Andy wondered if he should go to the police, because he thought you were being blackmailed or something, but I assured him everything was fine."

Samson scratched at his chin and the wood sliver that was clinging to his scruff. "I just need to make sure you're okay, though. You seem a bit off the last while, and I know sometimes Shelvin *forgets* about his subs. If you need someone to talk to, my ears are open."

Elliot let out a breath. No matter how alone he felt, it was nice to know that Samson had his back. He hadn't realized that delving into kink had opened up his life to new friends, too.

And it was the sweetest thing he'd heard all month. Samson's support even beat the little stuffed cow that Hunter had bought him for no particular reason. Elliot hadn't asked, and he didn't need to. Flowers or a stuffy, it didn't matter. As long as it was from Hunter, he would cherish it.

Shuffling his feet against the plywood, Elliot smiled, his chest warming a few degrees. Maybe he shouldn't have knelt at a job site. It wasn't professional, but he had needed it so badly.

"He's a good Dom, but you're right...sometimes he gets busy and forgets, but I do, too." Now *that* was a lie. He thought about Shelvin all the time, even the moments when Hunter was in his arms. Every call in the morning was the highlight of his day. He was never missing one again.

"Yeah, he's okay." Samson shrugged, giving him a wink. "I like a man who knows how to play doctor, myself. You ever try anything like that?"

Doctor? A Gynecologist was the first thing that popped into his thoughts, but he did not have the right parts for that.

Elliot shook his head, his eyes wide. He took a step closer, lowering his voice. Someone was coming down the stairs, the sharp sound of their whistle getting closer. "Like stethoscopes and stuff?"

Samson chuckled, his ears going red. "I figured with how many things doctors liked shoving up my ass, and how much I tended to like it, that I might as well try it out for fun. Who knew that I'd fall in love with it?"

Elliot wasn't sure if he wanted to know more. Doctor's offices gave him the shivers, but he was sure that cock warming would turn other men off, while that was probably his favorite thing...other than maybe the vampire gloves.

He'd looked the damn things up online after his punishment, cringing as he got his first clear look at them. No wonder they'd hurt like fuck, but at the same time, they'd felt so wonderful that he wanted to do it again—maybe not with an audience next time, though. His denial at the time had been such a bitter lie, but he'd been terrified of the snap of electricity. It had brought back too many bad memories.

"Offer stands." Samson leaned away, wiping his hands on his pants. "And don't forget breakfast."

* * * *

Twenty minutes later, Elliot let himself into his apartment, grinning when he saw Hunter's jacket on the hook. It would be time to completely abandon the spring jackets soon and replace them with the monogrammed umbrellas that they kept in the closet during the cooler months. Last year, he'd splurged and had gotten them both rainbow umbrellas with their names in looped cursive. Hunter's family had not been impressed, which made the hundred-dollar contraptions all the more worth it.

Elliot paused, Hunter's name frozen on his tongue as he caught the low hum of conversation. His heart thudded in his throat when he spied the extra pair of shoes on the mat and the jacket crumpled next to them. The shoes were filthy, with mud and sand jammed between the tread and making a mess all over the floor.

I'm home early and there's a strange man in the house. Don't panic.

He couldn't help it. He was a terrible husband, and he knew it. When was the last time he'd put Hunter first and made love to him with abandon? He could hardly bring himself to do it, even with his scenes with Shelvin. It just seemed…wrong somehow.

He'd fucked up, and there was no turning back. *Do I leave and pretend or go to the kitchen?* It would be hypocritical of him not to accept that Hunter had taken a lover, especially since he'd been fucked in the middle of a forest in the dead of night.

He slowly moved to the kitchen, dragging his feet with each step. The voices became clearer, but he still couldn't make out the words. He grabbed a glass of water, his hands shaking as he carefully added ice to it. It was only when he pulled the chair back from the table, his legs going out from under him, that he finally understood.

His heart pounded, his legs shaking as his hands started to tremble. *This is not happening.*

"I don't like what you're doing to him," said Hunter with the haughty edge that he only ever had when he was reaching the point of a tantrum. "It's not normal or natural, and you're just digging up his memories and using them against him. He's a whole different person since you strolled into his life and took him away from me." Hunter's voice went loud and shrill as if he were on the edge of tears. "Then you *dare* show up here and tell me *I'm* the one in the wrong?"

"Yep," Shelvin drawled, slow and soft like he always did. Elliot shivered at the sound of his Dom's voice, his body frozen in his spot. Next to his intense gaze, Shelvin's voice had been the first thing to draw him in.

"You...you asshole!" Something shattered as Hunter yelled, and Elliot wondered after the safety of his sole cat figurine he'd managed to smuggle into the house. It didn't match the décor, but neither did he most days.

"Oh wow, I'm so insulted." Elliot could almost picture the sarcasm rolling off Shelvin's words. "The thing is, I'm completely aware that I'm an asshole. That's where I thrive in life, and I'm sticking to my guns. But I would *never* belittle or shame someone that I loved, especially if I was married to them. I would do everything I could to support them, not stab a dagger in their back at the first opportunity."

Oh God. He's defending me? Why were they even talking about him? He'd fucked up with both of them…maybe even beyond repair. He'd already been drifting apart from Hunter, but now there was a Marianas Trench worth of unsaid things between them.

"I bought him a stuffed toy," Hunter huffed, his voice dropping. "I read online that people like him like that kind of thing. So there, I *am* being supportive."

So that had been the reason for the stuffed cow. Elliot had thought it was kind of cute and had put it on his pillow every morning when he left for work, but he actually found it a tad silly. He wasn't a little by any stretch, and Shelvin was not Daddy material.

"My sub is not a little, and there it is again with the 'people like him'. Do you really despise kink that much?" Shelvin sounded like he was getting riled, which was a feat in itself. Elliot had slapped him with his dick, and he'd remained calm then.

But it was a question that Elliot already knew the answer to. Hunter hated kink and everything about it. If he had his way, it would probably be illegal. He just didn't understand what a wonderful and freeing thing it was and how the community itself was more accepting than any Elliot had ever tried to be a part of.

"You know he was raped, right?" said Hunter, his voice dripping with rage unlike Elliot had ever heard it. "Repeatedly. He was beaten and raped over and over when he was younger. This is just some fucked up therapy for him that is dragging him back to where he was."

Elliot was on his feet in a moment, his stomach clenching as he fought the urge to puke. He grabbed the edge of the table, his vision blurring as his body shook. He bit his tongue, blood pooling in his mouth as sound rushed through his ears. It wasn't loud enough to block Shelvin's dangerous growl.

"That's not your story to fucking tell."

Something clattered to the ground, smashing next to Elliot's feet and shattering into a thousand shards of glass. Freezing water soaked into his socks, so reminiscent of something else warmer and brighter that reeked of copper. He could almost smell it and feel the old aches coming back in an instant.

Years of therapy disappeared as panic engulfed him.

Deep breaths.

"Sweetheart."

I know that voice. Elliot forced his eyes open, shuddering with instant relief when he saw Shelvin standing before him. His feet were bare, the shards from his cup probably digging through his skin. There was a touch of pink in the water now, the stain slowly swirling outward.

Oh God.

"Leave him be!"

Elliot shook his head, Hunter's voice slapping what little remained of his calm aside. *I can't.*

Shelvin seemed to let Hunter's screech roll right off him. How, when it slammed right into Elliot's shield, splintering it until there was nothing left.? His vision waivered as everything went dim, his breaths coming so fast but hardly filling his lungs at all. His hands throbbed and tingled, feeling like they belonged to someone else and not himself.

"I need you to breathe, sweetheart. Count with me, okay? In…out, okay again. In…out. That's good."

Elliot clung to Shelvin's voice, matching his breathing as his Dom guided him. Shelvin was still calm, his face open and honest like it always was. *Fuck,* he was beautiful.

"What's your color, sweetheart?"

Was this a scene? He had no fucking clue what the hell was going on. Panic was consuming him, his chest so tight that he was certain he was having a heart attack. Hunter's stricken face caught the edge of the vision, sending him straight back into hyperventilation.

"R-red." He wanted it to stop. He wanted Shelvin to whisk him away to a place where nothing would ever hurt him again and his memories would be tiny pinpricks of darkness in a bright life.

"It's okay, sweetheart. I'm here to take care of you, and everything is going to be fine. We're going to step away from the glass and go somewhere quiet. I need you to count for me, okay? You're doing good."

He leaned into Shelvin's hand as soon as he was touched, soaking up the warmth that seemed to leech the cold from his skin. Squinting at the light, he tried to lift his foot, the heaviness of his sodden sock dragging him down. It couldn't have weighed much more than normal, but it seemed monumental.

"Drag your feet, sweetheart. We'll shuffle out of the kitchen and into the bedroom where it's quiet. The lights are off, and it's nice and safe. I'm with you every step."

"Yes, Master." It was barely a whisper, but it was there, pulling more of the panic from his limbs as he gave himself over. The glass tinkled on the floor as he slowly moved, his feet feeling as if they were suctioned to the surface.

The distance of the kitchen to the bedroom had never felt so far, and he'd almost lost his strength by the time his toes met the transition of tile to hardwood. He made it one step through the door before his strength drained completely.

Shelvin tried to catch him, but he was no match to Elliot's size, and he ended up sprawled on the floor next to him in an undignified pile that would have been funny in any other situation. He seemed to recover in a moment, cradling Elliot's head to his chest and easing him closer.

Every moment burned into his memory, stretching as if it were moving in slow motion, and Elliot's body was the only thing that managed to keep time. But Shelvin was right there with him, his slow breaths like oxygen to his starving lungs.

"Count for me, sweetheart."

One, two, three. Elliot's lips formed the words, but he wasn't sure if he was saying them aloud or just in his mind. He pushed with his gut, trying to speak up so Shelvin could hear him. *I can be good. I can listen.*

"It's okay, baby. Don't force it. You're doing so good."

Elliot flinched as a sudden light blazed above him, whimpering and turning his head into Shelvin's chest. It burned his eyes, his panic rising as he was plunged into reality at full force.

"Turn the light off," came Shelvin's voice, as calm as ever. Seconds later, blissful darkness enveloped him again, shadows slipping over him. He let out a groan, his tense muscles relaxing one by one and easing further with Shelvin's hand in his hair.

"What happened?" Hunter whispered, his voice low but still panicked. *Is he okay?* Elliot struggled to look, but a hand on his cheek stopped him.

"Not the time," said Shelvin, shifting slightly. Elliot clung to him, willing him to stay. He couldn't be alone yet. *Not yet.* "Clean up the glass and get my sub some tea — no caffeine. Make sure it's cool enough to drink and put a straw in it as well."

Soft footsteps padded away from them, and Elliot let out a groan, his head suddenly throbbing as his vision cleared and he looked up at his bedroom ceiling. Shelvin stared at him, his face relaxed and his eyes dark. A smile touched his lips when he caught Elliot's gaze.

"You with me?" He tucked a lock of hair behind Elliot's ear before placing a kiss on his forehead.

Elliot leaned into the touch. His heart was beating its slow rhythm, and someone had removed his wet socks. His feet were aching, and the skin felt tight when he moved. He probably had a hundred cuts on his soles. "What happened?"

"You had a panic attack, sweetheart." Shelvin shook his head slowly as Elliot sucked in a breath. "None of that. It happens to us all, and you did so well telling me your color. You listened like a good sub and let me guide you back to us."

Some of the tension in Elliot's chest wilted. It was so wonderful to finally be *good* for someone.

"Hunter?" Elliot glanced around the room but didn't see or hear a trace of his husband. He wasn't sure if it was relief or disappointment that answered him.

Shelvin looked a touch strained, his eyes going tight as he appeared to fight a frown. Elliot immediately wanted to take it back. He tried his best not to mention

Hunter's name between them, not because he knew Shelvin would be upset but because saying it almost felt like a betrayal in itself.

"He's in the other room cooling down. He brought you some tea. It's probably not warm anymore."

A straw touched Elliot's lips and he opened them automatically, testing the metal tube with his tongue. Reaching for Shelvin, he didn't make it far before something shifted over him. He glanced down to the nearly dozen blankets piled over them, trapping their warmth before it could escape. It was no wonder he was so warm and cozy.

Taking a slow sip, he let the cool chamomile wash over his tongue, the slight bitterness chased away by a touch of sugar. Hunter always knew exactly how he liked it—just a bit sweet but so strong that the liquid was dark in the cup. He took another sip when he realized just how thirsty he actually was. His throat and mouth were parched, his lips so dry that they felt like they would crack at any moment.

"I'm sorry," he said when he finally came up for air. Shelvin only shook his head, his soft smile making a reappearance. It fit perfectly on his face, the same as the intensity in every scene.

"You make it sound like it's a chore to hold you," said Shelvin, placing another kiss on Elliot's forehead. The sensation hummed under his skin, the warmth spreading until the last of the ice melted. "I *want* to take care of you, sweetheart."

"No." Elliot frowned, glancing at his empty cup. A few dregs swirled in the bottom, dark and fractured just like his childhood. "I'm sorry I didn't tell you."

Elliot swallowed against the memories that suddenly seemed more distant. They had been so vivid in the kitchen, like he'd been there again in the closet with no way to escape.

He shook off the nightmare, focusing on Shelvin's face. His lips were pressed into a thin line as he sent a sharp look toward the door. The easy calmness had been sucked away. "It's your story to tell, Elliot, and you'll tell me if and when you're ready."

Elliot followed his gaze, spotting Hunter standing in the doorway. Hunter's face was stricken and pale, his eyes bloodshot and his nose red from crying. His hair was a mess and there was a spot of blood on the collar of his shirt with a pink bandage wrapped around his finger

Elliot had never seen him look quite so frantic before. Even on their wedding day, Hunter had been a picture of serene beauty, not batting an eyelash when it had started to rain.

"Did you want me to leave you two alone?" asked Hunter softly, sniffing and wiping his nose with the back of his hand. "I don't want to make you worse again."

Worse? Elliot bit his lip, looking at the blankets surrounding them. They smelled of him and Shelvin, with only a faint wisp of Hunter. Probably because Hunter hated them, preferring decorative pieces over the practical ones he'd piled away in Elliot's closet.

"That's up to Elliot," said Shelvin, smoothing his palm over Elliot's cheek. "But I'll make the decision for him if he's not up to it."

Elliot turned his head into Shelvin, breathing in his scent. He was leather and silk and the chlorine for his condo building. It was everything that had ever made him calm. There was no smoke or anything worse, nor the cleaning supplies that his house reeked of almost all the time.

"I can't be strong for you right now, Hunter. I c-can't." He clutched Shelvin, shuddering as a wave of emptiness crashed through him. Shelvin shushed him, holding him close. The emptiness eased, even as Hunter sniffed.

"I think you should stay," said Shelvin, shocking Elliot to his core. "You need to see how strong your husband is. He's been through so much, and he's been holding on for so long, but he trusts me enough that he can show the other side of himself. I think he would trust you, too, if you gave him the chance."

Oh. Of all the ways Elliot would describe himself, *strong* had never been one. He'd always been too needy, too broken and too desperate to be strong. But Shelvin had never lied to him.

Hunter settled next to them with a sniff and a whisper of cloth, the sweet scent of his vanilla soap blanketing him. Elliot reached for him, touching his light in the darkness of what his life had been. Hunter was so good to him, even if Shelvin couldn't see that all the time.

Hunter gripped him, his palm smooth and soft like it always was. Elliot breathed him in, humming in relief when his panic didn't surge forth again. Hunter had helped him from the brink before. Nothing had changed.

"What can I do?" came Hunter's whispered question, barely a breath in the quiet room.

"Just be here with us," said Shelvin, his voice rich and soft. He combed through Elliot's hair, easing the last of his strain. "It's time for you to be with us for everything. It's time for you to become the husband that Elliot believes you are."

Elliot let out a breath, sinking into the warmth and the whispers. *Everything will be okay.*

Chapter Seventeen

Shelvin

"You okay?" asked Clint for the third time as Shelvin paused mid-way through explaining one of the many rooms in the new Unkinked. It was nearly time for the drywall to go in, and the flooring was already stacked in a pile on the main floor.

A few crews milled about, Samson giving them a wave when he noticed them. Clint gave him a beaming smile in return, probably happy to meet another fellow kinkster on the job.

"I..." Shelvin scrubbed his eyes, grimacing when the itch only got worse. He'd hardly slept since Elliot's panic attack, checking his phone constantly just in case Elliot called. He had once, just to let Shelvin know he was okay and that he needed some time before he came back to work. Shelvin had told him to take all the time he needed.

Maybe that was too long. He'd never been impatient before. He'd seen a panic attack enough times to recognize the signs and help Elliot through it, but he'd been exhausted ever since. His heart went out to his sub, whose scars were buried deep beneath his skin.

He couldn't imagine what Elliot must've gone through. His beautiful sub didn't have a single mark on his skin, but emotional scars could be so much worse than the ones displayed for all to see.

"Have you ever not known what to do?" asked Shelvin, lowering his voice as one of the roofers slipped past them. Ducking into the future *Heal* room, he leaned against the wall where soon there would be stainless steel sinks and an examination table.

"What are we talking about here?" asked Clint, looking around the room in confusion. "The place looks great—much better than I expected, actually. Don't ask me about paint colors because I don't have a clue. Gray...just go with gray."

Shelvin shook his head, not even tempted to smile. Clint had been a mentor to so many in the community, but Shelvin hadn't been in town long enough to get to know him as well as he would have liked. Unfortunately, their families weren't that close, although they'd bonded at a family reunion.

"With my sub." Shelvin sighed, looking to the peaked ceiling. "It was a fucked-up situation to begin with, but now it's really fucked, and I have no idea where to go from here. He's taking some time to figure things out, but once he's back, I don't know if I can trust him enough to scene with him again."

That was what it came down to. Until Elliot got real and open about his limits, Shelvin wasn't going to push him past a bit of cock warming and humiliation. He'd been so close to having his sub safeword and he hadn't even known it because he'd gone in blind. His usual motto was *'fuck the details'* in everything but work, but he'd never dealt with a traumatized sub before.

The last thing he wanted was a trigger to send them both spiraling. But he couldn't exist on pins and needles, either.

"You do like them fucked up and out," said Clint with a wink before he scratched at his chin. He looked like he hadn't shaved in days and had gotten about the same amount of sleep as Shelvin. He'd been in that state since Shelvin had known him, though, and he still managed to be handsome. It almost made him jealous.

"True." He let out a sigh. "But Elliot is — and I can't believe I'm saying this — different. I *want* to spend more time with him, maybe even more outside of scenes and work. He's a good guy, and I can see our relationship going a long way, but…"

He trailed off and Clint waited for him to continue, letting the silence rest between them. Nearly a minute went by before Clint finally spoke. "Don't leave me hanging like that. But, what?"

"He's married," said Shelvin. It was probably the number one concern he had. "His husband detests kink and even seems to hate the fact that he's gay, which is just fucking weird. Gay is the way." Or maybe those worries were only the tip of the iceberg.

"That could be an issue," said Clint, sobering.

If only that was all. "He's traumatized beyond belief and has no support system other than said husband." Shelvin shook his head. *What a fucking train wreck.* "And my favorite part of all is that he won't take responsibility for anything in a scene."

Clint let out a low whistle before crossing his arms. "I've seen fucked up before, man, but that is *fucked.*"

190

"Great." Shelvin shrugged. "The local king of kink and even *he* thinks it's hopeless. I'm not dismissing him—no way. But what the fuck do I do? The last time I saw him he had a panic attack that took ages to come out of. The whole time I just wanted to stay with him, hold him tight and not leave him with his asshat husband. I had to force myself to leave."

"I didn't say it was hopeless." Clint waved his hand, going quiet as another person shuffled down a nearby hall. Their voices carried a long way in the empty rooms. "It actually reminds me of something I went through when I was first starting out in the lifestyle. I started sceneing with another guy named Ross who was in a relationship but looking for a third." Clint let out a fond smile, shuffling his foot on the ground.

"Ross' existing play partner was the clingiest bastard who I'd ever met and hated when we played together, so he tried to get Ross kicked out of a club by calling 'red' when they'd barely started a scene. Then he freaked out when Ross tried to give him aftercare. Fucker dragged Ross through the dirt, got him fired from his job and almost arrested."

"Holy fuck." Shelvin swallowed. So maybe his situation wasn't that bad. He'd heard of a few cases of people being outed in the kink world and treated like a leper at their day job. He'd been lucky on that front. His boss didn't give a shit what he did on his own time. *One of the perks of being self-employed.* "What did you do?"

Clint laughed, his eyes going bright. "I left the other guy in the gutter with a broken nose before I proposed to Ross. Shortly after, we got hitched and started our own club together."

Spluttering, Shelvin couldn't help but laugh. Clint had always been a bit of a mystery. *He's been a badass all along.*

"Well, I can't marry the guy," said Shelvin. He needed his space and his solo time, which he imagined would immediately disappear if he ever gave someone a ring. That, and the idea of marriage made him a bit nauseated.

Once he made a promise, he was keeping it. He didn't need a piece of paper and a gold band to remind him of that.

"He's your sub, right?" asked Clint, waiting for Shelvin's nod. "Then it's time that you *both* remember that."

* * * *

Clint is right. Shelvin hated being wrong, but he couldn't explain his way out of it this time. It was one thing to give Elliot his space, but it was another entirely to leave him without a support system, especially when he knew there was a chance that Elliot wouldn't reach out to him. They'd crossed that bridge before.

He'd been cursing himself for the last two hours, wrapping things up with Clint at the office before he'd driven to Elliot's building. He'd already knocked on the condo's door twice. He'd slipped in as another person had entered the building, so he wasn't sure if Elliot was even here, but where else would he be?

Rapping his knuckles harder, Shelvin shook his hand out as it throbbed, the skin already well on its way to bruising. The next building he designed would have doorbells for every condo. This knocking shit was fucking infuriating.

The lock clicked a moment before the door swung wide. Shelvin cursed internally a second time when Hunter stared back at him in nothing but a towel, looking more miffed than anyone had the right to be at four in the afternoon.

"What are *you* doing here?" Hunter raised one side of his lip, giving him a nasty sneer that left a bad taste in Shelvin's mouth.

Well, at least I know where I stand. I'm back to being shoe scum.

"What are *you* doing answering your door in a towel?" Shelvin shot right back, peering over Hunter's shoulder. Elliot's coat hook hung empty, his shoes missing from the mat. It had been chilly in the morning, so the coat probably hadn't been put away for the season quite yet. "Someone might get the wrong idea."

As far as Shelvin was concerned, the only time it was okay to answer the door in a towel was if you were starring in a late-night video or dream.

Maybe I should have called. He wanted to see Elliot, though, not just hear his voice.

"He's not here. He decided that we needed to take a break, not that I got any say in that," said Hunter, tossing his sodden hair over his shoulder. "I guess you must've told him that we should, since he doesn't want to make any choices on his own lately."

I will not kill him. Jail would not be fun. Shelvin gritted his teeth, narrowing his eyes when he caught sight of an unfamiliar pair of shoes next to Hunter's. There was a jacket on the floor next to the boot tray, too. *Fucker.* It didn't take much for Shelvin to connect the dots.

"He's not here, but your side-piece is?" asked Shelvin, dropping his voice into a drawl. Did Elliot know? Normally, Shelvin wouldn't give a fuck, but

Elliot was his sub, and he was going to take care of him, no matter what. He was sick of Hunter dragging him down at every turn.

Hunter scoffed. "Like you're one to talk. You take him to your kinky club and fuck him six-ways to Sunday, and he comes home and won't even touch me? I deserve to have someone else who isn't afraid to give me what I want."

I was wrong. I am going to jail. Shelvin grabbed the doorknob, pushing Hunter back into his apartment before slamming it closed in his face. He'd never slammed a door from the outside before, but it was even more satisfying than doing it to the religious group that had caught him unawares one day at his old place.

So close. One more second in Hunter's presence, and he would have lost his shit. It was the last thing he wanted to do with his precious sub on the line.

Reaching for his phone, he stalked down the hall, finally finding Elliot's number by the time he got to his car. He dialed, letting it ring to voicemail before he ended the call. With a wince, he sent a text message.

Need to talk. Where are you?

As soon as he pressed send, he wondered if it was a mistake. Did it sound too harsh? Maybe Elliot would be worried and take it the wrong way. And was he supposed to put punctuation at all? *Fuck*, he hated texting.

His phone buzzed in his hand, *'Office'* and an address displayed on the screen. It was a downtown address, and the streets were slammed with traffic, but he sped out into the mess, anyway, squealing his tires as he dropped the clutch around the first bend. A cop who had been hiding at the intersection flashed his lights in a warning and Shelvin clenched his jaw, gratingly slowing to a normal speed.

I'm no use to him dead.

The outside of Elliot's office was so underwhelming that Shelvin had to double-check to make sure it was the right address. The building was identical to the others around it, with yellow brick at the base that did nothing to enhance its style.

The flower beds were nice, though. Not that there was much alive in them at the moment except for a few tulips and daffodils. But still...'A' for effort on that front.

Shelvin ducked into the building, wincing at the gaudy logo and rich wood of the reception desk that was a stark contrast to the exterior. *Fucking engineers.* The guys never seemed to know when to put design before practicality and always had wood somewhere that it didn't need to be.

And were those exposed metal beams supposed to be a ceiling? *Fuck,* Elliot was never going to hear the end of his rant. As soon as Clint's build was done, he was designing a new office for Elliot's company, and there was fuck all they could do to stop him.

"Can I help you?"

Shelvin strolled over to the receptionist, noting that her pastel pantsuit fit in perfectly. Slapping a smirk on his face he unzipped his leather jack. The temperature of the building *was* perfect, even it was ugly.

"Shelvin!"

Shelvin turned toward the sound of his name, his chest flipping uncomfortably when he saw Elliot emerging from an elevator. He rubbed at his sternum, hoping that it was just the Chinese food that was giving him grief. The last thing he needed were butterflies.

But Elliot looked so *good* — good enough to eat, in fact. He was dressed in a button-down sweater and slacks that did wonders for his body, his shirt cuffs rolled up and stretched over his thick forearms. His eyes were bright and warm with none of the grief that Shelvin had last seen him with.

Thank God. He couldn't stop himself. Grinning, Shelvin held out his arms, laughing as Elliot's eyes went wide before he pulled him into a hug, regardless. He smelled like paper and candy with a touch of something else that Shelvin was sure he would never forget. He held on for a second too long before he finally relaxed his grip and let Elliot pull away.

His cheeks were stained red, his eyes glassy and his smile wide. The receptionist was staring at them uncomfortably, but Shelvin only had eyes for his sub.

"You look good," said Shelvin, skimming his hands over Elliot's shoulders. "I was worried about you." He felt good — just the way he remembered, only real and before him, and not a figment of his imagination.

Elliot made a face, shooting a look at the receptionist. "I'm fine…great actually. Come on, and I'll show you my office."

Elliot led him to the elevator, which was passable at best, before pushing the button for the thirtieth floor. The doors slid shut with a ding and Shelvin reached for Elliot's hand, squeezing once before he let go. Elliot shot him a smile full of relief. It was exactly what Shelvin needed.

After the excruciatingly slow elevator ride, the top floor of the building was revealed to be a touch more tasteful. Instead of cubicles, there were a maze of different offices in all shapes and sizes, some configured into squares and others like giant fishbowls made of frosted glass.

"It's bigger than I thought." There had to be at least a dozen people bustling about, and who knew how many on the other floors. *Why the fuck does anyone need so many engineers?* One was more than enough to deal with in day-to-day life.

"This used to be apartments until we took over and gutted the entire thing except for a few floors. It doesn't look like much from the outside, but the inside is a whole different ballgame. I had just started when they were doing the overhaul, so I got to pick out my office and design most of it."

That would explain the little details that Shelvin had started to see around the place. Elliot's signature wasn't exactly beautiful, but it was exotic in a practical sort of way. There were stark similarities between the office and the details that Elliot had added into the design for the new Unkinked.

They rounded a hall, and Elliot paused at the entrance to the corner office that had been obscured by frosted glass. The sunlight was streaming through the windows, flowing over the numerous plants Elliot had stashed in the room. Shelvin looked over them, his eyes going wide. "You like to grow things?"

Strolling to the miniature tree with something that looked a lot like small limes on it, Shelvin touched one of the leaves. It was soft but surprisingly thick, the shiny surface giving off a citrusy smell as he pinched it.

There were a few similar plants and a palm in the corner that cast a slim bit of shade over the desk. The rest was bright and open to the sunlight. It had to be a nightmare for Elliot to read anything on a computer screen.

"Yeah...I love plants, actually. Anything alive is like my therapy — plants, animals, even fish." Elliot pointed to the base of one of his plants that was in a glass bowl, the white roots exposed and immersed in water. A blue beta circled the roots, slipping through the strands easily before heading to the surface to grab a breath.

"You don't have any in your condo," said Shelvin, smelling the citrus on his fingertips, his mouth watering at the tart sweetness to it. "You must spend a lot of time here taking care of them." As much as he loved the look of them, a plant would probably never survive him.

Elliot's smile dimmed before he shrugged, looking out of the window where the sun was growing dim with the few clouds passing through the sky. The congestion on the street had thickened, horns honking and signal lights flashing as people rushed to get home.

"Where are you staying?" asked Shelvin, moving to the next plant and hissing when a thorn dug into his thumb. He brought his hand to his mouth, sucking the drop of blood that bloomed. It hadn't looked like the thorny kind, but there were a dozen or so prickly bits speckled along the stems.

"Careful," Elliot whispered, his gaze on the floor. The easy relaxation had disappeared. "Did he send you here?"

Shelvin moved close, wrapping his arms around Elliot's shoulders and leaning against his chest. They didn't fit perfectly...not like in a romance movie, but Elliot against him was one of the headiest feelings in the world. He loved feeling small and powerful at the same time, like he could take on the world with the one at his side.

"I'm not an errand boy," said Shelvin, placing a kiss on Elliot's collar. The door was still open, so he pulled away, sliding it closed before leaning his back against one of the exterior windows. It was cool against him, easing the warmth of the sunlight filtering in. "You're putting on a brave face right now, sweetheart. Don't do that on my account. I came to see *you*...not a mask."

Elliot let out a sigh, slumping his shoulders. Without the smile, he looked ten years older, stress lines carving their way over his features. Shelvin wanted to curse himself for not coming sooner.

"I'm staying in a hotel for now. I told Hunter we needed to take a break, and he didn't take it all that well."

"That's an understatement," said Shelvin, reaching for Elliot's hand and dragging him closer before letting the window take his weight. Elliot's hair shimmered in the sunlight, looking so soft that Shelvin wanted to lose his hands in the strands for days. "Are you comfortable at the hotel or did you want to stay with me?"

Elliot shot his head up, his eyes wide. "W-with you? I didn't think..."

You never do. Elliot always seemed to lose his mind while Shelvin was around him.

"Elliot, you're my sub, baby. I'll take care of you, no matter what. If you need a place to stay or if you don't want to be alone, you can stay at my place. If you aren't ready to sleep together, then you can have the guest room until you are."

Elliot's eyes went glassy as he caught his lip between his teeth. "I." He lowered his voice to a whisper, glaring at the carpet. "I don't want to decide. Tell me what to do, Shelvin. Fix it for me."

His heart broke a little as he shook his head. *I can't, baby.* He wished he could explain it in a way that Elliot understood. The was something he could do, though. "Get on your knees, baby. Will anyone come looking for you?"

Shelvin glanced to the door. The knob was unlocked, and people passed by the frosted glass every so often. He couldn't hear them clearly, but that didn't mean that someone wouldn't walk in at any moment.

Elliot dropped like a rock, shaking his head as hope filled his gaze. He had a faraway look in his eyes like beginnings of subspace, with no thoughts to the people beyond the glass.

His sub went there so easily that it was almost scary. Shelvin was so glad he'd found him before Elliot had stumbled into the wrong kind of Dom.

"Take my cock out and put it in your mouth." He shifted his legs wider, hiking up his shirt so he'd stick to the glass a bit and it would keep him from slipping. His legs ached almost immediately from the position, but it was worth it to see Elliot slide between his thighs.

Elliot made quick work of Shelvin's zipper, sealing his mouth over Shelvin's cock before he started to suck almost immediately. The groan in his throat almost broke down Shelvin's walls.

"Don't suck, baby, just hold me. I want your jaw to ache."

Elliot was almost under, tears on his lashes and cheeks rosy and hot. *Not yet.* He was so fucking beautiful, the moment of sweet stillness passing between them and stretching out, calming every nerve and making him whole again.

"Do you like that? Do you like holding my cock in your mouth, knowing that any one of your coworkers could come in here and see you on your knees? Your boss could walk in, and he'd know that you're a slut...*my* slut. Everyone would know you're mine, and they'd never dare touch you again."

Shelvin gritted his teeth as he struggled against the urge to thrust. Elliot's mouth was like heaven, and it was hard not to plunge his way through the pearly gates.

"What would Hunter think?"

Elliot's eyes went wide, and he started to pull back, but Shelvin grabbed him by the back of his head, dragging him into place. He'd *never* said Hunter's name during a scene because he'd known how Elliot would react. There was a huge difference between being humiliated and being ashamed.

But he couldn't go another moment with Elliot thinking he was doing something wrong. He'd always kept his end of the bargain, even if Hunter hadn't kept his.

"I'm your Dom, but I can't live your life for you," said Shelvin, easing his grip on Elliot's hair and letting him take a quick breath. "There are some decisions you have to make, and I can't let you hide behind me and hate me when things don't turn out the way you would have liked. Hunter is your husband, and I know you're loyal to him and you'd do anything to please him. What you need to decide, is how far you want to go. What would you give up for him? Do you need to break our contract for him, or will you allow yourself to hate the best part of yourself?"

Shelvin bit back everything that he wanted to say. Hunter was a manipulative, cheating bastard who put

Elliot down to bandage his own insecurities. In Hunter's opinion, Elliot would *never* be good enough, and Elliot was going to harm himself if he tried to be. He could only burn the candle at both ends for so long until the flame consumed itself and went out.

"I'm your Dom, baby," said Shelvin, his heart pounding as he said it again. Did Elliot know what that meant? *Really?* It wasn't just a contract or a hit of endorphins. It was everything. "Are you my sub?"

When Elliot jerked back, Shelvin let him go, tucking himself back into his pants as Elliot stumbled to his desk and leaned heavily against it. His chest heaved, his face flushed red and his eyes glassy with unshed tears.

Did I just lose the best thing that's ever happened to me? Shelvin's stomach twisted, his lunch threatening to make a reappearance. There wouldn't be much there, but he was sure his body would make a good effort on it.

Elliot bit his lip before he turned away, his gaze downcast.

I think I did.

Chapter Eighteen

Elliot

"Are you my sub?"

Elliot bit his lip, grabbing the edge of his desk and holding the thick plank of wood until his hands began to ache. His chest was tight, his core so cold that he must've been dipped in ice at some point.

Being a sub was what had started the first and last problem in his life. His need for submission had driven his husband away and had drawn him into a world and life that he hadn't been fully prepared for. Every moment was like a drug, leaving him high and only longing for more. The rest of his life had settled into a bleakness with no remedy.

He'd expected to kneel. He hadn't expected to love his Dom in the same way he loved Hunter. The issue was that now he craved Shelvin every day, not Hunter. He wanted Shelvin's touch on his body and his voice in his ear. He would hand every orgasm away for the rest of his life if it meant being with Shelvin.

But Hunter *hated* it. He couldn't stand kink, and he'd withdrawn even more since Elliot's panic attack. It had been like walking on glass around the apartment — stepping as carefully as possible, but still getting cut deep. Elliot hadn't been able to stay there another second with the tension so thick that it threatened to destroy his marriage before they had a chance to discuss a thing.

And Hunter had called him 'unfaithful'. His words were still ringing in Elliot's ears. *"You disgust me. How can I even look at you when I know he's just been inside you?"*

Maybe he was everything Hunter accused him of being. Maybe he was just using kink as an excuse to get fucked real good — until he couldn't bear to sit the next day.

But if his time away from Hunter had proved anything, it was that he was very good at putting on a smile and making people believe he was okay. *Fake it until you make it.* It took Shelvin's support to realize that it had all been for nothing.

"Do you still want me?" asked Elliot, letting out a breath before tracing a stain on his desk with his finger. They had a contract, but Elliot would break it in a moment if Shelvin didn't want him.

Shelvin's glare was nearly electric. He was still hard, his cock tenting the fabric of his pants, but Elliot couldn't look away from his eyes. "Are you doubting your Dom? If I say I'm your Dom, then that's who I am. Don't fucking question my loyalty."

Shelvin was all of five-seven, but Elliot trembled before him — the only one who wanted him, but Elliot was barely worthy. He couldn't deny himself, though. He *needed* him.

"I'm your sub." He slid to his knees, nearly whacking his head against the desk on the way down. The plastic mat for his chair thudded into his knees as he settled hard. He kept a clean office, but he knew his pants would be filthy. It seemed appropriate.

"Then drop your pants." Shelvin crossed his arms, tapping his foot when Elliot sent a glance toward the door. He didn't think anyone would come looking for him at this point. He'd been willing to risk it to get his mouth on Shelvin again, but this was different.

"In my office?" Elliot looked to the glass door. It was frosted, only showing shadows when someone got very close. Even as he watched, someone passed by, probably bustling to get the last few things done before they went home.

"Is it a limit?" Shelvin asked slowly, licking his lips when Elliot shook his head. The sun shone against his hair as he lounged against the window like a god.

Hands trembling, Elliot reached for his belt, undoing the buckle as his cock throbbed to life. He was so sensitive, his trigger probably thinner than a hair. He'd hardly come at all since he'd started seeing Shelvin, unable to muster anything with Hunter and refusing to jerk off unless the condo was empty...which rarely happened.

His heart pounded as he stared at the door, staying on his knees as he started to shuffle his pants and boxers down. His belt buckle struck the plastic with a thump of utter finality.

Someone could walk in and catch them at any time, and the idea of it had every nerve alive and singing. It was humiliating and thrilling, his heart pounding in time with his cock. He was already dripping pre-cum, his shaft wet with it.

"All the way off, Elliot." Shelvin circled him once before grabbing him by the hair and tugging him to his feet. His movements were all rough Dominance and none of the soft compassion that he'd shown Elliot in the past. It was exactly what he needed.

His pants dropped to his ankles as he stood, his hair prickling on his legs in the cool air. Having a corner office meant that the sun came from more angles, heating his room so the tropical plants thrived. But right now, he was freezing and so terribly exposed that he might as well have been in a cold cellar.

"Nice view. I wonder if they can see that ass of yours from down there and watch what I'm going to do to it."

Elliot looked over his shoulder in dawning horror. The windows within the office were frosted, but the exterior ones were crystal clear. Thirty floors, but they weren't that high, and with evening approaching, the office was almost brighter than the outside, the overhead lights like a beacon. If anyone looked from the surrounding buildings, they would see him standing at his desk with his pants around his ankles.

"We're going to have to talk about our limits again, but I don't think now is the time to go over everything." Shelvin reached around his hip, tugging Elliot's cock twice. Elliot hissed at the sensation, his hips bucking against his will.

"Is impact play still a hard limit?" Shelvin released him, circling the desk and leaning across it, his lips inches from Elliot's. "I want to beat your ass so bad, baby, and I don't want you to enjoy it."

Ah. His cock twitched as Elliot trembled, closing his eyes against the onslaught of pure pleasure that thrummed through him at Shelvin's words. He'd put impact in his off-limits because he'd been afraid of what memories might bubble up. The last thing he needed was to think about his past while his Dom was trying to push him into subspace.

"I'm afraid," said Elliot, leaning into the desk to try to close the distance between them. Shelvin pulled back with a smirk, wagging his finger back and forth.

"Do you trust me?" asked Shelvin, looping around and disappearing behind Elliot's back. Elliot craned his neck around, but Shelvin was right behind him, standing too close to make out his expression.

"Of course I do." *What kind of question is that?* He trusted Shelvin more than he trusted anyone else in his life. The man had never once let him down, even when Elliot had had a temper tantrum and a panic attack. "I know you'll take care of me, Sir."

Shelvin sucked in a breath a moment before he grabbed Elliot's ass with both hands, digging his fingertips into the firm flesh. Elliot winced, imagining the bruises that would fade from black to purple, then green. Hunter would see them and glare at him, turning away with his nose in the air while Elliot would burn with shame and something else that had stayed hidden for too long.

"What's your safeword?" Shelvin dug his fingers harder until Elliot groaned under the assault. It fucking hurt, and Shelvin had stronger hands than he'd been led to believe.

"Red to stop, yellow to slow down."

"Good." There was a jingle of a belt as Shelvin took a step back and every hair raised on the back of Elliot's neck. "Now I suggest you try to keep quiet. I wouldn't want somebody to hear you."

A slap split the air and Elliot jumped, a puff of air sneaking past his lips. He blinked, craning his head back in confusion when the pain didn't come. It hadn't even been the belt that he'd expected, but Shelvin's hand, with only enough force to make him tingle all over.

"Color?" Shelvin raised one brow, wiggling his fingers as Elliot watched them. "Did you expect me to beat you with a belt, sweetheart? I hate to disappoint you, but your ass is made for my hand."

"Green." Elliot pushed his ass out, lowering his head to the desk and moaning as a second slap landed. He bit into the fabric of his shirt, smothering the cry that longed to be let loose.

It stung...barely, and instead of memories, pure sensation wafted over him, crawling over his skin and dropping straight to his balls. He rocked into the next hit, even as Shelvin tutted.

"I think you're enjoying this too much," said Shelvin, reaching into one of the drawers on Elliot's desk. "Let see if I can find something to teach you a lesson. You've been very naughty doubting your Dom." Shelvin hummed under his breath, shifting through the drawer until he clasped something silver. "Perfect."

Elliot didn't get a good look at it through the shield of his arms, but he recognized the sound of it as soon as it struck his flesh. He'd used it for it's intended purpose countless times, even tapping it on his desk when he worked through a particularly difficult problem, but he never thought he'd be spanked with it.

"That's better." Shelvin brought the thin ruler down a second time, chuckling as it landed with a soft *thwap*. "It leaves a nice mark. I wonder if I can get the numbers to stick." He swung it again, this time at the lower cup of Elliot's cheek.

Elliot hissed, wincing as a zing shot through him. His skin prickled, the first hint of pain seeping through. It was barely more than a bug bite, fading quickly to warmth. "The numbers are painted on."

"There you go, doubting me again," said Shelvin, angling the ruler and taking another swing. "I'll just have to prove you wrong."

Elliot bit his lip, holding every whimper back with sheer willpower as Shelvin unleashed himself on his ass. The tingle morphed into a steady burn, which quickly became a flame. Gasping, Elliot rocked against the desk, curling his toes as one spank seemed to slice straight through him.

"Y-yellow." His voice was a quiver of nerves, sweat soaking into his shirt. He hissed as Elliot touched his ass, scraping his nails over the hypersensitive flesh.

"You did good. Can you stay still for just a second more? I want to put some cream on your ass before I take you home with me."

"Yeah." Elliot let out a breath, relaxing into the desk and resting his cheek on the polished surface. His cock was aching and dripping a steady stream of pre-cum onto the floor, but it was almost inconsequential. Hours before, he'd been at an all-time low of guilt and second-guessing, but now?

I feel good.

There was the sound of the belt again and the high drag of a zipper. *Is he putting his belt back on?* He'd only taken it off for show, after all. The zipper didn't make sense, though.

It hardly mattered, not when his innards were buzzing, and a smile stretched over his face that Elliot wasn't sure he could stop. His ass ached, but it was the best ache in the world...the same way his balls throbbed when he finally got to come after an hour of edging himself in the bathroom after a scene, with Hunter out of the house grabbing them takeout.

It was only when he heard Shelvin spit, and the slick sound of flesh on flesh, that he finally understood. Elliot craned his neck back, nearly drooling at the sight.

Shelvin had his cock in hand, jerking it roughly only inches from Elliot's ass. His breathing was harsh, pre-cum joining the saliva that he'd already slicked his way with. His gaze was locked on Elliot's ass and the red stripes that crisscrossed the surface like a checker board.

Cream.

Shelvin let out a low gasp and a groan, closing his eyes as he rocked his hips into his hand. A moment later, cum spurted from his cock, landing over Elliot's exposed ass. It was like molten lava on his heated cheeks, already starting to cool as Elliot whimpered.

"Let me rub it in, baby. It'll make you feel so much better." Shelvin licked his lips as he smeared his cum with his fingertips, even tracing Elliot's crack and dripping it over his hole.

It was hot and so fucking dirty that Elliot wondered if he would spontaneously orgasm...only he couldn't. That was his hard limit, right? He wasn't even sure anymore with how his head was swimming and his cock was throbbing.

Shelvin rubbed until his cum started to dry, tightening over Elliot's skin and leaving an uncomfortable mess. Sucking his finger clean, he tugged Elliot's pants on, reaching around and securing his zipper and belt. The cloth dragged over his skin with excruciating pressure, the cum already itching terribly. Elliot only shuddered as Shelvin patted his cock once before drawing back.

"Call your boss in here, sweetheart," said Shelvin, strolling over to the lime tree with an air of nonchalance before stroking one of the leaves. The hint of citrus was immediate in the air. "I've always wanted to meet the guy. I hear he has quite the eye for detail."

Elliot trembled, glancing at his desktop phone which blinked with a voicemail that he hadn't noticed ring through. Between the perfume of flowers and plants, he doubted that his boss would smell the slight twinge of sex, but Shelvin was right. The man never missed a thing.

Hand shaking, he reached for the phone, dialing Sillib's extension. The line connected with a soft click. "M-Mr. Manchester, could you come to my office for a moment? I have the architect from one of my project's here, and he wanted to touch base with you."

That sounds so wrong. The last thing Elliot wanted was for Shelvin to *touch base* with his boss. The surge of possessiveness was startling.

"Is everything okay? I know the timeline was tight, but you seemed to be on track the last time we spoke," Sillib replied, his voice laced with concern—probably because Elliot had rarely asked for help or a consult in his life unless things were ready to go sideways.

Elliot nodded, swallowing, even though his mouth was bone dry. Shelvin stared at him with one brow raised, his clothes neat and orderly, despite having just come. He wasn't even flushed. When Elliot looked down at himself, he couldn't believe how in order he appeared. On the inside, he was a disaster, his ass throbbing so much that it had to be visible through his pants.

"No problems, but he's an architect, so…" Elliot trailed off, cheering internally when Shelvin narrowed his eyes.

"I think I'm catching your drift. The last thing we need is another high and mighty strutting around and stalling the project. I'll be there in five."

Elliot hung up the phone, heaving in a gasp as Shelvin stalked over to him, his eyes dangerous. He had to struggle not to take a step back, even though his Dom was literally no match for him physically.

"You have a problem with me being an architect?" Shelvin drawled, wiping a bit of drool from Elliot's lip that he hadn't noticed. He sucked his finger into his mouth, licking it clean. Elliot shivered at the display, still so close that he ached.

"Only if you have a problem with me being an engineer." He tried to mirror Shelvin's smirk and pour confidence into his words, but it probably fell flat. Who could blame him? His knees were trembling, and his hands were shaking so hard that he was sure he wouldn't be able to keep steady.

"You should sit. I wouldn't want Mr. Senior Engineer to notice that situation of yours." Shelvin flicked Elliot's strained zipper, sending a zing all the way up his cock.

Elliot had barely dropped to his seat, hissing as his ass touched the surface, when Sillib stepped through the door.

He looked good for his age, with speckles of gray in his hair that he made no attempt at hiding. He was in shape, too, with a form-fitted suit that he usually kept for the office. If he hadn't been so straight and vanilla, he would have been Elliot's type. Shelvin's assessing look must have caught his thoughts because he shot

Elliot a glare before he stepped forward and offered his hand.

"Nice to meet you. I'm Shelvin Mainstay. I've been working on the project with Elliot, and it's coming along great." Shelvin seemed to grow two sizes as he clasped Mr. Manchester's hand, jumping into a long-winded explanation of their project. Sillib stared at him wide-eyed, sending Elliot a confused glance before he settled on nodding his head.

"So, that's it, really," said Shelvin, wrapping it up with a smile. "I just wanted to speak with Elliot's manager and *touch base*, so to speak. He's probably the best engineer I've ever worked with, not that my opinion counts for much." He sent Sillib a wink, who chuckled awkwardly.

As he left and the door slipped closed, Elliot let out a breath, collapsing against his desk and laying his head on the cool surface. He couldn't fucking believe it. He'd just called his boss into his office with cum all over his ass and his Dom praising him enough to have pre-cum slicking his pants. If he looked down, he'd probably see a stain at the front. How could he explain that away?

"You did so good for me, sweetheart." Shelvin's voice came from right behind him and a moment later there was a hand on his shoulder. He relaxed under the touch, giving Shelvin control as his life attempted to unravel. "Let me take you home."

Chapter Nineteen

Shelvin

Elliot stood at the front door, looking around with wide eyes with his hands tucked inside the sleeves of his jacket. It was frankly adorable to see the shock and awe on his face, and the surprise that came along with it.

Shelvin chuckled, hanging his coat on the hook and slipping on his fuzzy slippers. He pulled a second pair out of the basket for Elliot, tossing them toward him.

"I thought that other place was your condo," said Elliot, removing his shoes without looking, his gaze fixed on the custom chandelier that hung from the sixteen-foot ceiling. Shelvin had splurged like crazy on the thing, going for awe and visual appeal in the end. He hadn't considered how often he'd have to dust the damn thing.

It wasn't typical that he had people over, but when he did, he loved surprising the fuck out of them. People who knew him — really knew him — knew that he was a disaster in most things in life. He wanted to shock them.

If the marble accent wall didn't amaze them, then the massive fireplace usually did — that, and the open-concept kitchen made entirely out of worn timber beams carved with shelves of varying size for plates and cups.

"Nah, that was just my office. I sleep there more than I do here, but this is home." It had taken most of his savings to get a house this size in the city that was up to snuff. He'd done enough of his own changes that it was nearly unrecognizable from the original schematics. He'd started the project as soon as he'd moved to town, and it had taken him nearly six months to complete.

"It's...wow."

Shelvin helped Elliot out of his coat, placing it on one of the many hooks. Only a few were occupied. It matched the theme of the five bedrooms, too. Most of them were empty, but some Shelvin had stuffed with materials from old projects and artwork. He'd even converted one into a playroom, although he'd barely used it since he'd moved in.

"Make yourself comfortable, and I'll get you a drink. Is Coke okay?" Shelvin looked over his shoulder as he headed for the kitchen.

"Wine?" Elliot asked hopefully, pulling on his own pair of fuzzy slippers. They looked a bit small for him, but the pink frills matched him perfectly.

"Not if you want to get fucked."

Elliot gave him a quick look that melted away to a smile. "Coke would be great."

Shelvin snickered, grabbing two cans from the kitchen before heading to the living room. He had to stomp on the bubble of hope and desire in his throat when he came around the corner to see Elliot kneeling next to one of the couches. His feet were tucked under him, his hands on his thighs and his eyes downcast. It must've made his ass smart, but Shelvin wasn't going to stop him.

He doubled back to the kitchen, grabbing a straw before heading to the couch, sitting in front of Elliot with his legs spread wide. Cracking the pop can, he put the straw inside, bringing it to Elliot's lips.

"Do you want a pillow?" he asked softly, waiting until Elliot had taken his fill before setting the drink to the side and taking a sip of his own. Elliot shook his head, wiggling his ass before he winced and nodded.

"Here." Shelvin grabbed the closest one, handing it to Elliot, who slid it under his knees.

There really was nothing like having his sub at his feet, his cock recently sated and his mind blissfully blank. He could imagine the picture being even prettier with a fire roaring in the background on a cold night, and Elliot eating from his hand as they watched television together.

"Are you hungry?" He hated the idea of going to the kitchen for a snack, but he didn't want a hungry sub, either. Elliot shook his head again, his spine stiffening. "Then what's up?" Shelvin plunged his hand into Elliot's hair, trying to ease that tension with his fingertips.

Glancing around, Elliot only seemed to get more uncomfortable. "Am I staying here?"

Good fucking question. Shelvin shrugged, trying not to let his internal struggle break through. "I would like you to stay if you're okay with that. I want to continue our scene, too, but we need to talk about a few things first."

Elliot bit his lip hard enough that his flesh went pale, and he looked like he might break skin. "Was I bad?"

"Nope." Shelvin tried to sound as nonchalant as possible. It killed him that that was the first place Elliot's mind went. "And we can skip some of the heavier stuff tonight if you want. You can kneel here until bed, but I think you might need to talk. You've been avoiding Hunter, and I haven't seen you at the build site in days. I know you need time, and I want you to know that no amount of time is too long, but I'm also here for you."

Elliot let out a sigh, slumping his shoulders as he shifted his gaze. He must've been feeling the pain in his ass, suddenly distraught and uncomfortable. "I want to talk about it, but don't make me tell you the details."

I would never make you do anything. Shelvin held back the rant that perched on the edge of his teeth. This beautiful and powerful man before him had had his confidence shattered too many times. It would be a long process ahead of them to repair the damage.

"You can use your safewords, and I can ask the questions if you like. If I go somewhere off-limits, then say 'red', and we can stop or move on to something else."

At some point, Shelvin had become a therapist. *When the fuck did that happen?* He was *terrible* with treating people delicately. Hopefully, he didn't fuck everything up that they'd worked so hard for.

"Belts and electricity are hard limits for you, sweetheart. Is there anything else that would bring back memories?" It had been easy enough to narrow down the first two by putting the pieces together, and

Shelvin had to wonder how Elliot didn't have any visible scars.

"I would be tied up," said Elliot, his voice shaky and wet. "Ropes, but sometimes cuffs, too. I don't think I can be restrained."

Well, fuck. That explained why Elliot had lashed out when Shelvin had bound him in the *Feel* room. Somehow, it made him even guiltier. He'd thought they had been doing so well, but he hadn't checked in enough. As a Dom, he should have done better.

"That's good, sweetheart. I need you to know that I will never restrain you again unless you ask me to, and even then, we'll have some pretty hefty discussions first." Shelvin gave him a soft pet, cupping Elliot's cheek before placing a kiss on his head. "What about toys? Anything I should steer clear of?"

"No. He only ever used…" Elliot trembled, his teeth chattering audibly. He was so pale, his face suddenly gaunt and every year carved over his features.

"It's okay, baby. Deep breaths for me. I'm going to call red on that one. You don't need to answer." Elliot instantly relaxed and let out a shaky breath. "How about sleeping arrangements. Do you need your space or are cuddles okay?"

"Cuddles, please. The hotel has been really hard, but I set up a bunch of extra pillows on the bed so it would feel like someone was there."

My poor guy. Shelvin cracked his knuckles against his thigh. He was going to kill Hunter for pushing Elliot away and leaving him so vulnerable. Then, he was going to punch himself for not checking in sooner.

"There's one other thing I wanted to check in on before we go upstairs. Did you want to come? It's *your* hard limit, sweetheart, but it should be yours, not someone else's."

That rule hadn't sat well with him from day one, but Shelvin had shrugged it off. *He* should have been the one in control of Elliot's orgasms. They were a reward and a punishment rolled into one, and sometimes they helped push a person into subspace. He was done with Hunter haunting their scenes.

"I...but Hunter." Elliot looked up.

Is cheating on you. Fuck, he wanted to say it so badly, but it wasn't his place. His sub had already been through so much. Surely that could wait until morning.

"It's your decision, and it's the only thing you have to decide for tonight. I'm not going to go easy on you. I'm going to do things that will make you want to come so badly, then I'm going to torture the fuck out of you until it feels like you might burst. If you take it all, I'll let you decide. You don't need an orgasm to please me."

Elliot shuddered, and Shelvin didn't have to look to know that he was hard. "When you're ready, I want you to go upstairs and open the second door on the left. Strip naked and wait for me on the bench. I want your eyes closed and your mouth shut."

Shelvin leaned back, reaching for the remote. He was willing to wait the whole night for Elliot to be ready—or until the morning if he wasn't. One thing was for sure. He refused to fuck up again.

It was only twenty minutes before Elliot suddenly stood and rushed from the room without a backward glance. Shelvin grinned as soon as he was alone, flicking off the television and washing his hands. He wanted to be extra clean when he took Elliot apart piece by piece. And hell, they both needed it tonight.

He found Elliot lying on the table face-first with his spank-stained ass presented to the room. It did look a bit sore, even though Shelvin had gone easy on him. There were twenty implements in the room that could deepen that blush from red to a purple hue.

The main event of the room, other than his sub, was the black padded table that was perfect for play. The implements were tucked away in the cupboards around the room, hidden from sight and the mind of an unsuspecting sub.

The cum he'd spread on Elliot's cheeks had gone flaky, most of it missing and probably on the inside his boxers. From the way he squirmed, it must've been itchy — either that or he was looking for pressure on his cock. When Shelvin clicked his tongue in disapproval, Elliot immediately froze.

"Turn over." Shelvin kept his voice calm and cold. Usually he treaded on the softer side, but not tonight. "Show me that pathetic little cock of yours so I can lock it away."

Moving to one of the cupboards, Shelvin grabbed one of his cock cages that would fit Elliot just right. Even if he chose to come tonight, it wasn't happening anytime soon. When he looked back, Elliot had rolled over, clinging to the table as his sides heaved. His cock was hard and purple, pre-cum shining at the head.

"Get soft or I'll grab the ice." He had ice packs in his freezer for exactly this purpose, but it was so much better to watch Elliot's struggle as he furrowed his forehead in concentration. Waiting until he started to flag, Shelvin lubed up Elliot's cock, slipping his balls, then his cock through the tight rings of the metal cage before locking the rest into place.

"What do you think about to get soft?" asked Shelvin, mentally stepping outside of the scene for just a moment while he washed his hands in the sink and pulled a pair of latex gloves on. "Not the way I fucked you in the forest or painted your ass with cream in your office." He grinned as Elliot's cock twitched in its confines, straining at the unyielding metal.

"Food," said Elliot softly, his slick hands leaving marks on the padded table. "Gross food like canned peaches and olives — or high school. Awkward speeches and stuff always kill the mood for me."

Shelvin smirked, flicking one of Elliot's swollen balls. "Not anymore. You're still trying to get hard in there. Your cock doesn't know what's best for it." The cage made Elliot's balls look that much bigger, the skin stretched tight over the narrow base of one of the rings. One day he'd put a set of rings above his balls and stretch them right out until they turned red and bright.

Grabbing a case from another drawer, Shelvin slicked a urethral sound with sterile lubricant. He waved it in front of Elliot's face to show it off, his cock twitching when Elliot's eyes went wide. He'd gone shopping since their last scene, wanting to be prepared for the next time Elliot was ready for him.

"It's too big." Elliot's voice was barely a whisper, his knuckles white as he grabbed at the table. Sweat stood out on his body, dripping between his pecs and toward the dib of his abs.

"We're just getting warmed up. I'm going to leave this in until you beg me to take it out. You can't come with it… You won't be able to even relieve yourself on your own. Every bit of you will depend on me. You should hope that I'm in a generous mood."

The sound wasn't *that* big, but it did have bumps along the surface that grew larger toward the tip, that were sure to stimulate Elliot in a *thrilling* way. It was the idea of dependency that he wanted to plant in Elliot's mind. It was the only way to show him how strong he was and to make him realize that he had called the shots from the very beginning.

Elliot flushed, shuddering as he spread his legs wider. His cock was nearly purple in the cage, the tip complete with a drop of pearly liquid. The poor guy looked like he hadn't come in weeks, but he was still offering himself.

"Or maybe you just want me to tease you, then leave you here. Maybe you want me to stretch this hole wide until you can't hold anything back."

Elliot's hips jerked and he curled his toes, the rosy flush on his skin spreading to his chest. The sweat on his naked skin clung to his dark hair.

"I won't make you choose." Shelvin roughly grabbed the cage, smearing the lube over Elliot's slit. His hole was so tiny and unassuming, but that was about to change. He wasn't into permanent body modification, but there was nothing wrong with a little stretch.

Lining the sound up, Shelvin slowly pushed it inside, bracing his hand on Elliot's hip as he attempted to buck. The last thing he wanted was for him to get hurt. "Tell me how it feels, slave."

"It's too big." Elliot's eyes rolled back, and his mouth fell open as Shelvin advanced the sound another inch. His hole spread wider, closing over a bump as it slipped inside. "It burns."

Shelvin withdrew it all at once, despite Elliot's whimpers. Pouring another shot of lube over the sound and Elliot's slit, he eased it home again, making it a touch farther before Elliot started to squirm. Over and over he worked it deeper until it was almost to the base.

Elliot didn't cry out until the last bump disappeared and Shelvin locked it into place with a few slow twists. Flicking Elliot's balls again, he took a moment to admire them, so much more swollen than they had been without the cage. He could only imagine the pressure from inside and out, but Elliot responded to it beautifully, as always.

"I have to go." Elliot clutched at his cock, tugging on the cage.

"I'm sure it feels that way, especially with that pop I gave you. Poor thing." Shelvin pulled off his gloves, tossing them in the trash. "Turn on your stomach with your ass off the table. I want to see if I can make you come past that sound."

He grabbed his vibrator of choice — a powerful prostate massager that was almost brutal with the level of vibration it put out. He didn't bother prepping Elliot, slicking the vibrator and easing it into place. It settled almost like a butt plug with a flared base and wouldn't budge unless Elliot bore down.

"The last time I tried to give you this treat, we were interrupted. Let's see if you can even get your safeword out past the screams this time." Grabbing the remote, he selected the pulse mode, which would throb against Elliot's prostate like the worst kind of torture. Elliot bucked, yelling as he scrambled to keep standing as his legs presumably went weak.

Shelvin flicked it off for a moment, letting Elliot catch his breath and listening for the one word that would put an end to it all. He waited a few seconds before he turned it back on to a higher setting. "You asked for it."

Elliot writhed and kicked, his caged cock flopping between his legs and sweat glistened on his skin. There wasn't a single part of him that wasn't flushed or flexing, the table squeaking beneath the force of his movements. Shelvin clicked the toy higher, then higher again, reveling in Elliot's yell that morphed into a whimpering scream.

He shut it off abruptly and Elliot went limp, barely clinging to the edge of the table as his knees dipped toward the floor. Circling him, Shelvin watched the expression slipping over his face. Tortured astonishment bloomed as Shelvin flicked it back on, the vibrations giving off a low hum that he could hear even as he strolled away to lean against the wall.

"I-I can't! Please." Elliot finally begged, going slack as Shelvin cut the power again. Any longer and his sub would probably end up on the floor. *As much as that would make a pretty picture…*

"Get on the table with your cock in the air. And don't let that vibe fall out or I'll put a stronger one in." Shelvin growled, playing the part of the predator as his prey scrambled to comply. His cock was so hard that he was aching and would probably come before he even got the condom on.

"How would you feel about a blindfold?" Shelvin shuffled through another cupboard after he got his sub lying comfortably and arranged how he wanted. On his back with his knees bent and his legs spread wide and his ass hanging over the edge, it put Elliot at the perfect height.

"Green."

Securing the blindfold in place, Shelvin made sure it was tight enough that there would be no peeking. It was fur lined, so no light would be visible, but he never could be too careful. He glanced back to the drawer where it had come from, wincing at the array of toys he'd left in complete chaos. *So much for staying calm and cool.*

"Good." He took a deep breath of Elliot's skin, licking from his neck all the way to his nipples. Elliot let out a gasp, shivering as he teased until Elliot's nipples were rock hard beneath his tongue and fingers.

Now comes the best part. With Elliot moaning beneath him, Shelvin reached into his pocket, tugging two nipple clamps out by the connecting chain. He'd grabbed them earlier, securing them in his pocket while Elliot had been writhing. Sucking Elliot's nipples one last time, he carefully clamped them, licking his lips at the sight.

The clamps themselves were silver, their bark much worse than their actual bite. A newbie sub like Elliot would probably look at them in terror, not knowing their intensity was moderate at best. The chain dangled between them, sliding over his chest and practically calling to Shelvin's fingers. A single tug on that chain would probably open Elliot's world to a mass of sensations that he never thought he'd experience.

Elliot furrowed his forehead, squirming on the table as he clenched his hands into fists. Was it confusion or pleasure that flitted over his face?

"They don't hurt," said Elliot, almost in awe. "A bit, but not as much as I thought they would."

It was nice to hear his sub had been thinking about nipple clamps enough that he recognized the feel of them against his skin. There were two really good reasons that they didn't hurt, though, and the first was that Elliot was floating.

"Just wait."

Shelvin cranked the vibrating toy, and Elliot bowed off the table, kicking his feet as his legs seemed to spasm on their own. He gritted his teeth, the blindfold already soaked with sweat and tears. *Beautiful.*

"Would you like to come?" Shelvin tugged on the chain attached to the nipple clamps, adjusting one as it started to slip. Maybe he should have chosen a harsher pair. Both of them were too far beyond for light things at the moment.

"I-I..." Elliot threw back his head, his body spasming as his cock jerked and a drop of cum slipped past the sound. The tendons in his neck strained and he screamed loud enough for the noise to reverberate around the walls.

Shelvin shut off the toy, reaching for the sound and tugging it from Elliot's cock. A stream of cum followed it as Elliot jerked again, his tortured moan nearly enough to make Shelvin lose himself.

Elliot had come from the stimulation alone, even with his cock caged and plugged. *So perfect.*

"Did I say you could come?" Shelvin slapped Elliot's caged cock, cum splattering on his hand from the hit. Bringing his fingers to his shirt, Shelvin wiped them clean. Even with as much as he wanted to taste Elliot, with Hunter sleeping with another man, he didn't want to take any risks.

With the cum still wet on Elliot's cock, everything went wrong in less than a moment.

Elliot burst into sobs, curling on his side and bringing his knees to his chest. His quiet whimpers morphed into calls of utter agony as he broke down, shattering before Shelvin's eyes.

Fuck.

Chapter Twenty

Elliot

I came. I came. Oh, fuck.

With every bit of torture Shelvin had put him through and each moment of exquisite pleasure, he'd never risked breaking the only rule. He'd never been close to coming. It was impossible. His cock had been caged and under pressure that had been all-consuming, with his balls stretched tight. Even the plug should have done something to keep his cum where it belonged.

But he'd fucked it all up.

"I'm sorry." Elliot curled on his side, wrapping his arms around his knees as he cried into the dark. Shelvin was somewhere in the room, his cold voice like sweet fire on his skin. But he must've been pissed. By coming, he'd disobeyed his Dom and his husband—the two most important people in his world.

"I think you can do it again, slave. Show me how fucking good you can be and come again."

Oh. Shelvin didn't sound angry at all, but nearly as turned on as Elliot was. And Elliot *was*. Despite the devastating grief of his orgasm, he was still hard — well, as hard as he could be with the cage gripping him like a vise.

The hum started in his ass a moment later, the pressure brutal from the very beginning. Only now, his cock was empty of the plug, the tiny hole stretched so wide that he was surprised that he was able to keep everything inside where it belonged.

The burning was still there, though, exquisite in its torture but making him feel like he would lose control at any time. And now he was open and gaping. "I need it. Put it back!"

He forced his legs straight, then shifted until his back struck the sticky table. The smooth fabric was drenched in his sweat and probably other fluids. The blindfold kept it all a mystery. Shelvin didn't say a thing as his touch came at Elliot's cock and the pressure returned in full force.

Oh God. It was worse — so much worse. The sound felt huge, spreading him wide but sinking inevitably deeper until it had to be all the way inside. Each bump was torture, and the cage held him tight, forcing his cock into the bars. He couldn't stand it inside, but he couldn't bear the thought of being empty again.

"Fuck!" Elliot twisted, his mind gone as he cursed and thrashed. It was pure torture and Shelvin wasn't even touching him anymore.

"Open your mouth." Shelvin's voice came from somewhere above his head so Elliot dropped his mouth open, tilting his head back to give Shelvin access to whatever he wanted. He nearly choked when the taste of cock and a heavy weight slipped over his tongue.

"Bite me and I'll never let you out of that cage," said Shelvin a moment before he bucked forward and grabbed the chain on Elliot's nipples, tugging both clamps free.

What had been a strong and even pressure burst into flames, his nipples at the center of the inferno. He bowed off the table, and it took everything he had not to bite down. He shouted past Shelvin's cock as it suddenly plunged deep enough to cut off his air.

"Yeah, baby. Fucking take it," Shelvin growled, his cock flexing as he came down Elliot's throat, only drawing back to coat Elliot's tongue with a few salty shots.

The taste was strong, the thickness nearly choking him and sending fire across his skin. Without a single touch to his cock, Elliot came again, his balls tightening as his cum tried to escape.

It started deep in his gut, building in his groin and balls, despite the death grip on them. With nowhere to go, it stretched on and on, the vibrations against his prostate and the burn of his nipples lasting an eternity. Even as Shelvin pulled the sound free for the second time and his cum finally burst forth, the core-deep orgasm didn't fade.

One moment he was trapped in a never-ending bliss, and the next he was blinking at Shelvin, his blindfold gone and his body somewhere…else. Shelvin smiled, his face wavering in and out of focus as Elliot fought to keep breathing. He'd never been so relaxed in his life, even deep in subspace at Shelvin's feet. This was something different.

He came to slightly as Shelvin began to tug at the cock cage. Elliot flinched, grasping Shelvin's hand and stilling his movements. "Leave it. Please."

"Anything for you, sweetheart." Shelvin's voice was the softest he'd ever heard it. "Did you want a cloth or a shower?"

His mind buzzed and the answer was so far away that he wasn't sure if it would ever matter. Blinking at Shelvin, he smiled, reaching for his Dom's hand and kissing his wrist. The skin was soft under his lips and smelled so good that he didn't hold back from tasting it.

"Come with me, and I'll get you a bath. You deserve *so* much aftercare. You were the best fucking ever." Shelvin was speaking quickly, almost tripping over his words, and for some reason, that was absolutely hilarious.

He giggled as Shelvin helped him from the table, his loose limbs dangling this way and that as he tried to stand. They made it to the bathroom, and Shelvin sat him on the toilet as he ran a bath. Elliot looked down at the bowl, the ache in his cock and belly hitting him with full force.

"You can go, sweetheart. I won't hear anything over the water." As if to prove his point, Shelvin plugged the tub, jerking the tap until the water burst out of it at full force. He busied himself filling the tub and checking the temperature with his wrist as Elliot let go, his cheeks heating as another rush of emotions washed over him.

Shelvin helped him into the tub, easing him into the water that folded him in a warm embrace. He hissed as the goosebumps faded from his skin, leaving a tinge of bright pink in its wake. His eyelids dragged their way back down, so heavy that he couldn't hope to lift them.

"Stay awake just a little bit longer," Shelvin said softly as he grabbed a cloth and started washing him. Bits of cum along with the layers of sweat slowly lifted from his skin, leaving pristine warmth and sweet soap behind. Elliot sank ever deeper, leaving his body behind as he drifted. Everything was good, and there wasn't a worry in the world. Delayed fixtures for their project mattered as little as the itch on his big toe.

"Tilt your head back, and I'll do your hair. You know you're perfect, right? Every bit. You are the most beautiful man I know, and I think your hair is my favorite part. It's dark in the sun but turns almost blue-black as soon as I get it wet. It looks so good right now." Shelvin ran his fingers through Elliot's hair, suds following his every move.

Using an extendable shower head, he rinsed Elliot's hair before pulling the plug. Elliot immediately shivered, wrapping his arms around himself as the cold started to creep in.

"It's okay. I just want to get some fresh water in here for you. It was starting to get cold." Shelvin moved the shower head along his skin, rinsing the remainder of the suds away before he plugged the tub again and filled it with fresh water. Elliot sank into it, gasping at every touch of Shelvin against him.

"Did you want your cage off or did you want to sleep that way?" asked Shelvin, shucking his own clothes and slipping into the tub. Elliot shook his head, furrowing his forehead as he imagined his cock without it. It was a part of his dynamic with Shelvin, and he loathed the thought of taking it off.

"I love that you're making decisions, sweetheart. It makes me so fucking happy." Adjusting Elliot's caged cock, Shelvin slid between his legs, leaning his back against Elliot's chest. His hair tickled Elliot's chin, dry and smelling vaguely of sweat and strawberries.

"You want me to wash you?" asked Elliot, his voice a low grumble that he hardly recognized. He could barely lift his arms as he circled Shelvin's waist before settling on his hips. His Dom was still sticky, the evidence of his orgasm on his belly.

"Nah." Shelvin shook his head. "Right now is all about you. I'll have a shower once you're feeling level, but I'm not leaving you until then. I couldn't bear to see you looking so lonely."

Strangely enough, now that Shelvin said it, Elliot had been lonely—not only in the tub, but in the hotel, in his office and even in his home. He'd been lonely for so long that he couldn't remember the last time he'd felt whole.

Elliot sniffed, wiping his cheeks. They didn't make any sense. A moment before he'd been on top of the world.

"I have candles in here. Hold on." Shelvin leaned away, scrambling for a lighter that was leaning on the edge of the tiled tub area. The whole back was tiled, extending from the edge of the tub and leaving a place for numerous candles. The lighter clicked as he pulled the trigger, lighting the nearest wick.

Vanilla and lavender soaked the air as the flame curled toward the edge of the glass. Shelvin let out a sigh, settling against Elliot with a deep breath. "I had hoped that you wouldn't drop until tomorrow, but I like to be prepared. Did you want some chocolate? I have a stash in here, along with some pop and water."

Envy curled in his gut, turning his stomach until Elliot had to look away. It was one thing for Shelvin to prepare for *him*, but the entire night had been spontaneous. There was no way he could have had candles and chocolate ready for him. How many subs did Shelvin bring back to his home and strap to his play table? How many of them were younger or more experienced?

"It's not what you think," said Shelvin, turning to lay his cheek against Elliot's chest. "I always drop after I play, and I've learned to be prepared. It usually takes a few days to hit me, and it's not as bad if I get to see you after a scene. Chocolate and candles are a poor substitute."

Elliot hugged him tighter. Everyone always talked about sub-drop, with articles in every forum about it. No one talked about Dom-drop. "What's it like?"

Moving his hands to Shelvin's waist, he shifted until his fingers met the flaccid flesh of Shelvin's cock. If he had a single regret about their scene, it was that Shelvin hadn't come inside his ass. As far as he was concerned, his mouth didn't count.

"Guilt mostly." Shelvin shrugged, kissing Elliot's pec. "I second guess that you actually enjoyed yourself or if I forced you at all. Or sometimes I feel like I have the flu. If I get really down, headaches and muscle aches stick with me for days. I've learned not to push myself that far anymore, and I try to only play with someone in a contract."

Elliot fought the sleepiness, dragging his consciousness back to the surface. "Can I do anything to make it better? I don't want you to feel sick."

Shelvin shrugged again, letting out a sigh as he snuggled closer. "Just having you here and taking care of you is good for me. Aftercare really helps me through it, and even seeing you orgasm this time was amazing. I'm not going to forget that for a long time. Besides, you gave me your world and let me hold it for a while. That means so much."

"Okay." Elliot wished he could do more. Between the sweet torture from the scene and now the romantic bath with the scent of candles in the air, he felt like he was a king. The cage must've been his crown, and he had no intention of taking it off anytime soon.

"Why didn't you fuck me?" It was gnawing at Elliot, digging deeper than he cared to admit. Shelvin had only taken his mouth in their first scene, but since then, he'd kept Elliot's hole satisfied. He almost wondered if that had become more important than the kneeling, although both gave him an equal rush.

Shelvin instantly went tense, pulling away just a bit to look into Elliot's eyes. His lips were tight, the darkness under his eyes suddenly looking severe. "It's not the time to talk about that."

But... There were only a few reasons that would stop Shelvin fucking him, and most of them were terrifying. Erectile dysfunction couldn't be the case. Elliot's throat could attest to that.

"Are you okay?" Or maybe it was something so much worse.

That sexy smirk split Shelvin's lips, easing the worry building in his gut. "Of course. Just because I didn't fuck you doesn't mean you aren't mine. That ass belongs to *me,* and I'm the only one who knows how to take care of it. Now, let's move to the bedroom before we both pass out. You're having a drink and brushing your teeth before bed, and that's final. I can't have my sweetheart getting cavities."

Even as Shelvin dried both of them and helped Elliot into bed, giving his caged cock a tender kiss before pulling the covers over him, the worry continued to grow. There was something wrong, and it was bothering Shelvin enough that Elliot could see it, even through his mask. He could only hope that it didn't ruin everything they had.

Chapter Twenty-One

Shelvin

He *had* to tell Elliot. The whole situation was terrible, and he was like a grim reaper hiding the demise of his sub's marriage while they both went through the highs and lows of an amazing scene.

The scene itself had been perfection, and he'd almost found himself giggling as adrenaline had surged through him when he'd come down Elliot's throat. It was only fair that his drop was worse than most, especially with Hunter's guilt on his mind.

Elliot's presence helped to the point that Shelvin was ready to offer him one of the empty rooms. They'd slept together on the first night, but after that, Elliot had retreated to one of the guest rooms to sleep. It had irked Shelvin at first, but he also knew they had work to do, and if Elliot was in his bed, they'd both be up late.

Not that they were fucking. *Nope.* Until Shelvin got his head out of his ass and explained why they were going back to condoms and frequent testing, they weren't doing anything of the sort. Elliot had to know something was awry. When Shelvin had avoided sex, he'd looked a little taken aback.

But it was also hard to have sex with someone when they refused to remove their cock cage. Other than to clean himself, Elliot had insisted on wearing it, getting defensive when Shelvin tried to remove it. It had to hurt, the metal bars unforgiving against sensitive flesh, but if it was what Elliot needed, then he was happy to do it for him.

Usually, he kept toys to scenes, and he'd never treaded the waters of a twenty-four-seven dynamic. Not that he wasn't interested... Having a sub at his disposal at all times would be as hot as fuck — but only if he remembered them. Sometimes he lost himself for days in his work, only emerging to relieve himself and eat. A sub waiting for him in that situation would be an absolute disaster.

No, he wasn't made for full-time.

"Elliot?" Shelvin stood from the couch, strengthening his resolve as he headed for the kitchen. Last he'd seen, Elliot was in a cute apron while making a batch of muffins. That was the second reason he was going to ask him to stay. After he'd taste-tested them, of course. 'Handsome' and 'great cook' were two very important priorities.

"Hey," Elliot smiled, turning away from the stove where he was lifting the muffins onto a wire rack. Shelvin hadn't been aware that he even had wire racks — or muffin tins, for that matter.

He'd donned a purple apron to bake in, and even with it, he looked like a disaster. There was flour all over him and the counters, and a smudge had even made it to the end of his nose. Something sticky was on the inside of his wrist where he'd rolled up his sleeve. Shelvin couldn't hold back his chuckle.

"I was just going to come find you," said Elliot, opening the oven to take a quick peek. "Do you have any containers? I wanted to take some to Hunter. These are his favorite, and I can't cook them without giving him some." His smile was brilliant, if not a touch strained.

Shifting as his gut sank, Shelvin covered his unease with a smile. As far as he knew, Elliot hadn't even talked to Hunter since he'd left, taking the space thing to a completely different level.

"Have you talked to him lately? Hunter, I mean." Shelvin crossed his arms, immediately uncrossing them when he realized how defensive he was getting. "You seem really okay about your time away, but I was wondering how Hunter was taking it. The last time I saw him, he was a touch...occupied." *Coward.*

Doms were supposed to be brave, but Shelvin had missed that memo at birth—especially when it came to the drama side of things. Where was Clint when he needed him?

"I haven't, but I think it's time," said Elliot, his smile barely wavering. "I think I just needed time away to realize I missed him and how much I rely on him. I know you haven't had the best experience with him, but he really is a loving man."

Shelvin winced, tugging his hair by the roots. "But did he understand that you were coming back? Or when? How do you know he'd be faithful to you?" He couldn't outright say it, even if it was swelling so large in his throat that it threatened to choke him.

"The same way that I'm faithful to him and my Dom," said Elliot, placing the last muffin on the wire rack before pulling a second tray from the oven. They appeared a touch burnt, but the smell was heavenly.

"Yeah. Ah, fuck." *Spit it out!* His throat went tight. He was fine with humiliating Elliot in a scene, but he couldn't do it for *real*.

"Is that what the 'no sex' was about? I understand if you want to use condoms. I was kind of surprised that you were okay with raw, seeing as I routinely have sex with another man...or not so routinely." He looked thoughtful for a moment before he shook his head. "It's strange," said Elliot as he started lifting the muffins from the second tray. "At first, I wanted to explore kink as a part of fixing my sex life. I mean, I love sex and I always have, but I couldn't always be the one in control. Instead of kink fixing things for me, I barely fuck him at all. We've only made love maybe twice since I started seeing you. The other night was the first time I've come in weeks."

Shelvin adjusted his cock as he throbbed to life. He'd assumed that Elliot was taking care of himself outside of a scene, but if that wasn't the case, then *fuck*. Shelvin had owned that part of him, even if he hadn't known it.

"And Hunter is okay with that?" asked Shelvin slowly, knowing the answer but begging Elliot to see it for himself.

"He's my husband. I think he loves me more than my cock." Elliot flushed, looking through the cupboard until he stumbled upon some old Tupperware. "I think the cage might be a surprise to him, but he'll understand that, too."

Wait... "You can't keep wearing it, Elliot." Shelvin couldn't help but bristle a touch. Maybe he'd let it slide for too long. "That one isn't meant for long-term use. Even now you're pushing it. I can get you one that would suit better, but I don't have anything right now. Give me a day."

"But I like this one." Elliot pouted, drooping his shoulders as soon as he set the container down. "Just let me wear it for a little longer."

"Fuck," Shelvin said under his breath. Other than some chafing and soreness at night, he couldn't think of any reason not to let him keep wearing it. The little nubs on it would be a problem. There were already a few spots that Shelvin had noticed when he'd cleaned it the night before that looked raw and achy.

"If I say you take it off, you take it off. You don't get to decide if it's playtime for your cock or not. Get to the bathroom now, and if you aren't naked by the time I get there, you'll be punished."

Elliot's eyes went wide as he looked to the oven and at the fresh pans he'd just slipped inside. "The muffins—"

"I'll take care of them." Maybe the things would burn, and Hunter wouldn't get any after all. Shelvin derailed that thought as soon as it surfaced. Territorial was not his style, even if Elliot seemed to drag it out of him.

Elliot started toward the living room, pausing to look back as he reached the door. He stayed silent, casting one last glance before he turned away.

Shelvin paced the kitchen, glaring at the timer each time he passed it. It seemed to move so fucking slowly that he was ready to bite his tongue off by the time it finished. The truth was, he was pissed—not just at Hunter, but at himself too. He'd let Elliot get away with far too much, pushing the boundaries when he shouldn't have. If there was one thing he wasn't going to risk, it was the safety and health of his sub.

The muffins were still a touch soggy when the timer went, but he shut the oven off, tugging them out and tossing the pan on top of the stove. Stomping up the stairs, he prowled toward the bathroom, letting his footsteps thump against the floor. Intimidation was key.

Throwing the bathroom door open, he fought a wince as it bounced off the wall, probably putting a dent in the drywall. He didn't look, not when every fiber of his being was focused on remaining calm while giving the appearance of rage. If that's what it took for Elliot to listen, then that's what he would do.

"On your knees," Shelvin barked, sparing Elliot a single glance. He had listened, his clothes folded in the corner and his form covered in goosebumps. The flour and muffin mix had disappeared as well.

His cock did look red in its cage, straining at the uncomfortable bars with a drop of pre-cum at the head. "Did I fucking stutter?"

He whirled back and Elliot flinched, dropping to his knees. He was wide-eyed, but there was still defiance in the set of his jaw. Shelvin was going to *break* him.

"Close your eyes." Shelvin rifled through the cupboard, grabbing a few things from his kit that he kept there. He hadn't mentioned it after their last scene, but he kept a few other things there for when he dropped. Sometimes he fucked himself to get over the sinking feeling, and he liked the scent of the strawberry lube he had stashed within.

He clicked his tongue as he surveyed Elliot, who was barely holding his submissive pose. He shivered on the cold tile, his lower lip trembling as he clenched his eyes shut. Shelvin nudged his knee and lower back, fixing his posture with a few touches.

"I wouldn't take you to Unkinked looking like this. I have to train you all over again before you're presentable. The first thing to go will be that fucking attitude." He turned to the sink, washing the dildo, despite the fact that it was already sanitized. Shutting off the water, he coated it in a layer of soap, leaving the suds dripping.

"If you want to mouth off, then I'll give you something better to do. Clap your hands if you need to safeword and don't drop this." Bringing the dildo to Elliot's lips, he eased it into his mouth, pausing at a few inches. Elliot's face screwed up, drool and suds immediately dripping to his chin. "And no teeth. That's all the cock you deserve, and you'll treat it right."

Shelvin went to one knee, pulling the key to the cock cage from his pocket. He had a spare on a hanger on the fridge, but he'd kept one close to him while he'd waited for Elliot to be ready to take it off.

Elliot's cock looked so sore, and as Shelvin slowly removed the cage, he hissed at the sight. The small bumps on the inside of the cage had left pinpricks of pink polka dots up and down the shaft. Elliot's foreskin looked irritated too and his balls were a touch swollen.

He grabbed a cloth, warming some water and soaping it up before he brought it to Elliot's cock and cleaned every inch. Elliot whimpered past the dildo, wiggling his hips to the side as Shelvin scrubbed a particularly raw spot. He stiffened at the same time, swelling in Shelvin's hand until he was at full mast.

Wiping the soap away, Shelvin slicked his palm with lube, smearing it over Elliot's shaft until it glistened. The smell of strawberries warmed the air, and the dildo slid an inch out of Elliot's mouth before he grimaced and suctioned it back inside.

"Do you get to come?" asked Shelvin, stroking Elliot's cock absently. Elliot shook his head, whimpering. "That wasn't a question for you, slave. All you have to do is clap and this all stops." Orgasms were off the limits list, but Shelvin wanted to check in to make sure. He had no desire to fuck up during a punishment scene.

He jerked quickly and rhythmically, not bothering with anything fancy except to twist his hand over the head of Elliot's cock a few times. His shaft swelled in his hand, and it wasn't long before Elliot shuddered, the dildo almost falling from his mouth as he jerked his hips. A huge amount of cum painted Shelvin's hand, dripping to the floor as he eased Elliot through it.

"Your orgasm isn't your punishment," said Shelvin, wiping his hand on the inside Elliot's thigh before he coated him in a fresh layer of lube and started jerking him all over again.

Elliot twitched, clenching his hands, and for a moment, Shelvin wondered if it was all over. He slowed his movements, pulling the dildo from Elliot's mouth. "What's your color?"

Elliot took a long breath, licking his lips and wincing at the suds he found there. "Yellow." His voice was rough, like he'd already been fucked. "It hurts." He hissed as Shelvin tightened his grip.

"Good. Maybe you'll learn something then." Rubbing the dildo in the spot of cum on Elliot's thigh, Shelvin shoved it back into Elliot's mouth, sinking it inside until it had to be tickling the back of his mouth. "If you feel you can't clap, just drop the dildo. Otherwise, keep quiet. I don't want to hear from you until you're done being a stubborn brat."

There was so much lube that Shelvin's hand slid easily over Elliot's shaft, which hadn't fully softened. The reddened spots had bloomed a touch brighter, the marks from the bars standing out like fingerprints on *CSI*. His first stop was a silicone cage that Elliot would be able to remove in an emergency and that didn't have pressure points like the metal one. They always had a plastic smell to them, but it was better than damaging Elliot's cock.

"Give me another one in the next thirty seconds or I'm going to force two more out of you. Your balls still look so heavy. How much do you have stored in there? I'd be happy to find out." Shelvin shifted on the floor, adjusting his own cock, which was like steel. "Come, slave. *Now.*"

He'd never asked a sub to come on command before, but hell if it wasn't the prettiest sight he'd ever seen. Elliot quaked, moving his legs in a way that looked like it was against his will. His forehead creased, then smoothed again and he arched as a dribble of cum streaked from his cock and over Shelvin's knuckles.

"That was too easy. Another?"

Elliot shook his head, hollowing his cheeks in an effort of holding the plastic cock inside his mouth. He opened his eyes, tears streaking down his cheeks. His pupils were blown, his eyes bloodshot and practically begging.

Shelvin wasn't moved. "Hmmm. It looks like you haven't learned your lesson, so let me remind you. I *own* you, and I want another one, so that's exactly what you'll give me."

It was too bad that his biceps were burning, and his shoulder was starting to seize up or he would have continued to jerk Elliot through a third orgasm. Still, he liked to watch almost as much as he liked to touch.

"Make yourself come."

Shelvin dropped his hand, shuffling back before standing with a muffled groan. He had a playroom for a reason, with benches built to his height, but he didn't want to associate a punishment with that room. That, and he didn't want to get carried away by hooking up his fucking machine and unleashing it on Elliot's ass. No...that would be a reward, not a punishment.

Elliot winced as he touched himself, crying out as he gripped his cock. The dildo slipped from his mouth, and Shelvin's heart stopped for the brief second that it always did when he heard or saw his sub safeword.

Dropping every appearance of anger, Shelvin moved right back to his aching knees, clasping Elliot's hands in his and stilling his movements. Elliot's eyes were wide, tears running full stream down his face as he panted open-mouthed.

"I-I'm sorry. I didn't mean to drop it," Elliot appeared to struggle to get the words out as he tried to reach for the dildo.

"Hey, baby. It's okay. You did so fucking good for me. The scene is over, and your punishment is over. You're forgiven. You're always forgiven."

Elliot cracked before his eyes, splitting wide open as he started to sob. Relief poured from him as Shelvin held him close, his tears soaking into his shirt. If it hadn't been for the relief, Shelvin wouldn't have been able to stand it, but that simple emotion made it so worth it.

"S-sorry."

"Baby." Shelvin kissed the top of his head. "Let me take care of you. You're mine and nothing is going to change that. Don't feel guilty for being so good."

Letting out a trembling sigh, Elliot sank into him, Shelvin struggling to hold his full weight. He loved it, though. Every inch and pound that Elliot had on him, only made him feel stronger because Elliot was *his*.

"Okay," said Elliot, as he slowly closed his eyes. His tears had already started to slow. "But please don't touch my cock anymore. It really hurts."

Shelvin grinned, letting out a chuckle. "I won't, baby. Now let's get you cleaned up. I'll be as gentle as I can, and I'll let you wash your cock so you can avoid the ouchie spots."

Chapter Twenty-Two

Elliot

Elliot stared at the door, wondering if he was supposed to knock or just head inside. His key was in his pocket, but he hadn't used it in weeks. It was almost a stranger now, the small metal divots shiny from touching them over and over as he'd pondered his return.

Dragging his fingertips over the numbers on the door, he bit his lip. Like the rest of the building, they still appeared new, with none of their burnished bronze glow faded at all. There was a smidge of dust on them which he wiped away. *It's now or never.*

Turning the key in the lock, he pushed his way into his home with Hunter, closing the door quietly behind him. He paused, shutting his eyes to let the familiarity sink in.

The smell hit him first, the sandalwood soap and hint of citrus dragging a warm feeling from his gut. It was quiet, with the distant hum of the fridge and keys clacking in the office as Hunter probably typed away on his latest project.

Nothing had changed. It was almost as if he hadn't left at all, but he felt so different. There was a new power in his core — something that he could finally hold onto himself without Shelvin there as a support. He was truly alive for the first time in as long as he could remember.

"Hunter?" he called softly. The sound of computer keys instantly stopped, and Hunter's chair dragged against the floor as he presumably pushed it back. When he appeared at the edge of the hall, Elliot's heart almost stopped. Hunter looked like an angel.

He hadn't changed, either. While Elliot had gone through sleepless nights and questioning every part of himself, Hunter had still dolled himself up, his hair tangle-free and his lips shiny with gloss that smelled like cherries. The frown on his lips was the only thing out of place.

Elliot halted halfway through a smile, shuffling a step back as Hunter's frown morphed into a glare. Hunter put his hands on his hips, squaring his shoulders as he blocked Elliot's way into the condo.

He could remember when they'd bought the place together, his own presence like a mirage within the walls. Slipping into place had been easy, and so had hiding among the modern fixtures — until it hadn't been so easy anymore.

"What are you doing here?" Hunter's voice was biting, matching the look on his face. His cheeks were starting to flush, too, which was something Elliot rarely saw. "How did you even get in?"

Elliot looked to the key in his hand, wondering if maybe he wasn't supposed to have it. It was the same spare he remembered getting cut at the hardware store. The first one hadn't fit in the lock, so he'd returned to the store three times on the same day, asking them to cut new keys until one finally worked. "My key?"

Hunter furrowed his forehead for a moment before realization seemed to dawn. "That's right. Chet isn't changing the locks out until tomorrow. He got called into work early." A look appeared on his face that had no business being there. It was something far away and soft—something that Elliot had assumed was only ever for him.

There were so many questions without answers, and Elliot couldn't ask a single one. Who was he to question his husband, who had stood by him through everything and had understood what he needed?

"Did you want me to go?" Elliot asked instead, looking to the boot tray below the coat hooks. Both were occupied by things that weren't his. Was he that replaceable?

Yes. It was like a poison that seeped into his blood. When had he ever been there for Hunter? Or given *him* what he needed? He couldn't even remember the last time he'd bought him flowers or taken him out on a date.

Hunter rolled his eyes. "I don't understand why you're surprised, Elliot. You made your choice. *You* walked out on me and said you needed time. Thank God you did. It finally helped things make sense. Chet loves me more than you ever did, and he would do anything for me. He actually cares about me."

Elliot swallowed, struggling to keep the tears from falling. His eyes stung as he blinked, staring at the glass sculpture beyond the hall. Truth be told, he hated the fucking thing, along with the sterile walls and the decorations that Hunter had plucked out of the hottest magazines. Even the citrus shampoo burned his nose, a false imposter compared to his plants at work.

"I guess I'll go then." His chest went numb as he turned away, the tears evaporating in seconds. "You're right. I shouldn't have come back." *Stupid, stupid. Of course, Hunter moved on, I fucking left him!*

He reached for the door as Hunter let out a strangled cry, dragging Elliot's gaze to him. In a moment, he'd crumpled, his eyes going glassy as his cheeks bloomed with red blotches.

"You're not even going to fight for us?" Hunter screeched, his voice rising two octaves as he clenched his fists. It was the Hunter that Elliot's friends had warned him about before they'd been married, when he'd been so broken that all he wanted was the presence of a kind being. It was probably the Hunter that Shelvin saw, too.

Am I? Elliot set his jaw, glaring at the shoes in his spot. They were a size or two smaller than his and worn, one of the laces almost broken through. "Will you? I was gone for *weeks*, Hunter, not years. You didn't just meet Chet a few weeks ago."

"So?" Hunter crossed his arms. "You've got your — whatever you fucking call him — your *abuser*. At least Chet treats me right."

Elliot shook his head, something breaking in his chest as a veil was lifted from his eyes. *How could I be so blind?* "Everything we've been through together, and you still don't understand." He touched his hand to his forehead, trying to squash his building rage. "I don't want to fight."

He turned but Hunter grabbed him by the elbow, jerking him away from the door. Elliot stumbled, surprised by Hunter's sudden strength. Or maybe it was just that his own strength was buried beneath years of resignation.

"If this is about Chet, then I'll dump him. Don't leave me, Elliot." Hunter's eyes were wide and begging, but it only hardened Elliot's resolve. The truth was, he didn't give a shit about Chet. He was finally seeing the Hunter that everyone had warned him about. The man before him hated himself more than anything and took it out on those around him. He was no better than a bully.

"Goodbye, Hunter." He tugged his arm free, dropping his key to the floor as he turned the knob.

"But y-your stuff. You can't just leave it all behind. You *can't* leave me." Hunter dropped to his knees, pulling at his hair as tears rolled down his face. Had he always been so dramatic?

"You can keep it." Elliot rubbed his chin, looking into the hall. His files from his home office were saved on his work server, and he could always replace his clothes. As for the condo…Hunter could have it. "You can have the condo, but our savings is mine. I'll talk to my lawyer tomorrow."

"Fuck you," Hunter grumbled, pointing one finger at him. A month ago, Elliot would have cringed under that look, but now, all he could see was a brat having a temper tantrum because they hadn't gotten their way. "That money is *mine*. You can't just decide to leave, then take everything from me, too."

"This condo is worth more than our savings…*much* more." Elliot shook his head and stepped over the threshold, closing the door behind him and cutting off Hunter's shriek. The poor neighbors were probably wondering what the hell was going on. Hell, *he* was wondering.

Hunter is cheating on me? In all fairness, Elliot had done the same thing. Their one rule they'd set, he'd broken with Shelvin, coming even with a cock cage and a sound. He should have felt terrible about it...about everything, but he didn't. It was as if he'd known when he'd left the muffins for Hunter behind.

It was somewhat of a relief to know that he wasn't going to step back in that condo again. He hadn't realized how heavily it had been weighing on him, but now that it was gone, it was as if he were free.

He only had one place to go.

* * * *

He found Shelvin exactly where he'd expected, and the sight of him made Elliot's stomach flip and his cock strain against its cage. The smooth silicone held him tight, the comfort of it almost more than the constant ache of being restricted. He fucking loved it. Although, a sound would have certainly made it better...even just a little one.

Shelvin looked up from the makeshift table that had been thrown together with two sawhorses and a scrap of plywood. Paint was precariously perched on the edge, but Shelvin didn't seem overly concerned. After giving Elliot a brief smile, he turned back to his conversation with Samson, tapping something he had laid out on the plywood.

Ugh, a color palette. Paint colors were Elliot's nemesis, and he'd sworn off them for good, leaving that part of the project to Shelvin.

The rest of the house was eerily quiet, which meant that Shelvin had probably called Samson here on a day off, just to go over plans. *Fucking architects.* They had no sympathy for a man's day off.

"Hi, Elliot," said Samson, pausing to tilt his hard hat. Elliot was almost certain there was a bit of cowboy in his blood. The hat thing was the biggest clue, not to mention he was rugged as fuck.

"You okay if I talk to my Dom?" asked Elliot, shooting Samson a meaningful look. It was hopefully a clue for Shelvin as well, who still seemed way too occupied with thirty shades of blue.

Scratching his hand over his scalp, Samson shrugged before pulling his hat back over his head. He looked almost as tired as Elliot felt. They were all in need of a break. "You need me to take off?"

Shaking his head, Elliot cast a quick glance to Shelvin, who still hadn't looked up. He was beautiful when he was lost in his work, his eyes shining with a single-minded focus that he only seemed to have for building and fucking.

Elliot dropped to his knees, moving slowly so he didn't land too firmly on the floor. He'd learned that one the hard way. Knocking the hard hat off his own head, he leaned into Shelvin's thigh, closing his eyes and breathing deep.

Now *that* smelled like home. Shelvin was chaos, control and leather that sent Elliot instantly into a trance. His panic and terror melted away as his artificial calm burst, tears battling with the sobs he'd been hiding in his chest.

Hunter. Fuck. Elliot loved him more than any man in the world, and it fucking stung. Shelvin moved a hand to his hair as a sob let loose, and to his credit, Samson started the conversation up right where they'd left off.

"You want a pillow, or did you want to hurt?" asked Shelvin, leaning close to the drawing as he spoke and flickering his gaze to Elliot for a moment before he looked away.

The question would have sounded so strange weeks ago, and Elliot wouldn't have been able to make the choice either. Now he just *knew*.

"I want to hurt." He needed to feel the same way on the outside as he did inside, and the ache in his knees was pushing him in the right direction. There was a nail under his left shin, digging through his pants and poking right into his skin. It was a good thing he always kept his tetanus shot up to date.

"You okay with this, Samson?" asked Shelvin. Elliot clung tighter, refusing to look at Samson's face. His chest already hurt so terribly, and it was getting harder to breathe. What was he going to do? Where was he going to stay? He was approaching forty... He couldn't start over again. He'd already left his life behind once, and it had almost cost him his sanity.

"I mean," Samsun drawled, his voice just a tad deeper than normal, "it *is* a kink house. I hope to be at the opening party so I can find myself a good doc to fuck me up."

"Cool." Shelvin tugged his hair, drawing Elliot's attention. "You can suck me if you need to, sweetheart."

Elliot lunged for the zipper on Shelvin's pants, taking out his soft cock with shaking fingers and drawing it into his mouth. He was salty with musk that coated his tongue, the dizziness of the sudden pleasure almost derailing him.

"I still say we set these up in the basement," said Shelvin, addressing Samson as if his cock weren't jammed down Elliot's throat. Well, maybe not his *throat*. He was still sort of soft, after all.

"Clint didn't ask for these, but that fucker loves surprises. What will we need, like forty feet of rebar and a shit-ton of mirrors? We could repurpose those beams that were mis-shipped, too." Shelvin tapped the paper, even as Elliot attempted to suck him deeper.

It was almost insulting that he was hardly reacting, which was just what Elliot needed. Quiet care was always better for him than screeching, when he knew he still had Shelvin's focus.

"What are we talking about for weight capacity? Do we just want them solid?" Samson scratched his chin, the flush on his cheeks giving him away. He was watching, and Elliot couldn't have given two shits about it.

"Let's just say this." Shelvin tugged his hair. *Hard.* "I want to hang this fucking brat from it and not let him down until he passes out from coming so much. I want it to hold him up as I fuck him, dangling by the ropes tied through it."

Samson cleared his throat, running a hand through his hair. "Uh, yeah. That sounds good...really good." He looked at Elliot, who blinked back at him, tears starting to blur his vision.

"He's a slut, you see," said Shelvin, licking his lips. He closed his eyes, furrowing his forehead before he seemed to be able to get control again. His cock pulsed in Elliot's mouth. "And every slut needs to be reminded of who they belong to—even if I have to breed his ass every day, whether he's asleep or not."

Samson flushed, but Elliot burned, his chest flaring as fresh tears streaked down his cheeks. He turned his head, letting Shelvin's cock fall from his lips. He licked it absently, making sure it never went dry. Shelvin hadn't been able to resist him, his shaft fully hard and throbbing as it bobbed with every lick.

"Did you know?" asked Elliot softly, tucking his fingers into Shelvin's front pocket. His jeans sagged, almost dropping from his hips before Shelvin tugged them back up, doing the button with his cock still hanging out.

"Yeah. I couldn't tell you, sweetheart. It wasn't my place." Shelvin drew his lips into a frown, finally looking away from the plans. Samson gratefully stayed silent.

There had always been someone in Elliot's life, telling him what to do, where to go, which job to complete and how to fuck. If Shelvin would have told him, maybe it would have been just another layer...someone else trying to turn Elliot against Hunter as he clung tighter.

How many family reunions had he been to where Hunter's family had left him feeling ashamed and listless? The sideways looks, the little jeers and comments that seemed to slide over Hunter to land squarely in Elliot's lap.

"Why would Hunter want someone like you?" Gay, damaged, broken? It didn't matter.

Shelvin had been the first one to show him that he wasn't broken—that he could hold his own, set his rules and explore his life and body in the way he'd always been meant to.

Except for maybe the urethral sounds. They would have to stay for special occasions only. It still burned a bit sometimes.

Letting out a sigh, he rubbed his cheek on Shelvin's leg, his tears soaking into the thick fabric of his jeans.

"Thank you." *Is it my imagination or does Shelvin look relieved?*

C h a p t e r   T w e n t y - T h r e e

Elliot

He was trembling beneath his robe, the people around him dressed like a rainbow of kinky celebrators. Leather caught his eye, along with a corset and a kilt, for some reason. He spied the plaid skirt and the hairy legs underneath that were almost as thick as his. Shelvin flicked his chin, sending him a wink to draw his attention back.

The house was packed, every implement in place and the paint freshly dried. It was massive, but the house was still stuffed to the nines as people scened, fucked and celebrated a new Chapter for their community.

The way it had come together was beautiful to its core and as kinky as fuck, each themed room like another world where couples could play together. And at the center of it all was Clint, standing on the main stage that Elliot and Shelvin had created together. His grin was wide, the light in his eyes like no other.

The most surprising part was the dress clothes he had donned for the occasion, going all out and even brushing his hair. Sweat still beaded on his forehead, and Shelvin was chuckling out something about a tie that Clint had hacked off as soon as members had started to arrive.

Every wall, they had built together, their sweat and blood in the very foundation. Their time and the last remnants of Elliot's marriage was stuffed along with the insulation.

Elliot cast a glance Shelvin's way, smiling at his Dom, who was talking animatedly with two massive men who had more tattoos than Elliot had ever seen. They were two of the most intimidating men he'd met that night so far, and they were twins to boot.

When it came to hard work, though, Shelvin wasn't one to get his hands dirty, unless it was with pencil or chalk. *Fucking architects.* He did have to admit, though, that Shelvin had elevated a simple house into a fucking ensemble of kink, even if they had finished a week or so behind schedule.

"Hello, fellow kinksters!" Clint called from the stage, grabbing the microphone and surveying the room. He bubbled with energy as he hopped to the edge of the stage. "And can I say welcome!"

The crowd applauded, a few chuckling as Clint stumbled, nearly tripping off the edge. He rubbed his head sheepishly, effectively killing his perfect hair. Maddy stood at the corner of the stage, shaking his head at the display.

"When Ross and I started Unkinked, we had big dreams for horny people everywhere," said Clint, followed by a few snickers across the crowd. "But I never could have imagined *this*. Unkinked became a home for so many, and I knew someday we would outgrow the bar. But this place..."

He stared at the hall, gawking in the same way he had when Shelvin and Elliot had done their final walkthrough with him. "This is better than anything I could have imagined. If Ross could see what he helped build" — Clint shook his head as he swallowed — "he'd be slightly less pissed about me spending his inheritance on it."

Elliot laughed, turning to Shelvin, who was grinning. The final price had been...a lot, but Clint had paid it with the same grin he always seemed to wear.

"I hope everyone gets a good tour tonight, unless you get distracted by our show. We still have our themed rooms, only they are bigger and better equipped now, and we've thrown in a few...surprises." Clint winked as Shelvin chuckled. The hair on the back of Elliot's neck prickled. He'd seen the basement, and that chuckle did not bode well for those who happened upon it.

"So welcome home, everybody! Our show tonight will be put on by the very men behind the vision of this place. It's only fair they get first dibs."

Elliot gulped, zoning out as his heart pounded. There were *so* many people, and he knew a lot of them now. They'd spent a fair amount of time in the club clothed, talking to people as they made their final preparations for the move to the new house. Most of them had seen him naked, too, but not all at the same time.

It was a big step. It was also the greatest thrill of his life.

Shelvin raised one eyebrow, shooting him a look. "Why are you still wearing clothes?"

Some of the crowd had started to disperse, others moving to the chairs that had been set up for the show. *His* show. His first public scene since officially ending his marriage.

Sliding his robe from his shoulders, Elliot hung it on a hook at the entrance, shivering in the warm air. If it had been possible, his cock would have been rock hard from the gazes that strayed his way. But even that part of him looked pathetic, locked away and tiny.

He was almost certain his cock had shrunk. Shelvin called it cute. Once he'd called it a 'clitty' but Elliot had safeworded right away. That was a limit, along with the brazier that Shelvin had wanted him to try.

The lacy panties were a full go, though.

"Aww, look at how fucking cute it is," said Shelvin, flicking Elliot's caged cock. The blow stung as it lanced up the sound stuffed into Elliot's cock. "We'll be ready to go down another size soon."

Elliot closed his eyes, letting that wash over him. He clenched his stomach as his gut spasmed, his cock twitching in its cage. Shelvin's voice dropped into a growl as he stepped close to Elliot and whispered into his ear.

"If I had my way, you'd be plugged all the time, begging me for even the tiniest things. I'd have your cock caged so tight that you'd almost be flat. All I need is that hole anyway." He slipped a finger between Elliot's cheeks, prodding his lubed entrance. "And you have a spare if I break that one tonight." He tapped Elliot's lips.

Oh fuck. Oh shit. Elliot took a deep breath, trying to calm himself as his cock tried to harden again, every part of it screaming from its confines. It didn't hurt as much as it did when he woke sometimes, his dreams driving him to the edge of orgasm, so he had to knock on Shelvin's door in the middle of the night and beg to be released.

Shelvin sometimes let him out, jerking him off before capturing him in his cage again. Or sometimes he just fucked Elliot, leaving him aching. Elliot hadn't decided which he liked more.

Nah. That was an easy one.

He went to his knees, lowering his head as he spread his legs and placed his hands on his thighs with the palms facing out. *Kneeling* was still his favorite.

Patting him on the head once, Shelvin strolled toward the stage, revealing a bench and a fucking machine that had been draped in cloth. Clint stepped forward to help him as they rolled the machine across the stage toward the bench.

The bench was unlike any that the bar had had before. The surface wasn't padded at all, and instead of stained wood or metal, it was made of resin that was as clear as glass. It meant that every part of the person on it would be displayed from above and below. *Nowhere to hide.*

Shelvin had shown him the thing after he'd ordered it and had promised at the time that he would strap Elliot to it one day. And the name he'd had for it...*breeding bench for my horny bitch.* Even the memory made him flush

After five trial runs, he'd taken restraints off his limit list...hopefully permanently.

"This is going to get kinky as fuck," said Shelvin, addressing the crowd with a swaggering smirk. His movements were so languid, as if he didn't have a care in the world. "So if you don't like that shit, there's the door."

A few laughs and one cheer went up in the crowd, and Elliot stared harder at the spot on the floor as he tried not to lose his nerve. There was a small speck of dust between his knees that had probably been left over from construction. He glared at it, licking his lips.

Snapping his fingers, Shelvin pointed at the bench, not bothering to look at Elliot to see if he would comply. He didn't need to look. He knew that Elliot would streak down main street for him or impale himself on a stranger's cock to please him. A breeding bench was *nothing*.

Elliot laid himself on the bench as he reached it, resting his head and belly on it while leaving his ass and legs over the side. The heavy cage dragged his squished cock down, the strain even worse as it pulled at the piercing that held the sound in place. He rocked his hips a few times, just to feel the burn.

"Stop." Shelvin slapped his ass, the touch making his skin prickle. Shelvin had nearly burned through every one of his impact limits, although he was almost certain that he'd never get there with a belt. A good spanking made him achingly hard now. He rocked his hips again, pushing his luck as much as he dared.

"Your sounds are mine. That's the only thing they can't have. If they want to line up and fuck your ass, though, it's fair game." Shelvin slapped him again on his other cheek and Elliot stilled, panting as he laid his head down and turned so he faced away from the crowd. There were so many of them.

Shelvin produced a black ball gag, shoving it past Elliot's lips and securing it behind his head. Checking the strap, he pulled it one notch tighter, forcing Elliot's mouth open to accept it. His jaw would probably ache for days, and every time it throbbed, it would bring him back to this moment. Shelvin had probably planned for exactly that.

"Look at them, slave. Don't try to hide now, not when we've worked so hard for this."

Elliot turned his head, inhaling sharply as he looked at the crowd. A few of them were flushed, and one in particular at the front had his sub in his lap, a hand down his sub's pants.

But he was really only here for one man.

"I hope you didn't stretch this fuck-hole out. Any looser and I won't be able to use it anymore."

Elliot groaned, arching his back as Shelvin slipped one finger into his hole. He *hadn't* stretched at all, merely squirting a bunch of lube inside and doing his best to hold onto it. Shelvin hissed, shoving his finger deeper.

"Still good and tight…for now. Just you wait."

Something blunt lined up to Elliot's hole as a low hum filled the air. The bluntness eased forward as the fucking machine purred to life, the dildo attachment sinking past his ring and working its way inside. The fake cock that Shelvin had put on the machine felt huge, splitting him wide enough that he'd probably be left gaping after only a few minutes.

When Shelvin had first suggested a fucking machine, Elliot had almost come on the spot. Add a crowd to that, and the cage and sound were the only things holding him back.

Deeper. *Deeper.* Elliot bit the gag as it sank into him farther than anything ever had. It was thick, but flexible, bending inside him. He arched his back on his tiptoes to try to get away. It was too much. Tears streamed down his face, and Shelvin tapped him on the cheek, smirking down at him.

Shelvin pushed a button and the machine paused, the hum going quiet.

Elliot dragged in breaths through his nose, trying to fill his lungs as he started to sink into that space that he only fell into around Shelvin. Sweat coated his skin, the warmth of the room nearly excruciating.

Shelvin leaned in, licking the shell of his ear. "I seem to remember something, slave. Something about a little name you like to call me when you think I can't hear you."

Elliot quivered, his toes slipping on the floor. The toy moved deeper, and he let out a choked gasp. Fuck it was good, breaking him from the inside as Shelvin took over everything else.

"Oh, that's it." Shelvin tapped his chin as he chuckled. "'*Fucking architect*', that's what it was. Well, slave, I'll show you what this 'fucking architect' can do."

With a click of a button, the toy withdrew all at once and Elliot nearly stumbled, chasing the feeling of overfullness. It only lasted a breath before it was sinking back inside, so slowly that it nearly killed him. His gut ached from the strain, his cock throbbing. *Fuck. Deeper.* He met its thrust as the pain evaporated into pure pleasure.

"What a fucking slut." Shelvin dragged a finger down his spine, fingering his hole that was already spread so wide. The toy withdrew, leaving him empty as Shelvin toyed with his rim, swiping through the lube that was dripping from him.

"There we go…almost broken."

Hitting another button, the toy surged ahead, its strokes much faster and shallower—and aimed directly at his spot. Elliot bucked, trying to get away, but

Shelvin pinned him with one hand on his back. His caged cock leaked past the sound with such an ache that Elliot screamed against the gag. It was going to burn for so long, and he was going to love every second of it.

"What's your color?" asked Shelvin softly as he palmed his cock that was still hidden away beneath far too many layers.

Elliot knocked twice against the table with his knuckles, the action taking every smidge of his focus. *Twice for green.*

He couldn't count how many times he'd been gagged or choked on cock as they'd scened lately, and they'd quickly developed alternatives for verbal check-ins. And since Shelvin loved testing limits, Elliot had had more than one occasion to safeword. It hadn't been nearly as terrifying as he'd thought it would be.

"Good." Shelvin turned away before tossing Clint the remote. Clint fumbled to catch it, and he must've touched one of the buttons because the machine suddenly sped up, bucking into Elliot without mercy. He shook as an orgasm raced through him, building but not escaping as he was battered.

"Watch it for a second, would ya? I need a drink." Shelvin stepped off the stage, heading for the back where he'd left his bag with a few bottles of water.

Elliot gripped the table, sweeping his gaze over the crowd once before he stared after his Dom. Was he leaving? His palms slicked the surface, battling his hold. Sucking air through his nose, he let his eyes drift shut.

There were so many people, and his humiliation was complete as he let himself go. His body throbbed once before the haze crept over him.

"Breathe, baby." Shelvin touched his cheek, releasing the buckle on the gag and pulling it from his mouth. Elliot opened and closed his jaw slowly, groaning with how much it throbbed.

"You came back, Master." Tears rolled down his cheeks with relief as he fully sank into the scene.

"Such a puppy." Shelvin patted his head. "I'm gone for two minutes, and you think it's an hour. You should know that I always come back for what's mine."

Hilarious. Elliot giggled, leaning into Shelvin's palm in the same way a pup would. A whimper pushed through him a moment later as the machine started to slow, its thrusts growing longer and deeper again.

"You like getting fucked deep?" asked Shelvin, slapping Elliot's ass as the toy withdrew.

Elliot nodded, rocking back to feel the ache within. The toy eased ahead, still slick and dripping.

"So many things to fuck you up with," Shelvin said absently. "I should find my longest toy and have you kneel over it all night so you won't feel empty. "Would you like that?"

"Yes, Master. *Please.*" Another shudder rocked through him, stealing his breath.

"Okay. Let's work toward that then."

The toy stopped and the humming of the machine finally went silent before Shelvin patted his hip, lingering to caress his ass. "Up you get, slave. I want to see the rest of the house before I take you home."

Elliot leaned back, lube seeping from his hole as gravity took over. He'd put *a lot* inside in preparation, but he must've been gaping, because it slipped past his entrance even as he tried to clench. It left him even more empty than he already was. He *needed...*

"Oh, I almost forgot." Shelvin held up a thick plug, circling around Elliot and easing it between his cheeks. His rim stretched over the base, and he was certain he would break until it finally narrowed and sank inside. He groaned as it settled against his prostate almost painfully. It had to have been swollen from the abuse, because it was fucking *tender*.

"Wouldn't want all my hard work to go to waste. Come along, slave." Shelvin took his hand, catching him when Elliot's feet almost went out from under him as the plug started to vibrate.

Leading him to the back of the stage, Shelvin pushed through a door to a private room. Throwing down a towel and a blanket, he helped Elliot sit, pressing a straw to his lips before commanding him to drink.

"How are you feeling, sweetheart?"

Elliot fisted his hands in the towel, squirming against the toy. It was big, holding him wide and too large to push out on his own. He must've been really stretched. He reached down, touching his rim and shuddering at the swollen slickness he found.

"Green."

"You did so fucking good. You are perfect." Shelvin grinned, cupping Elliot's cheek and bringing their lips together.

"Do I get to come?" Elliot palmed at his cock, which had never hurt so much. He'd been wrong. The cage was much too small for him. He couldn't imagine going down a size.

Shelvin chuckled, taking a cloth and wiping at some of the slick on Elliot's legs. "Depends on how you answer the most important question in the world. Right answer, and you get to come."

"Wrong answer?" asked Elliot, sucking down another sip of his drink as he spread his legs to give Shelvin better access.

"That plug stays in and on all night, and I keep that little cock of yours plugged. You'll have to beg me if you plan on relieving yourself any time soon."

What kind of choice is that? Shelvin's smirk spread wider, his eyes alight.

Elliot wasn't sure when it had happened, but he'd started to imagine his future with Shelvin in it. There was no reason for him to move when there was a room at Shelvin's house with all his things. Why would he ever want to leave?

"Okay." He relaxed, falling into the vibrations of the plug. He couldn't last all night with them…not without losing his mind.

"Which is the best? An architect or an engineer?"

Elliot narrowed his eyes, glaring at his smirking Dom. *Fucking architects.* Maybe he could survive the night with the plug after all.

E p i l o g u e

One year later
Shelvin

Shelvin spread his legs, leaning against the back of the couch as he let his eyes fall partway shut. Elliot was on his knees in front of him, his cheek resting on the edge of his thigh. His hand was perched on the knee of the man next to them, his fingers looking so tanned against the pale white fabric of his jeans.

"How can you wear white?" asked Shelvin, sluggishly turning from the television. Lucan stared right back at him, raising one eyebrow as he eyed up Shelvin's ratty jeans.

There was nothing wrong with his jeans. The holes added character and the original color didn't matter nearly as much as what they'd faded to.

"I look great in white." Lucan crossed his arms, even as he smiled, turning his attention back to the screen.

True. The guy looked great in almost everything, including a bath robe or sneaking a snack from the kitchen in the nude. Elliot certainly knew how to pick them.

Shelvin could still remember every word of their conversation when Elliot had told him that he was ready to start dating again. He'd been elated for his sub, but also a little terrified that his next step would be moving out.

They'd picked out fucking curtains together, and as far as Shelvin was concerned, that shit was permanent. He didn't need a contract anymore, not when Elliot was his in every way that mattered.

But they weren't exactly romantic about it. Shelvin was pretty sure he was actually allergic to candlelit dinners and wooing someone. The thought of it certainly gave him hives.

Since Elliot had officially moved in, he'd had his own space, his own room and his own bed. He even went as far as to label their containers in the fridge to make sure that Shelvin didn't accidentally grab something with too much spice in it. It was cute and terribly domestic.

Sometimes Shelvin would wake in the middle of the night to find Elliot standing at his door, his eyes downcast and his lip between his teeth. He always asked Elliot the same question.

"Do you need to be my slave or my sweetheart?"

When Elliot had started dating again, it had almost been a relief. Elliot needed affection almost as much as he needed to kneel, but Shelvin was fucking shitty at the former. That, and he couldn't be a good lover when he didn't come home for a week because he lost track of time at the office.

The first guy Elliot had brought home had been taller than him with a set of shoulders that Shelvin wanted to gnaw on. It had been their third date when Elliot had decided it was time to introduce the guy to Shelvin.

Shelvin winced at the memory. It hadn't gone well. And the second suitor had had a similar outcome. Not much heartbreak, but Elliot had been disappointed. Shelvin always let him come those nights, rewarding him for trying and for being so fucking *good*.

Then Lucan had strolled into the house on their fourth date and spotted Shelvin on the couch with an apple halfway to his mouth.

"Wait…I'm confused. Is this your roommate or your boyfriend?" Lucan had asked, toeing off his shoes as Elliot flushed and fiddled with his fingers.

"Shelvin is my Dom and my Master…and I guess my roommate, too."

Elliot had looked so fucking beautiful that day, but Shelvin had been focused on Lucan, watching every move. To say he'd become protective of Elliot was an understatement.

"Cool." Lucan had shrugged, and that had been the end of the tension and the beginning of a whole new fucking book. Shelvin still couldn't believe it some days. Lucan was hot, too, which helped, even if they weren't fucking. Eye candy had its merits. Maybe one day he'd ask to watch.

Taking a sip of his drink, Shelvin offered the straw to Elliot, who took a small sip before resuming his position. His knees must've been aching from his time on the floor because he'd been squirming for almost ten minutes straight. He had his pillow, though.

"You watching the game this weekend?" asked Lucan, reaching into the bowl of popcorn between them and shoveling a few pieces into his mouth.

Grabbing another piece, he fed it to Elliot, who accepted it with a hum.

"Nah." Shelvin stretched, his back cracking. "There's an event at Unkinked this weekend for the first anniversary. They have some pretty awesome shit planned. You're welcome to join."

"No thanks." Lucan smiled, patting Elliot's head as he squirmed again. "Just means more chicken wings for me. I might invite a few of the guys over if you don't mind, though—trash the place while you two are away."

Okay...so maybe Shelvin loved the guy a little. He knew for a fact that Elliot had already said the words and he was probably planning to get a ring sometime soon, too. Shelvin had made him promise that he would be asked to be the best man...or the ring bearer...or *something*.

Elliot wiggled his hips, drawing Shelvin's attention again. *Oh.* So maybe it wasn't his sweetheart's knees that were the problem after all.

"I think it has to go," whispered Lucan, sending him a wink.

Just the fact that he was cool with their dynamic was a hundred points in his favor. But he also managed to remind Shelvin of things that he sometimes forgot when his mind wandered.

Like how he had plugged Elliot's cock with a sound...and how much pop Shelvin had been making him drink.

"You have something to say, sweetheart?" Shelvin tapped Elliot's cheek to get his attention. He was drifting pretty good, and he wasn't going to push him much further.

Elliot shook his head, the barest hint before settling back down. His back was tense, though, along with his thighs, and his eyes were red-rimmed. He'd be floating hard soon.

"Five more minutes," said Shelvin, grabbing another handful of popcorn. Elliot whimpered, a tear rolling down his cheek. "Okay, fine. Let's go, sweetheart. You did so fucking good for me. After a nice bath, you can let it all out."

Sometimes he wasn't sure when it had become so easy being a sadist.

Elliot sobbed, one hand dropping to his caged cock.

"Come on, sweetheart, let's go. Let your Master help."

Lucan didn't even blink, grabbing the remote and flicking the channel. He had his own key to Elliot's cage dangling around his neck, although he left the sounding up to Shelvin. It was probably for the best.

"I'm changing the channel. I can't watch another second of curling without expiring."

Shelvin narrowed his eyes. Curling was fucking A-level material. Where else could you yell 'hard' all day and get away with it?

"You should marry that fucking guy," he whispered softly in Elliot's ear before reaching for Elliot's cock and unhooking the sound from his piercing. He tugged the sound free, tucking it into his pocket to be sterilized later. "I changed my mind. I'll meet you up there in a second and get you all bathed up. Don't dribble before you get there, sweetheart." He tapped Elliot's ass once, urging him forward as he scrambled to the bathroom, doing his best to pinch the tip of his cock through the cage.

Seeing Elliot so desperate would always satisfy him.

He turned on Lucan, shooting him a mild glare as he pointed over his shoulder to where Elliot had just disappeared. "You should marry that guy or something. He's fucking perfect for you." He grinned as Lucan's mouth dropped open.

"How did you know I bought a ring? Did you look at my Mastercard statements? I swear to God, that's a limit, Shelvin."

These guys. I swear. We are fucking made for each other.

Want to see more from this author? Here's a taster for you to enjoy!

It's a Kink Thing: On Kink's Edge
M.C. Roth

Coming September 2023

Excerpt

"Yes, Sir. No, Sir. Thank you, Sir." Keady rolled his eyes as he strolled to the bar, slipping through the middle of a scene that looked like it was about to get intense. The Dom shot him a glare at the interruption, the sub hardly noticing from his position on the floor.

That glare was like a taste of the thrill he'd been seeking for months. Too bad he wasn't welcome.

The Dom had no right to be pissed at him. That was what happened when you set up a scene in the middle of the bar area. There was an open play area in the club for a reason.

But at least that Dom was looking at him with something other than mild contemplation—not that Malone, Keady's own Dom, didn't *look*. He was just too sweet, too careful and too fucking gentle. It drove Keady insane. Instead of 'Yes, Sir.', 'Go fuck yourself, Sir' had been on the tip of his tongue before he'd excused himself and headed for drinks. Malone had only smiled and nodded obliviously, sending him another patient look.

He didn't get it — or Keady — and it was infuriating. There were so many couples at Unkinked — a club for kinky bastards like him — and they all seemed so much happier than he was. They all appeared to know exactly what they wanted, when he was still tripping over limits like some newbie.

If lust had a smell, it was Unkinked, with music pounding off the bodies that were all searching for the same goal. Sweat and sex mixed with the latest cocktail, coating his tongue and skin. Some members came to get drunk, and others wanted to submit, but the outcome was the same. They all left satisfied. *Except me.*

Leaning against the bar top, Keady bit his lip before looking over his shoulder. Malone was looking his way, speaking with another Daddy Dom like him. Keady had thought that maybe he was little, but now he wasn't so sure. He loved to color, could play video and board games for hours and the thought of wearing a diaper was positively thrilling.

But it didn't push on him the way he wanted to be pushed, and after a few months of being his 'Daddy's boy', he'd reverted to 'Sir'. He'd hoped that Malone would punish him for it, but he never had, taking it all in stride and grabbing him another coloring book from the store to doodle in.

"What can I get you?" Clint sidled up to him from the other side of the bar, and Keady sent him a smile filled with relief. If there was any person he'd spill his guts to, it was Clint. Owner of the BDSM bar Unkinked and former nurse, Clint had patched him up enough times that he knew almost everything about Keady — *except for the part that matters.*

"Anything…please. I'll double the tip if you spike it with something fun." Keady lowered his head into his palm, scrubbing the sweat from his skin. "And for

Christ's sake, turn up the air conditioning. It's packed in here tonight."

Clint only chuckled, slipping him a ginger ale and a smile. "Don't want to get you in trouble."

Keady grasped the fizzy drink, struggling down a swallow while wishing for something so much harder. He must've been insane to sign a contract that prohibited alcohol. Then again, he'd been pretty fucking desperate at the time. He'd pissed off more than a few Doms before he'd finally settled for Malone.

"But could you?" asked Keady, his voice surprisingly desperate. Usually, he was better at hiding it, but tonight was getting under his skin in the worst way. The packed bar, sweet smiles and the sound of pain from other subs weren't helping, either.

Clint paused, narrowing his eyes and giving him another once over. The dishcloth in his hand was well-loved and worn, the color all but faded away. "How long until your contract is up?"

Clint knew as well as he did that Keady would never break a contract. He was serious about kink, and he'd been in the lifestyle since he'd graduated high school — before high school had ended, really, if he counted the few choice boyfriends he'd put through the wringer.

"Three months." *Fuck,* that sounded so long. Ninety days of 'Sir' at the end of every sentence and unfulfilled orgasms... Ninety more days without subspace and probably more, if he were honest with himself... He hadn't been that deep in...years.

"That's not so bad." Clint scratched his chin where three days' worth of growth was. On most guys, unshaven and worn clothes would look sloppy, but on Clint, it was endearing. He was hard not to love when he spread his heart around to everyone. "We'll be in the new place by then, and who knows? Maybe you'll find your dream Dom."

The rumors that Clint was leaving the bar behind and building a house of kink instead had been circulating for months. It was nice to finally hear the gossip confirmed. It was also a little terrifying.

Unkinked had become a home to so many kinksters like himself, and the thought that they might be uprooted put him on edge. It wasn't so much the bar, the open play area and the themed rooms, but everything else. *The people.*

Keady snorted, taking another sip of the sweet bubbles. It reminded him of the days he'd spent sick on his mother's couch, flat ginger ale his companion when nothing else worked. Once they'd figured out that he was allergic to meat, the stale soda had become a thing of his past.

"You know I won't." He swirled his glass, tapping his foot as the song switched to something low and throaty. Hopefully, the new place had better music with speakers that could blast his eardrums out.

"I thought we talked about this," said Clint, swiping at a bit of moisture from the bar top with the cloth. Another man stepped up to order, but Clint ignored the guy. "Your dream Dom and your nightmare are pretty close to the same thing in your fantasies, but this is your life. I need you to be safe, okay? I don't want to go down that road again."

It was the road that had left Keady with a few scars on his back and a stern talking-to from Clint. He'd been terrified that his membership to Unkinked would be rescinded, but Clint had taken a different path. Six months of voluntary domestic servitude was something of Keady's worst nightmares, but he'd done it—cleaning the rooms at Unkinked and helping Clint with set up and take down on the nights he could.

It had driven them even closer to one another, and Keady had met Maddy along the way, a person whom he could call his bestie. Too bad Clint wasn't his type. *And off-limits.*

"Yep." Keady stared at his glass, his stomach rolling. "That's why I'm here." Sticking to Unkinked meant that his heart didn't pitter-patter during a scene, but he didn't end up injured or dead, either.

"Someone will come up," said Clint, tilting his head to gesture down the bar. Keady followed his gaze, gritting his teeth when he saw who Clint was trying to point out. "I imagine Cutler will be looking for a new sub again. His last one only made it twenty-four hours."

Keady shuddered, eyeing up the man in question. If serial killers had a look, it was Cutler's. Even his *name* sounded dangerous. He was tall and lean, his face twisted in a perpetual frown and a scar over his lips that had to be from some kind of fight to the death. The thick-rimmed glasses completed his look like some sort of Clark Kent disguise.

Keady wasn't sure if it was a coincidence that Cutler had just shown up one day without a sub or a back story. Maybe he'd changed his name to run from the police, his hands still stained from a fresh murder. It didn't explain why Clint vouched for him, though.

Subs rarely lasted more than one scene with him since he'd arrived, and word was that he'd been kicked out of other kink communities. *But why?* He couldn't have disrespected someone's safeword or he would have had his ass handed to him by the Dungeon Master.

The peek Keady had caught of one of his scenes had been intense, but Malone had dragged him away before he'd witnessed much more than a heavy flogging and screams.

"He looks like a goddamned serial killer," whispered Keady, quickly averting his eyes when Cutler looked his way. A flush settled over him and his belly went tight. He could *feel* Cutler's eyes on him, raking through his skin to the vulnerability underneath.

Do I like it? He couldn't answer.

"Huh. I thought you would have been into that," said Clint, shrugging before he turned to grab the newcomer his drink. "Think on that one."

Bastard. Pursing his lips, Keady looked back to his Dom, frowning at what he found. Malone was still waiting patiently, his perpetual smile driving his nerves past what he could stand.

The worst part was that Malone had become a friend, which was the last thing he wanted in a relationship. A 'friend' couldn't give him what he needed. No, that took someone very special.

He glanced at Cutler, ice traveling down his spine when he caught his glare. That look was a thousand promises and threats all rolled into one, with a side dish of terror. Swallowing, he grabbed his drink, rushing back to his table. He felt Cutler's eyes on him with every step.

About the Author

M.C. Roth lives in Canada and loves every season, even the dreaded Canadian winter. She graduated with honours from the Associate Diploma Program in Veterinary Technology at the University of Guelph before choosing a different career path.

Between caring for her young son, spending time with her husband, and feeding treats to her menagerie of animals, she still spends every spare second devoted to her passion for writing.

She loves growing peppers that are hot enough to make grown men cry, but she doesn't like spicy food herself. Her favourite thing, other than writing of course, is to find a quiet place in the wilderness and listen to the birds while dreaming about the gorgeous men in her head.

M.C. Roth loves to hear from readers. You can find her contact information, website details and author profile page at https://www.pride-publishing.com

PUBLISHING

Sign up for our newsletter and find out about all our romance book releases, eBook sales and promotions, sneak peeks and FREE romance books!

www.ingramcontent.com/pod-product-compliance
Lightning Source LLC
Chambersburg PA
CBHW021512240626
47154CB00002B/599